BY DIA CALHOUN

Firegold

Aria of the Sea

White Midnight

WHITE MIDNIGHT

WHITE MIDNIGHT

Dia Calhoun

Farrar, Straus and Giroux
New York

Acknowledgments

I would like to thank both my editors on this book, Wes Adams and
Francesca Crispino. Thanks also to Rinda Byars, Margery Cuyler, Julie
Smith, Joan Soderland, and Jan Ward for reading drafts of the manuscript. Special thanks to Lauren Wohl for finding the manuscript a new
home. Finally, thanks as always to my husband, Shawn Zink.

Library of Congress Cataloging-in-Publication Data
Calhoun, Dia.
    White midnight / Dia Calhoun.— 1st ed.
        p.   cm.
    Summary: While barbarians threaten the land, mysterious visions help guide fifteen-year-
old Rose when she is given the chance to free her family from servitude, if only she will
provide a wicked old man an heir fathered by his deformed grandson, "the Thing" locked in
the attic.
    ISBN 0-374-38389-8
    [1. Toleration—Fiction.   2. People with disabilities—Fiction.   3. Social classes—Fiction.]
I. Title.

PZ7.C12747 Wh 2003
[Fic]—dc21

                                                                        2002035939

For James and Eva Calhoun,
and for the crew of the *Kursk*

Contents

Part Three

Part Four

Prologue

The night she witnessed the terrible thing, the moon woke her. She slid out of bed, opened the cottage door, and blinked at the moon-button shining in the sky. Was it sugar—sweet silvery sugar—that made the moon shimmer? She stuck out her tongue to lick it clean.

A warm wind tugged at her nightdress, and the leaves on the apple trees waved at her—*come out, come out and play!* She skipped up the path where branches scribbled shadows on the ground. Her toes jiggled the mud. Then a worm popped up to admire the pictures the moon had painted on the night.

When she came out of the orchard, she saw the gigantic house guarded by the fence of jagged white teeth. She stopped. Reckless flowers; magic flowers; crimson, gold, and silver flowers grew between the gaps in the teeth.

Here! Over here! they called. She ran through the open gate.

"Hello, rose," she said, laughing, and picked one. It bit

her fingers, but she did not care because, down in the black pockets between the petals, secret worlds beckoned. The instant her breath touched the petals, a crash shattered the night. She looked up.

Beneath the roof peak, a round window glowed like a second moon—a golden, candlelit moon. She frowned. Were those moths beating against it? Or hands? Was something trapped inside the attic?

She remembered a scary song, a scolding, a scream in the night. They all sang together in her mind as she stared at the golden moon.

> The three-headed Thing
> Grabs you while you dream.
> The three-headed Thing
> Eats you while you scream.
> Nah! Nah! Nah! Nah!

She choked. Was that . . . ? Could it be . . . ? The night swirled. The sky cracked like an egg around the moon, and the stars dripped down, burning her skin.

A door banged. Footsteps pounded across the porch. She crouched beneath a rosebush. Again the door banged, and with a *bump-bump-tap* a heavier set of footsteps chased the first. She tried to shrink, tried to be as tiny as the worm. The footsteps came closer. One shadow panted; the other took quick, raggedy-doll breaths. They struggled together, one small and one big. Her heart beat as fast as one of the chicks' in the barn.

"I won't go back!" a voice shouted.

"See this?" a deeper voice asked. A knife swept up, a silhouette in front of the white moon. "See it? Nasty little beast, I should kill you. But I can keep you from escaping again."

"No!" A white hand stretched toward the golden moon. "Lee-lee—" A scream rang out, then stopped, muffled.

She squeezed her eyes shut. Beside her, inside her, the rose she had picked grew big and black, whirling faster and faster, its petals snarling until at last it swallowed her. Her breath stopped. She tried to burrow down, to hide in the earth, hide from the terrible thing that was happening beneath the two round moons that glared in the night.

PART ONE

1

The Thing in the Attic

M e? Work in the Bighouse?" Rose dropped a dirty wooden bowl, which clunked onto the floor. She held her breath, the stale air filling with dread.

"It's a lucky chance for you," said Gerald, her father. "Coming to Mr. Brae's notice like this."

Lucky? Rose's throat tightened.

"I don't like it," her mother said, "not one bit." She bent, grunting with the effort, and picked up the bowl. "Chipped," she muttered, then drowned it in the dishwater. "I know him. He's up to something."

"Now, Maggie," Gerald said, "you're too suspicious."

"And with good reason." Maggie scoured the bowl. "Knowing what we know, knowing what lurks up there in that attic. Or have you forgotten, Gerald?"

"Of course not," he said.

Rose clamped her tongue between her teeth. How could her parents ask her to work at the Bighouse when the Thing lived there in the attic? What if it began its horrible screaming or broke down the attic door or dragged its monstrous body down the stairs or . . . Rose pushed between the bench and the oak table, where she sat down across from her father.

"But why me?" she asked.

"Beth's moving up North Valley to get married," Gerald explained, "and Mr. Brae needs someone to help Mrs. Schill with the housework. He says you're a hard worker. A 'fine girl' was how he put it."

"I'll *fine girl* him," Maggie said, brandishing a wet spoon. Drops spattered Rose's face. "Why, once when I was younger, he tried to—" Maggie stopped. Her lips pursed, sucked into her cheeks. Her mounds of fat seemed to swell like biscuits rising in a pan.

Rose reached for the thick beeswax candle standing unlit in the middle of the table. Her hands shaking, she tore off the drips curdled on the sides. She could never work near the Thing, never. But how could she convince her father of that?

"What about my job with Donney?" she asked, wishing she were outside leading the old ox around the northwest well.

"Any bondgirl on the place can take over your shift," her father said.

"But Donney likes me," Rose argued. He was one of the few on Greengarden who did, but she did not say that. Instead, she tried to think of another excuse—fast. Her mother, who had finished the dishes, slapped a jam jar stuffed with lupine onto the table.

"I chipped that jar, too," Rose said. "I'm always dropping things. Remember, Ma, how I dented your wedding plate?" She nodded toward the three pewter plates hanging on the stone chimney above the hearth. "I'm no good at housework. And up at the Bighouse, with real china—I'd surely break something." Rose flicked another bit of wax into the pile beneath the candle. "If Mr. Brae thinks I'm too old to lead Donney anymore, let me work in the orchard like the other girls my age. I'm good at that."

"We've been through this time and again," Maggie said. "It's bad enough you work with those trees on the Faredge Wall. Fieldwork's not for you, Rose. Not with your condition."

Rose scowled at her mother's words. She loved fieldwork, loved the rows of apple trees with their leaves and their buds and the rough bark of their trunks.

"As for housework," Maggie added, "if you'd just learn to settle your nerves, you wouldn't be so clumsy. Earth's Mercy!" She slapped Rose's hand, then scooped up the candle bits. "I've never seen such a fidgety girl. Leave be!"

Rose clasped her hands in her lap until her knuckles turned white. But soon her fingers crept out and folded pleats in the flour-sack apron that covered her long brown skirt. On the bottom of the apron was a ruffle that her mother had added; the absurdity of a frill on a flour sack made Rose wince. Or was it the absurdity of a frill on her?

Gerald leaned forward. Wrinkles bunched beneath his eyes.

"I know you're scared of the Thing, Rose," he said softly. "But it's locked in. The door is stout oak and reinforced with iron—I've seen it myself. Besides, you'll only be working on the first floor, nowhere near the attic. Mr. Brae promised that."

An invisible hand seemed to squeeze Rose's chest. Not now, she pleaded with it; go away! The slats on the rocking chair threw bars of shadow across the pitted pine floor, paths of darkness that led into the hearth's black mouth.

Rose pushed back the bench and walked over to a barrel draped with a red doily—the end table for the sagging sofa. Above the sofa hung a painting, a cast-off from the Bighouse that was Maggie's greatest treasure. Men and women wearing diamonds, satin vests, and swirling lace gowns danced in a room blazing with seventy-seven candles. Rose had counted them. She took a match from the tin on the barrel.

"Already?" Maggie asked. "It's only dusk. And such a nice spring night."

But Rose scraped the match on the kitchen table. When she held the match to the candle's wick, it sputtered, and a flame leapt up.

Maggie sighed. "Buggy creatures will be in, with the light, and the door open."

"Listen, Rose," Gerald said. "Besides doing housework, you'll tend the garden out front. Mr. Brae admires your skill with plants. I know how much you like those roses."

"*Will* tend the garden?" Rose hugged her knees to her chest. "Then you've already decided? I have to take the job?"

Her parents exchanged glances.

"If you don't, you stupid mouse," a voice said, "Pa and Ma could lose everything." Rose's brother, Dorrick, leaned against the doorjamb. "Even *you* wouldn't be selfish enough to risk that," he added. "Though it wouldn't surprise me if you were."

Rose wondered how long he had been eavesdropping. He stood with his arms crossed and his fists crammed into the sweat-stained armpits of his shirt.

"Pa could lose his job if you cause trouble," Dorrick said. "Mr. Brae can make him a common worker again quick as that." He spit outside.

"We'd lose the house," Maggie added.

Rose knew her parents had worked hard for this three-room cottage with its loft upstairs. Even though they were only bondfolk, her family had a decent house because her father was second-boss here at Greengarden Orchard. He even bossed freemen. Some folks said that if Gerald Chandler were not a bondman, Mr. Brae would make him first-boss. Bondfolk were bonded to the land; they had to purchase their freedom for the unimaginable sum of one thousand dollars. Mr. Brae could throw the Chandlers into a shack any time he chose; a one-room shack with a dirt floor. It would kill her mother, Rose knew.

"Risk or no, I don't like it," Maggie said. "A girl near fifteen years old alone with him. Not to mention that Thing in the attic."

Rose flinched. The invisible hand squeezed her chest again, and her throat closed. *The Thing in the attic! The Thing in the attic!*

"Stop frightening her," Gerald said. "I tell you it can't get out! Besides, she won't be alone. Mrs. Schill's there."

Maggie sniffed. "Lot of good she'll do, passed out from drink half the day."

"The old man should just kill the Thing and be done," Dorrick said.

"That would be unnatural." Gerald swatted a bug.

"Unnatural?" Maggie raised her eyebrows. "To kill a beast?"

In the silence that followed, Rose's chest lifted and fell too fast. She coughed. A gust of wind rushed through the doorway, and a moth darted into the candle flame, where, with a hiss and a sputter, it burned up.

"Come in and shut the door," Rose told Dorrick. "The bugs are terrible."

Dorrick snorted. "Nice excuse, Miss Baby-'Fraid-of-the-Dark."

A faint, smoky stink filled the room; Rose coughed again. Dorrick came inside and sprawled on the sofa, but left the door open.

"There's something else you should know, Rose," said Gerald. "Mr. Brae's offering good wages."

"I'll bet." Dorrick laughed. "She's not worth much. She's lucky to get her nickel a week for walking that flea-bit ox. What's he going to pay, a dime maybe?"

"A dollar," Gerald said. "A dollar a week."

Rose sat completely still.

"A dollar!" Dorrick exclaimed. "For a wheezing twit of a girl? That's double my wages!"

"Well, that changes things," Maggie said, nodding. "Why didn't you say so in the first place, Gerald? I could fix up this place. Maybe buy them pretty dishes off Mrs. Willow."

While the others talked, Rose pulled on her fingers: the first finger, the middle, the ring, the pinkie, and then the first again. Even if she gave her parents half her wages, as Dorrick did, the remaining fifty cents a week would add up quickly. She could buy Golden Flames, a new variety of apple. Ever since she had tasted the sweet, vanilla-flavored apples from the North Valley, Rose had dreamed of growing them. She had questioned the fruit merchant until she became convinced that the Golden Flames could survive here in the warmer south. With fifty cents a week, in three months she could earn enough to buy branches for several dozen grafts.

She turned to her father. "If I take the job, can I still work with my apple trees along the Faredge Wall?"

"Why not?" Gerald leaned back, grinning now. "The way you've trained those Appelunes—and the bushels of fine fruit they give—it's the talk of Stonewater Vale."

"There'll be talk all right," Maggie warned. "That much money. What will Bartla say? People might think he . . ." She looked at Rose, then looked away.

"Who's to know what Mr. Brae's paying," Gerald said. "Unless someone tells our private family business to his girl." He looked hard at Dorrick, who scowled. "So what do you say, Rose?"

Rose reached into the jam jar, picked a lupine—tinted the blue-purple of the sky before dark—and then rubbed it against her cheek. She did not want any trouble with Mr. Brae, and she did want the Golden Flames. But no matter how strong the oak door with its iron bars, the Thing might still get out. And then? Her skin turned cold.

"I'm sorry, Pa," she said. "I can't. I'm scared of . . ." When she tried to take a breath, only a thread of air flowed in. She cramped with dread.

"Who cares if you're scared?" Dorrick snorted. "You're always scared. This is your chance to get you a place. Who do you think's going to take care of you when Pa and Ma are gone? Me? Not a chance. I'll be second-boss, married, and living here with Susa—alone."

"Now, Dorrick," Gerald said.

"I'm just speaking the truth, Pa. No one's going to marry her with her wheezing spells. A man might overlook it if she weren't as timid and ugly as some chewed-over mouse, but she is. She doesn't even have eyelashes! And Ma coddles her so much she never does a day's work."

"That's not . . . true!" Rose clasped her arms around her chest, struggling to breathe. "You don't care about Pa and Ma. You're afraid . . . if I don't obey . . . Mr. Brae'll hold it against you. Then you won't . . . get to be second-boss some-day! You're . . . selfish!"

Dorrick jumped up and strode toward her with his fists clenched. His forearms bulged beneath his rolled-up sleeves. Rose shrank back.

"Dorrick, stop!" Gerald said. He stood, and the bench toppled beneath him. He ran around the table. Dorrick swung at Rose, but Gerald struck him from behind, deflecting his blow.

"Gerald!" Maggie cried. "Don't hit our boy!"

At that moment, what Rose had dreaded, what she always dreaded, happened again. The invisible hand squeezed, and this time it did not let go. Spasms gripped her chest; spasms kept her from speaking, from breathing. She wheezed until only two things existed: pain and the hunger for air.

They twisted one around the other, air and pain, pain and air, until green spots danced before her eyes. Or were they leaves, sun-dappled with light and dark? Leaves fluttering on newly planted trees? The spasms seemed like roots taking hold, roots grappling down into the land, and the land was her body.

"Blighted Earth," Maggie swore. "You've frightened her into a spell—a bad one, too. Gerald, I won't have this ruckus. Tell Mr. Brae it's all off."

"Wait," Rose gasped, curling into a ball. "Tell him I'll . . ." as she struggled to speak, the wind gusted, the door slammed, and the candle went out.

2

The Bighouse

Rose scrubbed the front hall in the Bighouse on her hands and knees. She hummed softly, making figure eights with the brush, and tried to ignore her fear of the Thing two stories above. Not once in the past two weeks had she seen or heard anything strange, but her nerves were as raw as a newly plowed field. She hummed louder.

"Silence!"

Her hum slid into a shriek. Rose looked over her shoulder as Mr. Brae swung his oak walking stick; it whistled through the air and struck the floor an inch from her foot. Rose jerked back.

"I am paying you to work!" he exclaimed. "Not caterwaul."

"I'm sorry, sir," she said. "I thought . . . I thought you were still away." Mr. Brae had been in Middlefield ever since Rose had begun working in the Bighouse. Once Mr. Brae had been a straight, handsome man; now his shoulders rounded as though protecting a wound in his chest.

"It does not matter whether I am here or not," he said. "I will have quiet in my house." His ears lay so flat against his head that on first glance he seemed to have no ears at all. His square chin had turned flaccid; behind it, a second chin hung, as though from a face hidden beneath the first.

"Do I make myself clear?" he asked.

"Yes, sir," Rose said.

Mr. Brae ground the heel of his boot against the damp floor until a smear blackened the wood.

"Is this your idea of clean?" he asked. "This is not a barn. Chandler assured me you learn quickly, but you are slower than a snail—and careless, too."

"I'll do better, sir."

"Yes, you will," Mr. Brae agreed, his thumb probing the mouth of the silver coyote head atop his walking stick. He appraised her as though she were a goose being fattened for dinner. "I see that my memory of your ugliness was not exaggerated." He laughed. "You are an ugly enough rose to serve my purposes well."

Rose clutched the scrub brush. What purposes? What did he mean? Soapy water dripped onto her skirt.

Mr. Brae frowned. "What a slattern you are! What if I were entertaining important guests?"

"Guests?" Rose knew that guests—landowners like him, anyway—never came to Greengarden for parties as they had when her parents were young. People kept away because of the Thing, and because Mr. Brae hated everyone. "If guests are coming," she said, "I'll go out to the kitchen." She started to get up.

"Don't be ridiculous," Mr. Brae said.

Rose sank down again. In the corner, the grandfather clock ticked away. She counted the strokes of the pendulum—twenty, forty, eighty—while Mr. Brae stared down at her.

"Let's have a little chat about the Faredge Wall," he said at last. "Where did you get the idea to plant the Appelunes so close together? And what made you think of grafting a big apple onto a small rootstock?"

Rose blinked. "Well, I thought . . . with littler trees closer together, I'd get the same amount of fruit in the same amount of space—as we do with big trees planted farther apart."

"I see no advantage to that."

"Well . . . smaller trees are a lot easier to take care of. I don't have to move ladders around, and I can reach everything real easy."

"But without strong roots," he said, "the trees will blow over."

"I figured the wall would protect them from the north wind."

Mr. Brae pulled a loose thread from his cuff. His finely tailored brown suit was immaculate, except that all the buttons were missing. The buttonholes gaped like hungry little mouths.

"I find it highly unlikely that you thought of all this yourself," he said. "You undoubtedly cannot recognize an opportunity when you see one, or appreciate when you are well off. Some foolish notion seizes you, and you immediately forget your duty to your family. You're just like my wretched daughter." He swung his stick toward Rose's head. "Stupid, ungrateful girls!"

Rose shrank back, scooting across the wet floor on her bottom, trying to put the bucket between them.

Mr. Brae laughed. "Get on with your work!" Then, his oak stick tapping, he walked away toward his study.

Cold bloomed against Rose's thigh from the water seeping through her skirts, but she stayed huddled on the floor. Mr. Brae was even meaner than folks said. Why hadn't her parents warned her? Most likely, they did not know; otherwise, they would never have allowed her to work here. Then she remembered the urging in her father's voice, remembered her mother's fondness for pretty things, which was even greater than her fondness for sweets. Maybe they did know.

The front hall seemed suddenly vast. Two full-length mirrors hanging on opposite walls reflected each other endlessly. In them, Rose could see the top of the grandfather clock with its revolving dials showing the phases of the moon. Each had a painted face that bounced back and forth between the mirrors, back into unfathomable regions. Rose hugged herself and looked away. For as long as she could remember, she had feared the moon.

Slowly, picking up the bucket, she tipped water onto the floor. It ran into a finger of light from a sunbeam. She scrubbed, moving from the shade into the light and back into the shade. If only she were out in the orchard, where dirt was soil and meant something good. Here in the house, dirt was only filth to be endlessly washed away.

Rose attacked the boot print with her brush. Soon, looked at in one light, the print seemed to be gone, but when she looked at it in another light, she could see a faint trace— like a bruise. Although she scrubbed until her wrist ached, the bruise remained.

* * *

After lunch, Rose found the feather duster. She tied a kerchief over her nose and mouth to keep out the dust that might trigger a spell. Mrs. Schill had ordered her to air the drawing room every month, but until now Rose had not even been inside. She crossed the hall and opened the door.

White sheets shrouded the furniture, which looked like mounds of snow on the blood-red carpet. An empty chandelier hung from the ceiling. From their portraits on the wall, three elderly people stared at Rose as she opened the gold brocade drapes over one of the tall windows. Wheels of dust spun toward the carpet, which was crimson now in the sunlight. In spite of the sheets and dust, Rose knew this room well. It was the room in her mother's treasured painting, the room where the Braes had held their parties twenty years ago when Amberly, Mr. Brae's only child, had been a young woman.

Rose lifted one of the sheets and saw first a carved wooden leg, then a gleaming table with a row of black and white strips. A musical instrument? She raised the sheet higher. A silver candelabrum on a shelf seemed bereft without its candles. To the right was a painting of a smiling little girl in a ruffled white dress. She had to be Amberly. Her shining brown eyes looked at Rose as though they shared some wonderful secret. It was hard to believe the girl was dead.

Rose looked back at the instrument. When she touched one of the white strips, it gave under her finger and sent a beautiful sound through the air. She stepped back, pressing the kerchief to her face as the sheet drifted down. Had anyone heard? Mr. Brae had left after lunch. Mrs. Schill? Nothing woke her from her afternoon nap. Verda—a great dray horse of a girl who did the heaviest housework? But she only came mornings. That left . . . the Thing. Rose listened, but the house was quiet. She took a deep breath and lifted another sheet.

Something screeched overhead.

She froze. The sound came again: a long-drawn-out metallic screech, human, yet inhuman. Rose looked up. Above the ceiling was the second floor, above that was another ceiling, and above that . . . was the Thing.

Rose closed her eyes. When she was a little girl, Dorrick, Susa, and the other children had dared each other to run up and touch the Bighouse while the rest watched, chanting:

The three-headed Thing
Screams across the night,
The three-headed Thing
Eats you with delight!
Nah! Nah! Nah! Nah!

Rose had always been too frightened to play. And now here she was, standing inside the Bighouse with the Thing only twenty feet away.

"Don't let it get out," she whispered. She threw all her thoughts toward that six-inch-thick door, reinforcing its strength with her own. "Earth's Mercy, don't let it out!"

How could she bear this place? First Mr. Brae and now this. Rose wanted to run home and never come back. If she did, though, no more coins would fill the jar beneath her bed, and the Golden Flames would never grow beside the Appelunes along the Faredge Wall.

Although the house remained silent, the silence had a listening quality, as if some presence strained to hear through the cracks in the walls. Rose crept to the drawing room door, opened it an inch, and scanned the hall. It was empty. She hurried toward the back porch to get the gardening tools—she had to get out of the house. The drawing room could wait.

By late afternoon, Rose had finished weeding around the Ecstasy rosebushes inside the picket fence. She stepped to the next bush, a Cur King, and began stripping off aphids. An early flower bloomed; golden stripes radiated from the center of the red blossom.

A chill rippled from her neck to her cheek. She turned and looked up at the Bighouse, which stood as white as a cloud against the blue sky. The first story had a broad porch. The second had tall windows. The third, which was the attic, had a round window of thick brown glass beneath the peak.

Over the window curved wrought-iron grillwork—fancy bars, really. The scrolling seemed to form a shape, but Rose had never been able to make it out. She could not help staring; the Thing might be watching her this moment, and she would not even know.

"Rose," Gerald called, walking out of the orchard. He crossed to the yard and stood outside the fence, smiling. "Fine day, isn't it? You must be happy here. I know how much you like those roses."

Rose looked down. She did not like them; she did not like them at all, yet for some reason her parents persisted in thinking she did. She disliked them because of her name—the awful irony of being an ugly girl named Rose, and the endless teasing that went with it. Mr. Brae's comment that she was an ugly enough rose to serve his purposes was exactly the kind of taunt she had been enduring all her life. He was not teasing, though. What had he meant? What was she ugly enough for?

"You do like them?" her father asked.

"They're thorny," she said. "I have to be careful or they'll draw blood."

His smile faded. "You're not thinking of quitting, are you?"

"I miss Donney," Rose said. If only her father would say she could quit, if only he would say it . . . but he did not. "I guess I'll keep on."

"Good. You won't mind so much once you get used to it."

Rose hoped she would never get used to someone swinging a stick at her head or to inhuman shrieks shattering her ears, but she said only, "When's the fruit merchant coming?"

"Tomorrow. Why?"

"I want a bundle of Golden Flame branches."

"But I told you, they won't thrive here, even grafted to the Cheldys."

"Not the Cheldys, the Appelunes. I've thought of a way to—"

"The Golden Flames need a northern climate; I don't care what you graft them to. You can't change the way of things, Rose."

She pressed her lips together. "Nobody thought the Appelunes would grow either."

"Oh, all right," Gerald said. "You're as stubborn as a clump of pigweed. I don't know where you get these ideas. You've had nothing but plants in your head since you began poking peas into the ground as a babe." He sighed. "It's your money. But you'd be better off saving it, I think."

Again Rose felt that odd sensation stinging her neck. She glanced up at the attic window.

"Have you ever seen it, Pa?" she asked.

"What?" He followed her gaze. "Oh. No. And I hope I never do."

"Sometimes when I'm working out here, I feel like it's watching me."

"I don't even know if it has eyes."

"No eyes?" Rose said with a rush of horror and pity. "It has a mouth, though. I . . . I heard it shriek today. It was terrible."

"Shriek?" Gerald gazed at some distant point over her shoulder. "Oh, I doubt that. We had a lot of wagons out. Likely you just heard a wheel that needed oiling. Or Mrs. Schill moving some furniture upstairs."

"But when I was little," she said, yanking off a leaf, "I remember hearing it—"

"There hasn't been any of that carrying on for years now. Your imagination's getting the best of you. Just pretend nothing's there, and you'll be fine." He walked away. "Your ma's got bacon for dinner," he called back over his shoulder. "Your favorite."

Rose did not answer. Instead, she ripped the leaf in half

and then in half again as she stared up at the round window. Ugly enough for what? she wondered again. Then something moved behind the glass, and as her hands jerked apart, she saw the shape in the scrolling bars. It was a black wrought-iron rose.

3

The Dalriadas and the Golden Flames

In the cottage that night, Rose lowered a candle hanger and dipped four candles into a pot of beeswax. She tried, as her father had advised, to pretend the Thing did not exist, but she could not. Instead of wax swirling around the tapers, she saw the blur of movement behind the attic window; instead of her mother humming, she heard an inhuman screech.

Rose raised the dripping candles. Her attempts to learn to sew had failed, to her mother's despair, but Rose's candles were straight and true, if plain. She had just lowered the tapers again when the cottage door burst open. Dorrick ran in.

"Fire?" Gerald sprang up from the rocking chair.

"No!" Dorrick said, panting. "News—a messenger just rode in. The Dalriadas raided another farm last night." In the past few months, the Dalriadas, a barbarian race who practiced dark magic in the Red Mountains, had begun attacking the Valley folk again.

"Where?" Gerald asked.

"Copia," Dorrick said.

"So close!" Rose jerked up the candle hanger and sent hot wax spattering across her apron.

"Is the messenger sure?" Gerald asked Dorrick. "The barbarians haven't been seen that far south since . . . the Council War."

"The man swore," Dorrick said. "Mr. Brae wants you and Mr. Terth to get down to the crew shed, Pa, and assign guard shifts." Mr. Terth was first-boss. Gerald grabbed his coat and followed Dorrick out. After Maggie bolted the door behind them, she turned and leaned all her bulk against it.

"Dalriadas," she said. "Earth save us. The tales I've heard, the tales I could tell . . ."

"You already have," Rose said, and she closed her eyes. When she was little, sometimes her parents had told her to clean her plate and do her chores because otherwise the Dalriadas would get her. Usually, though, they had threatened her with the Thing instead.

* * *

When the fruit merchant arrived the next day, everyone crowded around his wagon, asking whether he had seen any sign of the Dalriadas on his road south.

"Not a one of those crop-cursing barbarians," he said. "But let me tell you, I sure hot-footed it—Copia may be twenty miles north, but folks, I ask you, what's twenty miles to a barbarian on a magic horse?"

"Not bloody far enough," said Kurt Sowerbee.

"That's right." The merchant pushed back his felt hat to reveal a sunburned nose. "I feared they'd curse my wares. Last thing we need's an outbreak of verblight. But I did hear that the High Council at Middlefield is mustering an army. They're calling up men from the North and South Valley to join up and fight the barbarians. We'll show 'em. You'll see."

After he had finished his business with the others, Rose asked if he had any Golden Flame branches for grafting.

He grinned. "If it isn't the girl who planted the little trees one on top the other, and made a marvel of it, too. I've told plenty of orchardists about your trick, dearie. And how are the Appelunes doing this year?"

"Full bloom, no frost damage," Rose said.

"Glad to hear it! So happens I've got a bundle of Golden Flames right here. Nice ones, too—just going begging. Getting an orchardist around Stonewater to try something new is like trying to teach a turtle to fly."

Rose smiled.

"New is the future, dearie, and you're smart to see it. I'll give you a good price, too. And if you pay some in advance, I'll trust you for the rest over time. Your pa says you got a good job."

Rose opened the canvas-wrapped bundle and brushed off the damp sawdust. She ran her fingers along one of the branches; it was straight, year-old wood about a finger thick, with well-formed buds. Perfect.

"I'll take them," she told the merchant, and gave him a dollar.

After gathering her tools, Rose carried the bundle out to her family's plot beside Greengarden's northern boundary, the Faredge Wall. The stone wall was six feet high and a quarter of a mile long. Along half of it ran a row of mature Appelunes; the white blossoms looked like lace against the old stonework. The new leaves were a pale, leaping green. Along the other half of the stone wall was a row of two-foot-high Appelunes that she had grafted onto dwarf rootstock only a year ago. She would join the Golden Flames to them.

Rose began to cut the branches into scions—pieces with two or three buds each that were cut at an angle on one end.

When she dropped them in the water to stay fresh, they pinged against the pail. Now and then she glanced at the Red Cameo apples across the lane. Suckers strangled the trunks. On the branches, unproductive shoots called water sprouts shot up like thickets of long, grotesque fingers. The orchard was slowly deteriorating from neglect. Rose slapped her knife against the whetstone, angry to see Greengarden failing. How she wished she could save it!

"I do what I can," her father had told her once. "But Terth is getting on. And Mr. Brae quit caring about everything when Amberly—when she died." The freefolk and bondfolk did not care either because they believed the Thing's presence had cast a curse over the place. Why work hard when the land was doomed?

"Why do *I* care so much?" she asked softly. The land had always called to her. Even now she could hear it in the roar of the Mirandin River threading through the valley. Land was the secret source at the bottom of her heart. Rose dreamed of owning land, a dream that she told no one, a dream that, for a bondwoman, was as dubious as living forever. At least the Golden Flames were hers. No one could take them away.

Footsteps swished in the long grass.

"It's cruel," a voice said. "I don't know why we have to mow when there might be barbarians lurking in the orchard." Two bondgirls, Susa and Opal, walked out of the Cameos with scythes in their hands. Long pieces of grass bent like drunken stripes on their skirts.

"I bet they're planning to carry off all the prettiest girls," Susa said. When she saw Rose, she stopped and wrinkled her forehead.

"I guess Rose Chandler won't have to worry, then," Opal said, "will she?"

Rose's hand tightened on the knife.

Giggling, the two girls nudged each other and then sidled up to Rose. Though they were fifteen, only a few months older than Rose, they had never befriended her.

"Did Mr. Brae kick you out of your fancy job in the Bighouse already?" Susa asked. "Can't say I'm surprised. You're much better suited to walking that filthy ox around the northwest well."

"It's my half day off," Rose said as she picked up another branch.

"Wish I had such an easy job," Opal said.

"Easy?" Rose glanced up. "Scrubbing floors? Cleaning chamber pots? Waiting on—"

"Beats fieldwork," Susa said. "Of course, we all know you have to take it easy because of your little 'spells.'"

Rose's knife slipped and cut her finger. The scion lay splintered on the ground. She knew that almost everyone, Dorrick included, thought she faked her spells to get what she wanted.

"Clumsy as ever, aren't you, Rose?" Susa plucked a daisy from her hatband and twirled it. Yellow pollen drifted out. Susa's honey-colored hair swooped low over her ears and twisted up beneath a straw hat with a split brim. The top six buttons were undone on her dress, exposing her throat and, lower, her cleavage. Beneath her left collarbone, a mottled strawberry mark stood out like a brand.

Dorrick, Rose thought, tying her handkerchief around her finger. He and Susa must have been gathering wild honey in the hills, what folks called sweethearts carrying on.

"How can you stand to work in the Bighouse?" asked Opal, who was tall and pale and had chicken feathers stuck in her black hair. "I'd be too scared. Have you seen anything? Or heard anything of . . ."

"Of what?" Rose, still seething, pretended innocence.

"You know what," Susa said.

Rose twirled the knife. "You mean . . . the Thing?"

They nodded, breathless.

"Sure," Rose said. "I've seen it lots of times." Opal's lips parted. Susa's eyes opened wide.

"Tell us," they said together.

"Well . . . I'd like to, but . . ." Rose shook her head. "I'd better not. Mr. Brae trusts me to keep the family secrets."

Susa threw the daisy at her. "Aren't you getting high and mighty all of a sudden, Miss Chandler."

Rose wiped pollen from her lips.

"Well, I'd be careful if I were you," Susa added. "We all know what happens to *fine* ladies up in the Bighouse, don't we? You might end up like Amberly and bear a bastard, too—a mad, misshapen Thing."

An invisible hand squeezed Rose's chest, a spell coming on. Her eyes locked with Susa's—five seconds, ten, until a muscle twitched in Susa's cheek.

"Come on, Opal," Susa said. "Rose Chandler's addled, just like Kalista." They turned and walked down the lane.

Rose leaned forward and took slow breaths, lengthening the exhalations. Sometimes that forestalled a spell. The daisy lay on the ground, its petals torn and twisted. Rose shuddered. Why had Susa said such a terrible thing?

When the tightness in her chest eased, Rose finished cutting the scions. Then she snipped off the top of a young Appelune, keeping the first graft intact. She slit the trunk, inserted the angled end of the Golden Flame scion at the edge, and bound them together with a strip of linen. How strange to be joining trees from the North and South Valley, so that something new could grow in the land. She sealed the graft with softened beeswax.

While she was wrapping the fifth graft, footsteps approached again, but from behind her this time, coming down along the wall. Rose kept her eyes on her work, hoping whoever it was would leave her alone. She needed to finish all the grafting today.

"Why aren't you cleaning my house?" Mr. Brae demanded.

Rose dropped the linen, which uncoiled like a spring.

"It's my half day off, sir," she said.

"Day off! Another week of your slovenly habits, and the house will be a pigsty." He peered at the scion. "What variety is that?"

"Golden Flame, sir."

"Never heard of it."

"The fruit merchant brought samples from the North Valley a few months back."

"Oh, those. You are wasting your time. They are susceptible to insect infection in this climate. And there are compatibility problems with rootstock as well. They will never grow here."

"They might."

"Don't contradict me!" he said, then twirled his walking stick. "Explain."

"I'm using an intermediate graft." She told him her idea, in more depth than she had told anyone else, because, to her surprise, he listened.

"Why didn't Chandler mention this?" Mr. Brae asked when she finished. "This could be profitable. Does he think to deceive me?"

"Oh, no! Pa doesn't think it will work. It's . . . it's my idea."

"Your idea?"

"I have lots of ideas about orcharding."

"Doubtful. Most likely you are thinking about young men and marriage like most flibbertigibbets your age." He watched her wind the linen. "Those branches must have been expensive. Whoever authorized their purchase without my consent will be fined."

"I'm paying with my own money," Rose said. "That's why I took the job in the Bighouse."

He stared. "But—why would you want trees?"

She finished wrapping the graft, thinking of these two snips of wood that would become a tree laden with fruit, and the miracle of that glowed inside her. But she was unable to explain. And never would she tell him about her secret dream to own land, or even about her wish to save Greengarden from ruin.

"It's just, well, the land," she said at last. She nodded toward the flourishing row of Appelunes. "I like to help things grow."

There was a silence.

"My cursed daughter planted the rose garden," he said. "She, too, had a way with growing plants—another of the many gifts she threw away."

Rose softened the beeswax in her hand.

"You look something like her," he added.

"Me?" Rose asked, startled. "But . . . wasn't she beautiful?"

"Extraordinarily. She was beautiful and you are ugly, but in an odd way, when the light falls just so, you resemble her—as that tree's shadow resembles the tree."

Rose dabbed the beeswax onto the graft.

"I have reached a decision." Mr. Brae dug his stick in the dirt. "Since you evidently have too much time on your hands, starting tomorrow you will add the second floor to your housekeeping duties."

She looked up, her eyes wide with fright. The second floor was too close to the Thing.

"But my pa said . . . you promised . . . I wouldn't have to work upstairs."

Mr. Brae raised his eyebrows. "You have only been working for a few weeks. I doubt you have paid for those branches yet."

"No," Rose said slowly. "I'm paying over time."

"Then, unless you wish to lose your job, and thus these—these—trees, you will do whatever I tell you." He walked back along the wall, staring at the perfectly pruned, perfectly trained Appelunes while his buttonless coat flapped in the wind.

4

Amberly

I'm sorry, Rose," her father said early that evening, "but if Mr. Brae wants you to work on the second floor, there's not a thing I can do to change it." He was sitting in the rocker smoking his pipe. Rose sat on the sofa, unwrapping a bundle of muslin.

"He shouldn't have gone back on his word," she said. She pulled away the last of the muslin and handed her father the oval portrait of Amberly.

"Earth's Mercy! Where did you get this?"

"In the drawing room," Rose said. "Under a sheet on the . . . spinet." Mrs. Schill had told her the name of the musical instrument.

Gerald's eyes shone. "I thought Mr. Brae had burned them all."

"I know you and Amberly were friends when you were little," Rose said. "I figured you might like to see it."

Gerald laid his pipe on the barrel end table. "You figured

right. But your ma will be back from her late shift at the dairy any minute. Don't let her see it."

"Why not?" Rose asked. When he did not answer, she leaned over the back of the rocker and looked at the painting. "She looks—sparkly."

"She was. When Amberly was little, she was like a spinning top. We played for hours down in the old oak field. Must have climbed that tree a hundred times." He smiled. "She'd own land one day, and I never would, but it made no difference then."

Rose straightened. Land always made a difference.

"Even after Amberly grew up and got all fine," Gerald said, "she was still kind to me—though by then I could only look at her and . . . Well, you can't change the way of things." He ran his thumb along the tarnished silver rosebuds twining around the frame. "I named you after her," he added; "well, after her favorite flower, anyway."

"I didn't know that," Rose said.

"Neither does your ma—and don't you go telling her." Gerald picked up his pipe, took a puff, and let the smoke stream out.

"When Amberly was a girl—those were good days," he said. "The orchard thriving. And then . . ." He sighed. "After war broke out with the Dalriadas, Mr. Brae took Amberly to the High Council session in Middlefield. He was a council member then. He had to go for the peace talks. But why—" Gerald hit the armrest, and ashes flew from his pipe. "Why did he have to take her?"

"Was the man she ran off with a council member?" Rose asked.

"That's what people said. I think he was one of the negotiators, because after they ran off, the peace talks broke down. I hope this war won't be as bad as that one."

"Why didn't they just get married?"

Gerald shook his head. "All I know is, Mr. Brae tracked

them down. Some say he killed the man. The man wounded him—gave him that limp. After Mr. Brae brought Amberly home, she tried to run away, so he locked her up in the attic."

Rose shuddered, imagining that sparkly little girl trapped in the dark attic while her fists beat against the door, and her cries echoed through the house. But, of course, Amberly would have been a woman by then.

"Amberly Brae betrayed her family," Gerald said harshly as he gave the portrait back to Rose. "She was an indecent woman. And she paid for her wanton ways—with the birth pain. Four days it took."

Rose winced. She had heard those stories. Some people said all the Thing's extra arms and legs had killed Amberly. Others said it was the three heads. Still others said she had died because Mr. Brae in his anger had allowed no midwife, not even her old governess, Emily Harsgrove. He had kept the doors bolted and the women away while his daughter had screamed and screamed.

Someone knocked on the cottage door.

"Hide that," Gerald whispered. Rose stuffed the portrait under the ragged sofa cushion.

"Come in," Gerald called. The door creaked, and when Joff Will stepped in, Rose's hand fluttered up to smooth her braid.

Joff Will was eighteen, a freeman, and as handsome a man as Rose had ever seen. Every young woman on the place, including Rose, fancied him. A man who could not bear the sight of a lost creature or a creature in pain, Joff looked after injured livestock and wild animals in a shed behind the Greentale pears.

"Why, Joff," Gerald said.

Joff took off his hat. His almost white blond hair made his dark eyebrows and lashes look even darker.

"Evening, Mr. Chandler," he said. Most freemen did not use "Mr." when addressing a bondman, even if that bondman was second-boss. Joff nodded politely at Rose, but she knew he did not really see her. "Mr. Terth's in bed with rheumatism again," he said. "And a man's come to see the land Mr. Brae wants to sell. Will you talk to him?"

Rose forgot her shyness. "Mr. Brae is selling more of Greengarden?"

"Just those three rocky acres by the ravine," Gerald said. "They don't amount to much."

"But where will it end?" she asked. "If he keeps selling off bits and pieces?"

Joff looked at her, surprised. "I've wondered that myself."

"Don't worry so much," her father said. He left with Joff, who kept looking at Rose until he was out the door.

She stood silently. The way Joff had stared—was she that ugly? Dorrick was right: no one would ever marry her. But what difference did it make? She did not want to get married; she wanted land. Rose retrieved the portrait of the beautiful little girl from beneath the cushion and looked at it, baffled. They were nothing alike. Amberly had sacrificed everything: her reputation, her family's good name, and, most astounding of all, her land. And in the end, it had killed her.

Why had she done it? Rose polished the frame with a corner of her apron. If she had land, she would not give it up for anything. She turned her head sharply and looked out the window as the two men disappeared into the orchard, dun green now in the fading light.

If she had land . . .

* * *

"Never cross that threshold," Mr. Brae told Rose the next morning. He stood in the second-floor hallway pointing at the dark stairs that led up to the attic.

Rose nodded. She would never go up there. Never. She glanced at the ceiling, fearing it might shake when the Thing lumbered across the attic. The door is thick, she told herself, the door is thick.

"If you do," Mr. Brae said, "I will severely punish you and your family." Then he told her which rooms to clean and which, including his, to leave alone. "Is that clear?" he asked.

"Yes, sir."

"Then why do you look daft?"

"Daft? Oh, I . . ." Rose took a deep breath. "I heard you're selling three acres by the ravine."

"So? Is that any reason for this bovine look?"

"Would you sell one acre to me? And let me buy it over time?"

Mr. Brae stared, then laughed so hard he clasped both hands over the coyote head on his walking stick and doubled over.

"Fool," he said when he straightened at last. "Golden Flame branches are one thing, but you cannot purchase land on a dollar a week."

"But that slope's so steep it isn't worth much, is it?"

"Those three acres are priced at three thousand dollars."

"Three thousand . . . dollars?" Rose asked, astonished.

"You see? Even one acre would take you years to purchase. But amuse me. What did you intend to do with it?" Again he had that appraising gleam in his eyes.

Rose pulled on her fingers and wondered how to explain. Even one steep, rocky acre would be something, would be land, her land. Nobody could tell her what to do with it— imagine! A place where nobody could tell her what to do. She would transform it from sagebrush into a green bounty of food and life. It would be a beginning toward—what? A farm? A bondwoman who wanted her own farm would seem outrageous to him.

"I would terrace it," she said at last. "And grow potatoes—it's perfect for potatoes. Then I'd sell them in town. So I could pay you back lots faster than a dollar a week."

"Potatoes?" Mr. Brae asked. "Potatoes! For a cash crop at Greengarden?" His face turned red and his voice rose. "And disgrace me again? Make me an even bigger laughingstock in Stonewater Vale than you did before?" He swung his walking stick. "Wretched females!"

Rose backed away.

"Always causing trouble!" he shouted. "Always disobeying your father!"

"I'm sorry!" Rose cried. "Never mind. Just stop shouting! Please, stop!"

Mr. Brae blinked rapidly, shook his head as though a wasp were buzzing around it, and then stood with his mouth hanging slack. Without another word, he walked away down the stairs.

Rose sagged to the floor. Why had he yelled at her? What had she done? She scowled at the hall. She hated it here, she hated it all—the dark woodwork, the dusty niches, the metal sconces shaped like the heads of fantastic beasts, each with its candle sprouting like a horn from its forehead. Rose looked down and saw that she was not sitting on the floor at all but on a step, the first step leading to the attic. She jumped up.

Rose tied a kerchief around her nose and mouth, then picked up the broom. She swept hard and fast. For half the night she had lain awake dreaming about those acres, hoping that if she saved every cent, she could buy one. But years! Rose jabbed the broom into a corner. Years for one steep, rocky acre! Imagine how much flat, fertile land would cost. It had been a stupid, stupid dream.

She would never own land.

You can't change the way of things, her father always

said. Bondfolk did not own land, and now she knew why. Anyone with enough money would buy freedom first.

"As soon as I pay off the merchant," she muttered, "I'll never set foot in this awful house again. I'll go back to Donney and the well."

When she had finished cleaning the hall, Rose yanked open a door and saw a small, bright room with a dormer sloping over a single bed. It had a headboard and footboard of curving white wrought iron. Lying on the white quilt was a red straw hat, like a heart on snow. She was tempted to try it on, but the room was sweltering, so she opened the window instead. A breeze blew the lace curtains; they fluttered across wallpaper with rosebuds on a white ground that had dulled, here and there, to ivory. All the furniture was painted white and coated with dust.

Footsteps plodded up the stairs. Rose stiffened—not Mr. Brae again. No, the footsteps were coming from the other direction, coming down the attic stairs. She froze.

A shadow fell across the doorway, and Mrs. Schill slunk into the bedroom. Her straggly brown hair was twisted into a knot. Spatters of egg, milk, and grease stained her apron.

"Frighten you?" she asked.

Rose lowered the kerchief. "A little."

"I bet." Mrs. Schill's lips slid back along her teeth into a smile. "You don't know the meaning of the word. How'd you like to be me? Taking that Thing its food . . . sitting outside its door until it's done slavering . . . " She leaned close, the smell of applejack sour on her breath. "Never knowing when it might break down the door and throttle me with its three arms." She cackled.

"But," Rose said, "I thought its meals went up on the dumbwaiter in the pantry?"

Mrs. Schill ignored this and glanced around the bedroom. "He tell you to clean in here?"

"Yes, ma'am."

"Hmm." Mrs. Schill laid her bony hand on a low chest of drawers that was painted white and decorated with golden curlicues. "I remember the day this folderol came," she said. "Amberly got so wound up she made herself sick. He spoiled her with such things."

"This was her room?" Rose asked.

"Only till she was fifteen. Then she moved to that big room across the hall—the one that's always locked." That was one of the rooms Mr. Brae had told Rose to leave alone.

"I heard the old goat shouting at you again," Mrs. Schill added, looking Rose up and down. "Wonder what he wants with you? You don't look like much. Not a curve on you, not like poor, pretty Beth." She smiled slyly. "Know why Beth had to leave?"

"Pa said she got married."

"Yes. Yes, she had to—quick."

Rose stared. "You mean . . ."

"You'll find out soon enough—in four or five months, sure as the cock crows." Mrs. Schill laughed and left the room.

Outside, a bluejay squawked, a woman scolded a child, and a wagon creaked; all of these sounds tumbled into a din in Rose's mind. Had Mr. Brae gotten Beth with child? Rose remembered the appraising gleam in his eye and then her mother's unfinished warning: *Why, once when I was younger, he tried to . . .* And Susa: *You might bear a bastard, too—a mad, misshapen Thing.*

On top of the chest of drawers, a white handprint gleamed where Mrs. Schill had lifted the dust away. Rose grabbed her duster and obliterated the print. Her mother had taught her to clean from the top down, so Rose dragged a chair to the wardrobe and climbed up. She whisked the top so fast that a fine, grey cloud rose like a ghost. Then the duster bumped something near the back—a wad of cloth wedged between the wall and wardrobe. She seesawed it up and out.

It was linen, a sampler worked with an oak tree and a border of oak leaves. Six identical brass buttons lined up across the top. Below them, words were cross-stitched in pink:

> If a young lady is good and meek,
> She obeys her elders without a peep.
> If she bends her self to wiser wills,
> Then with sweet love her heart soon fills.
> —A.

This had been crossed out with a big X stitched in red. Above the tree, in rough, red needlework, were the words:

> If a woman chooses her own path,
> she lights a candle
> with the moon.
> If a woman shines darkly bright,
> she sees with her breath,
> her soul, her heart.
> If a woman beholds the well of life,
> she loves with its same
> starry depth.
> If a woman loves with her soul's dance,
> She leaps every mountain
> Between her and her beloved.
> If a woman chooses, shines, beholds, and loves,
> Then, in her midnight hour,
> Love will be her Light.
> —A.

Below Amberly's initial was a big crystal button with a black rim. Rose tilted the sampler and watched the light chase across the crystal. Then a board creaked in the ceiling, only six inches from her head. She crushed the sampler. The creak came again. Was she dreaming? Rose looked up at the ceiling—the floor of the attic—where something thudded and dragged, thudded and dragged.

The Thing was above her.

Rose jumped off the chair. She ran into the hall, tore down the stairs, and wrenched open the front door, forgetting that bondfolk were forbidden to use it. She burst onto the porch, then ran past the rose garden and out through the gate. Even in the orchard, she kept running, first through the Penna pears, then through the Redheart apples, until at last she reached the old northwest well that irrigated the bondfolk's vegetable plots. There a little girl was leading an ox—harnessed to a boom connected to the pump—around in a circle.

"Go home," Rose told her.

"Huh?"

"Go!" Rose shouted and grabbed the halter. The girl ran off.

"Come on, Donney." Rose urged the old ox forward. "It's me! It's me!"

She led him around the circle. The boom was like the spoke in a great wheel, turning the pump, pulling the water up through the cracks in the earth. And around again she led him—five times, fifty times she retraced her steps, leaving footprints, obliterating footprints, until her entire self was contained safely there in the deepening circle of mud. Nothing outside existed. Only the rope rasping her palm. Only the *plop*, then the ripe steam of Donney's droppings. Only the squelching of his hooves.

She would never go back, never. Here she was safe.

Yet, at the center of the circle was the dark well, which, in spite of all she could do, kept pulling her in, pulling her downward.

5

A Terrible Proposal

One night, after another two weeks had passed, Rose shut the kitchen door of the Bighouse behind her and stepped out onto the dark porch. She had returned to her job in the Bighouse after all, even though each day was a struggle, because she could not bear to lose the Golden Flames—especially now that her dream of owning land was gone forever. The loss still stuck in her throat like a lump that she could not swallow.

She clung to the porch rail, annoyed that Mr. Brae had made her stay late to clean up pages he had torn from old books. Which route home would be worse? The path through the front yard, where the Thing might see her from the window, or the back lane, where she would be out longer in the dark?

Her answer came as the full moon reared above the eastern hills. Rose pulled her shawl over her head to hide from the horrible white face, then cut through the front yard, hurrying past the roses, which had burst into bloom with the long June days. Thorns spiked like wildcat teeth. When she turned to close the gate, Rose did not look at the round window. She had heard the thud–drag three more times since she had cleaned Amberly's room, but instead of fleeing the house, she had hidden in the hall closet.

Now Rose ran toward the orchard. As soon as the trees enclosed her, their leaves concealing the moon, she slowed to a walk. Her heart kept pounding until she saw the cottage, where ribs of light splintered through the cracks in the shutters. She opened the door. Her parents, who were sitting at the table, stopped talking. Maggie looked up, her raisin eyes dazed and bright above her fat cheeks.

"Rose." Gerald cleared his throat.

"Sorry I'm too late to help with supper and washing up, Ma," Rose said. "Mr. Brae kept me."

"That's all right, Rose honey." Maggie waved one hand. "We're eating late tonight."

Rose frowned. Usually her mother would have been banging pots and scolding if she had to do all the cooking and washing up herself. And Maggie never called her "honey."

"But it's after eight," Rose said. "What's going on?"

"We need to talk," Maggie said just as Dorrick's boots clomped outside.

Gerald glanced at the door. "It had better wait until after supper."

Rose sniffed. "Something's burning."

"My biscuits!" Maggie cried and bustled to the oven.

All through supper, Rose wondered what she had done wrong. Had Mr. Brae complained about her—or, worse, learned that she had sat on the attic threshold? *If you do, I will severely punish you and your family.* Had her father lost his job as second-boss because of her? But would her mother be glowing if Mr. Brae was about to evict them from the cottage? Gerald neither talked nor looked at anyone, and he made boxes out of his mashed potatoes instead of eating them.

"Have more bacon, Rose honey," Maggie said. "Fried it up special for you."

"I've had plenty, Ma. Thanks."

"You need more meat on those birdy bones. Eat up." Maggie plunked three more strips, charred in some places and white in others, onto Rose's plate.

"I've something to say," Maggie added. "You young ones listen. Me and your pa have your best interests in mind—though you might not see it. You two should put the good of the family first, too. No matter what." She wagged one finger, a little out of breath. "No matter what. Me and your pa do."

Rose put her fork down. A chill crept over her.

"What's wrong with you, Ma?" asked Dorrick, spearing a chunk of raw turnip on his knife. "You forget how to cook? And you're babbling so much I can't get a word in edgewise."

"Never you mind," Maggie said. "Not everything's your business."

Dorrick rolled his eyes and then looked at Gerald. "A group of men from Stonewater are riding north to join the army fighting the Dalriadas. I'm going to ask Mr. Brae if I can go."

"No!" Maggie cried.

"What?" Gerald asked, looking up from his plate. "Oh, that. No, you're not going."

Dorrick scowled. "But we've got to stop the barbarians before they get any farther south. They're raiding every week. They're defiling Valley women—think of the half-bloods."

"Abominations!" Maggie shuddered. "They'll have to be done away with."

"I want to help, Pa." Dorrick leaned forward.

"I said no." Gerald slathered butter on a burnt biscuit. "You're too hot-headed. Besides, I need you here."

"Right here," Maggie echoed.

"But I'm good with a bow," Dorrick said. "I could pick off dozens of the worms."

"You're talking about killing people," Gerald said. "Different from us, and enemies, yes, but still people. Call things what they are." He glanced at Rose, tore off a chunk of biscuit, and chewed it fast.

"People!" Dorrick scoffed. "Red-haired barbarians with horns growing from their heads? People? Who eat raw human flesh?"

Rose looked at a gobbet of curly white bacon fat and put her hand to her mouth. The room spun. The pewter plates above the mantel whirled; curving lines of silver light reflected off their rims.

Gerald threw the biscuit onto his plate. He stared at it, then picked it up and ate the rest in one bite.

"Pa, listen—" Dorrick said.

"Blighted Earth!" Gerald swore, crumbs spewing from his mouth. "Enough! You wouldn't know what to do! You wouldn't know what was best!"

Rose stared at him. Maggie's hand stopped halfway to her mouth. Dorrick slammed down his cup, and milk frothed over the table. He pushed back the bench so hard that Rose had to grab it to keep from falling off. Then he stomped out of the cottage.

"Just as well," Maggie said. "Now we can talk." She nudged Gerald, but he was watching the milk drip over the edge of the table.

"Gerald?" Maggie prompted.

He did not answer.

"Well." Maggie heaved herself up. "Dishes first, then."

Usually Gerald cleared the dishes, but tonight he lit his pipe and sat smoking at the table. Maggie washed. Rose dried, turning the plates beneath the cloth until every drop was gone. Even then, she clung to them, comforted by their familiarity, their earthenware brown, their weight in her hands. When all the dishes were put away, Maggie plopped down beside Gerald.

"Rose," she said, "you scrub that shelf much more, there'll be no wood left."

"I'm coming." Rose wrung out the washrag and sat down across from her parents.

There was a silence.

"Mr. Brae came to see us today," Gerald said at last.

"I knew it!" Rose exclaimed. "I've done nothing wrong, Pa. I—"

Gerald held up one hand. "No one said so. As a matter of fact, I'd say you've made quite an . . . impression on him." Gerald paused. "He's made you a proposal."

"A proposal?"

Gerald nodded, blowing a smoke ring into the air. "Of marriage."

"Of . . . marriage!" Rose exclaimed. "Me? But I couldn't. I'm too young to get married. Besides, Mr. Brae's way too old for me and he's a landowner and I'm bonded and . . ." Her stomach shifted as she pictured his sardonic eyes. "Oh, and I couldn't."

"You'll be fifteen in two weeks," Maggie said. "Lots of girls get married at that age. I did." She smiled at Gerald, but he did not look at her.

"No." Rose crossed her arms. "I'd throw myself in the well before I'd marry Mr. Brae. He's horrible."

Gerald stood up and walked to the sink. With his back toward them, he pumped water into a cup. When the cup was full, he kept pumping while water spilled over and over into his hand. Finally he drank the water down in one long swallow—as though it were whiskey.

He turned toward Maggie. "Maybe—"

"It's best, Gerald." She pursed her lips.

Gerald sighed and sat down again. "You wouldn't be marrying Mr. Brae—exactly. He made the proposal for . . . his grandson."

"His grandson?" Rose frowned. "But he hasn't got a grandson."

"I'm afraid he does," Gerald said.

Rose looked from one of her parents to the other. "You mean . . . you can't mean . . ."

They would not look at her.

"Earth's Mercy." Rose grabbed the table. The world seemed to be falling away, as though the cottage had no walls, as though she were outside, alone, naked in the dark under the blazing moon—no, two moons, for a second moon smoldered beneath the first. The invisible hand squeezed her chest. Each beat of her heart shook her body. She laughed wildly and chanted like a child, "Marry the Thing! Marry the Thing! Nah! Nah! Nah!"

"Calm yourself," Maggie said. "You'll have a spell."

"A spell! A spell!" Rose cried. "A magic spell—so the ugly rose can marry a monster!" She coughed. "What a good joke!"

"It's no joke." Gerald shook his head. "It wouldn't be so bad once you got used to . . . it," he said, exchanging a glance with Maggie. "Really. I'm sure it wouldn't be."

"But why should I marry the Thing?" Rose's voice grew shrill. "And why would it want to marry me? Will it get down on one knee to propose? Three knees? Does it even have a knee? Why, why should I marry it?"

"Several reasons," Gerald said. "The first is that Mr. Brae wants an heir."

Rose stared at him, but he was watching the smoke curl from his pipe. She turned to her mother, but Maggie was fiddling with her apron strap. Had everyone gone mad? Not just marry the Thing, then, but actually lie with it, lie with a monster? Bands came winding around Rose's chest, wrapping tighter and tighter, like a winding-sheet. Why did they want her to die? What had she done to deserve this?

"If Mr. Brae wants an heir," she said, "he can get married again himself."

"Can't," Maggie said. "He's tried. No landed woman will have him 'cause of the . . . his grandson."

"They're afraid their babies might be deformed, too," Gerald said. "There's bad blood in the Brae line."

"And Mr. Brae's too proud to marry beneath him," Maggie added.

"I know this sounds crazy," Gerald said. "We were shocked at first, too. But think, Rose." He leaned forward and looked straight into her eyes. "You would be the Mistress of Greengarden."

"What?" Rose whispered. Her hands opened on her lap, then her fingers opened, as well, as if to hold what she had heard. *The Mistress of Greengarden?* If she was Mistress of Greengarden, she could save the orchard. She would own land, and not just any land, but Greengarden itself! Then the thud–drag of the Thing lumbered through her mind and her hands closed. How could she save Greengarden if she was dead?

"You would be free, Rose," Gerald added. "Free."

"Us, too," Maggie said. "He'll free us all. Think—my Dorrick a freeman! And Mr. Brae will make your pa first-boss."

"Pa . . . first-boss?" Rose echoed, more afraid than before. The change in her family's fortunes would be staggering—too staggering. Something had to be wrong, somewhere, because she was not worth all this. Yet, how could she stand against such bribes?

"There's more," Maggie said, smiling. "We get the Guest-house—with all the furnishings! Mr. Brae took me over. Tables, carpets, draperies, lamps, and oh, the prettiest little chair with—"

"Furnishings!" Rose exclaimed. "You'd see me die in exchange for a house and some stupid furniture?"

Maggie turned pink.

"A pretty chair for an ugly daughter!" Rose shouted. "Who got the better bargain, Ma?"

"Now, Rose—" Gerald said.

Rose stood. She stared at her parents; they seemed like strangers.

"You're serious," she said. "You want me to marry a monster. How do you know it can even have children? How do you know they won't be monsters, too?"

A drop of sweat smeared Gerald's forehead. "Mr Brae says his grandson—"

"Why are you calling it his 'grandson' all of a sudden?" Rose's breath grew ragged. "It's always been *the Thing*. Isn't that what you told me when I was little? 'Go to bed, Rose, or *the Thing* will get you. Eat your mush, Rose, or *the Thing* will eat you.' " She kicked the table. "But now that you want me to marry it, you're pretending it isn't a monster. Then why is it locked up? It will kill me!"

"It won't," Gerald began, "Mr. Brae promised—"

"Curse Mr. Brae!" Rose shouted. "I'm sick to death of Mr. Brae! I won't marry the Thing—ever!"

She ran into her room. She lunged toward her bed, but her feet slipped. She reached up, falling, rushing into a realm without air, where the spell swallowed her.

6

The Spell

"L ight," Rose called in her delirium late that night. "More light."

Her parents dragged three benches into her room. They lined them with candles—tapers and pillars of tallow and beeswax—round ones, square ones, tall ones, short ones; the candles Rose had dipped and molded and rolled. She called for more, always more, until she lay in bed guarded by a wall of flame. All through the dead hours, she watched her room tremble with light. She thought nothing, felt nothing. There was no room inside of her for that; there was barely room for her breath to rasp in and out. Only the force of her will kept the flames from dying, kept the dark at bay.

She heard a creak. Her mother moved her massive body into the bedroom doorway and stood silently. Maggie was watching the light, too—for fear of fire. When dawn came, Rose slept fitfully through the day, weakened by the spell. She ate nothing. At dusk, she woke to another night of silence and flame.

Rose blinked. Then sunlight from the window fell across her hand. It was morning. She sat up, exhausted and hungry, and was startled by the sight of the melted gobs of wax crusting the benches. She stayed in bed all day while Maggie dosed her with barley soup, plumped her pillows, and piled on blankets until Rose lay sweltering in the June heat. No one mentioned the proposal. By the third morning, Rose felt stronger. She sat on the edge of her bed and reached for a black stocking. When it was halfway up, she drew her leg to her chest, pressed her forehead to her knee, and rocked.

During breakfast, she ate her griddle cakes while Dorrick talked about the latest Dalriada attack—in Larch, a town only fifteen miles north.

"Mr. Brae picked eight volunteers to join the South Valley Defense," Dorrick said. "And I'm one. You can't stop me going now, Pa."

"Seems not," Gerald said. "I don't know why he's sending so many. We'll be shorthanded, for guards and work. This war has thrown everything into an uproar. In town yesterday, Jord had to wait hours to get the horses shod because the blacksmith was too busy making spearheads and shields for the army."

"We're going to win, Pa," Dorrick said. "You'll see."

"Don't tell your ma you're going yet—she's got enough on her mind." Gerald glanced at Rose.

"I'll find out if the barbarians really have horns," Dorrick said. Rose shuddered. Dorrick turned toward her, grinning. "And blood dripping from their fangs," he added as Maggie walked out of the larder.

"Breakfast sitting easy, Rose honey?" Maggie asked.

"So-so," Rose said.

Dorrick eyed her. "Wish I could get out of work as much as you do, Wheezer." And, clutching his chest, he pretended to choke while his tongue lolled from side to side. "I can't breathe! Help me! Oh! Oh!"

"Shut your mouth!" Maggie slapped him hard. "You know nothing of what it is to be a woman! Nothing!"

Dorrick's jaw dropped as a spidery red blotch crawled over his cheek. Rose's own cheek tingled in sympathy. She had felt that slap many times, but she had never seen her mother strike Dorrick before.

"I pity your poor Susa," Maggie said. "Do you hear me? Pity her. Now get out!" Dorrick grabbed his work gloves, stomped toward the door, and slammed it behind him.

For the first time in days, Maggie met Rose's eyes, but Rose looked back at her plate. However guilty her mother might be feeling now, Rose knew that her mother did not like her and never had. An ugly daughter was a sore trial for a woman who craved pretty things.

A few minutes later, Rose left for her day's work. The nearer she came to the Bighouse, the more her arms and legs ached, as if she were lugging buckets of rock uphill. When the Bighouse came in sight, her eyes locked on the barred round window. Her mind jolted out of blankness, and she turned and ran.

Marry the Thing! Marry the Thing! The words shouted inside her, and she clapped her hands over her ears.

"Oh, stop, stop!" she cried. "Make it stop." She ran up Coyote Road toward the sagebrush flat above the orchard. Whorls of dust kicked up by her feet billowed behind her and settled on the sagebrush. Without irrigation, the land dulled into tan, olive, umber. A cow lowed in the distance. Wind creaked through the spiked grass that drove sharp seeds through her stockings. When she reached the top and looked down, Greengarden in all its glory lay below her.

Acres of fruit trees rolled out as if they were nubby emerald stitches on Amberly's sampler—all crisscrossed with brown roads. On one of them, a group of men crowded around an overturned wagon. To the south, near the shacks where the bondfolk lived, a girl chased a goat with a red shirt flapping from its mouth. The Faredge Wall looked like a narrow line a child had drawn as part of a game. Rose looked at the barns, corrals, and work sheds, the cottages of the freefolk, the Bighouse with its roses like jewels.

She could be mistress of all this, Mistress of Greengarden. After Mr. Brae died, she could restore the orchard, make it thrive as it had when her father was young. She could renovate the irrigation system, replace old sprawling trees with new varieties planted close and low, correct the pruning . . . Then Rose tried to imagine Susa, Opal, and Mrs. Schill calling her mistress or Mrs. Brae. The people would never accept her. Didn't Mr. Brae realize that? Besides, she would die before him; the Thing would kill her. And yet . . . If Mr. Brae believed the Thing could father an heir, then he must also believe it would not kill her.

Across the valley, the silver vein of the Mirandin River throbbed like the pulse in her throat. Rose felt as if she were the land, the land wakened and looking at itself. This unimaginable marriage was her only hope to own land. She would never earn enough to buy a single acre. But the price. Rose forced herself to look at the attic window. The sun glittered off the glass, shooting Susa's words straight into her soul.

"Earth's Mercy," Rose whispered. "What if I have a monster, too?" What if the Thing begat another Thing and she died birthing it just as Amberly had? Her baby—a monster? Mad? Misshapen? Rose bit her knee, tasted dust on her skirt. No. She would not marry the Thing, not for land, not to save Greengarden, not even for . . .

Her family. "Put the family first," her mother had said. "No matter what." Rose groaned. The Guesthouse, first-boss, freedom—each blessing was another stone dropped into a sack to drown a kitten. Compared to so much good fortune, the life of one ugly, nervous girl who feared the dark was a small sacrifice. And if she refused, what would her life be worth afterward? Every day her family would look at her and think, But for her we would be free.

Behind Rose, a meadowlark burst into song in the bitterbrush. She jumped to her feet, startled. A Dalriada might be aiming at her even now. Although she had never dared explore the foothills behind the flat, Rose knew there were hundreds of canyons where the barbarians might hide. She looked north. Beyond the foothills, the Red Mountains encrusted the horizon. The snow-covered peaks, baring here and there a ridge of red rock, looked like teeth streaked with blood. How could anyone live in such desolation? How could anyone live away from the Valley?

Rose hurried down Coyote Road, averting her eyes from every pine tree, every knoll and bush, because a Dalriada might leap out from behind it. Back in the orchard, she walked among the Penna pear trees and frowned at the water sprouts growing from gnarled nodes on the branches. They reminded her of old Erdin's hands, clawed with bone-ache, swollen at every joint. With proper care, the trees could yield three times the fruit.

She came out of the orchard near the Faredge Wall and squinted in the sun bombarding her family's garden. Here she had played as a toddler, poking seeds into the soil, constructing miniature stick orchards complete with irrigation canals. When she turned seven, she had begged for her own corner. Each year she had experimented, expanded, until now she grew the best garden on the orchard. Yet, in spite of her success, Rose still had to argue with her family about every new idea.

She scooped up a handful of the rich valley-bottom soil, shaped it into a patty, and took a bite. When she was little, her parents had threatened and cajoled her to break her habit of eating earth. *It's dark in your belly. Swallow it and the*

Thing will swallow you. Rose spit out the dirt and grabbed a hoe. She attacked the weeds skulking through the carrots. An hour passed while she worked and worried and cried.

"Women are always too stupid to know what is good for them," said a voice.

Rose looked up and saw Mr. Brae standing with one hand on his hip.

"Do you want more?" he asked. "Is that it? Or are you too feebleminded to understand what I am offering you?"

"I understand." She straightened, her sweat-soaked dress pulling along her back.

"Then what is the problem? Isn't it worth a little unpleasantness? Believe me, the prospect disgusts me as much as it apparently does you." He turned sideways to her. "This is what I have come to! Bribing worthless bondfolk to get an heir! Why should I care? Let Greengarden go to blazes."

Rose pulled a weed.

"But then, then, without an heir," Mr. Brae muttered, "the cursed Village Council will get their hands on it—Landers, Dakken, Dean. I will not give them the satisfaction. I will not let her win."

Her? Rose wiped her face with the back of her hand. Whom did he mean?

"You've been planning this since I first came to work in the Bighouse," she said. "Why me?"

"I told you your ugliness had a purpose. No one will suspect—or care if they do. If I had chosen Susa, that voluptuous bitch—you see? A riot on my hands. But no man will mourn an ugly girl wed to a monster."

"But there are other ugly girls," Rose said. "Why me?"

"I have watched you." Mr. Brae jerked his head toward the garden, then pointed his walking stick at the Faredge Wall. "I have seen what you have accomplished here—despite the interference of idiots. You have a strong instinct for the land and for farming. That instinct will strengthen the Brae bloodline."

Startled, Rose leaned on the hoe. He wanted her skill? Then she would not have to wait until he died to start improving Greengarden.

"I must have an heir," he said. "And you are the only person who satisfies all my requirements. Parents who can be bribed. A conscience. Ugliness. The right agricultural instinct. And—here we come to the crux"—he bent and picked up a handful of dirt—"you have a secret wish that only I can fulfill."

Rose stared.

"I know you," he said. "I know what you want down in that timid heart of yours. What a presumption for you even to have imagined it."

She felt something hard in her throat.

Mr. Brae held out the handful of dirt. "You want Greengarden."

How had he known?

"The perfect bait for you, isn't it? But there is only one way you can get it. So the only question is, What is stronger? Your hunger for land, or your fear of"—he smiled—"of monsters?"

Her lips pressed together, Rose lifted the hoe over her head.

Mr. Brae laughed. "Your struggle is extraordinarily entertaining. Like a mouse after cheese, aren't you, but afraid of the cat?"

She hacked a clump of pigweed, wishing it were his foot, then raised the hoe again.

"You are different from my whore of a daughter," Mr. Brae said.

Rose stopped the hoe in midair. She looked at him, but he was gazing south toward the Red Cameo apples.

"Amberly gave up Greengarden." Mr. Brae swept his hand in a circle, and the dirt flew out. "She gave up all this—unthinkable! For a disgusting love. You, however, are willing to give up all hope of love for this."

Rose stood completely still. Love? She looked at the woolly hills, at the carrot tops frothy as green lace, at the Appelunes with their shadows rippling over the stone wall, and at the tiny stick grafts that would someday burst into Golden Flames. She thought of Amberly's sampler. *If a woman chooses her own path . . . If a woman loves with her soul's dance, she leaps every mountain between her and her beloved.*

Mr. Brae was wrong. Rose was not different from Amberly at all. They were the same. Amberly had loved a man; Rose loved Greengarden.

She put down the hoe. A crumb of earth had stuck near the corner of her mouth. With the tiniest flick of her tongue, Rose licked it off and swallowed.

7

The Covenant of the Earth

Y ou look pretty," Maggie lied three weeks later as she pushed one last hairpin into the garland of wildflowers on Rose's head. "Prettiest bride ever." She turned Rose toward the mirror, and the white ribbons hanging from the back of the garland swirled out. "Look."

Rose did. She wore a made-over blue dress of her mother's—needle holes showed where the old seams had been ripped out. However, Maggie had done wonders with tiers of ruffles along the skirt, and puffs and tucks across the bodice. Above that sea of blue froth, Rose saw a girl with a wide mouth and pinched brown eyes, a scrawny girl, a girl who looked far too young to be getting married. Her thin hair, which Maggie had bound in rag curlers last night, was swept up in a ridiculous gob on her head. Rose blinked at herself. Without eyelashes, her eyelids made her look frog-like—ugly.

Maggie smoothed the apple blossoms she had embroidered around the neckline. "I'm the best seamstress in Stonewater Vale, if I do say so," she said. "Isn't she fine, Gerald?"

He did not turn from the window. "That's my daughter."

"She won't be wearing hand-me-downs much longer. Soon our Rose will be dressed like them"—Maggie winked at the painting above the sofa—"in velvets and lace."

Rose shook her head. She did not want fancy clothes, only Greengarden.

"It's time." Gerald picked up two burlap sacks: one held Rose's belongings; the other, the candles that she had spent the last weeks frantically making.

Rose turned and tripped over a crate filled with dishes her mother had bought from Mrs. Willow. Three more crates stood around the room, all packed for the move to the Guesthouse. Everything was changing too fast—even she had changed. She was fifteen now, and in a few minutes she would be married, married to . . . She shut her eyes.

"You're sure about the papers?" Maggie asked Gerald. "Sure everything's signed and proper?" Regardless of the cost, she had insisted that Councilman Dean, a member of the Village Council in Stonewater, draw up the marriage papers.

"Yes," Gerald said. "I've told you ten times already."

"Well then," Maggie said, her voice pitched high. "Mustn't be late, right, Rose honey?"

Outside, Maggie took Rose's left arm, Gerald her right; Dorrick followed behind. As they walked through the orchard, Rose wanted to break away and run—back to the cottage, up to the canyon, over to the Faredge Wall—anywhere but where she was going. The wind blew hard. Rose placed one foot in front of the other and imagined she was leading Donney around the northwest well. Each of her footprints spoke a word in her mind: land, land, land.

When the Bighouse came in sight, Rose gasped. Over a hundred people swarmed around the path—and not only people from Greengarden.

"You told!" Rose turned to Dorrick. "Nobody was supposed to know the day!"

"I didn't tell anybody," he said. "But you couldn't expect something this crazy to stay a secret."

Maggie twitched her skirt. "You hold your head high. Before sunset, you'll be their mistress."

"Oh, Ma!" Rose whispered. "You didn't . . ."

"It's my right," Maggie said. "To have my friends see my one girl married. See her so important."

The fifty feet between the orchard and the picket fence seemed like the longest distance that Rose had ever walked in her life. Usually the folk cheered a bride going to her bridegroom, but now everyone was silent. Their glances devoured her. Something crunched beneath her shoes. Corn, dried corn—for fertility. Horrified, Rose looked up. The attic window watched like a dead eye. With a lurch, then a grating sound, the curving black bars seemed to turn, pulling her in, whispering, "Tonight, you will be inside . . ."

"The poor babe!" old Erdin, in her wrinkled brown dress, wept into her wrinkled brown arm. Mrs. Willow dabbed her eyes with her handkerchief. The wind whipped the white ribbons around Rose's face, and she felt like a cow being led to slaughter. Some of the young men, like Kurt Sowerbee with his sneer, eyed her with the same hungry look they gave every bride, but others stood with their arms slack, their Adam's apples sliding up and down.

"She's so young," Bartla said.

"Sew black! Sew black!" cried crazy Kalista. "Stitch a vision on her poor, bare back!"

A little boy screamed, "Mama, the Thing's gonna eat her!"

Rose stumbled.

Joff Will stepped in front of her and took off his hat.

"Marry me," he said.

"What?" Rose asked.

"Don't do this." Joff hunched one shoulder at the Big-house. "Marry me instead."

Opal shrieked, as did several other girls in the crowd.

Rose stared up at him. She felt as though the sun had risen and cracked the ice in her chest, felt as though her lungs had suddenly room to breathe. The finest young man on the place, a man who could probably marry any girl he chose, wanted her? Of all the strange things that had happened in the past weeks, this seemed the strangest.

Something jabbed her ribs—Maggie's elbow. Although Rose would be freed if she married Joff, her family would not.

"Thank you," Rose told him. "It's very kind of you, but—"

"Everything's set," Maggie interrupted.

Joff looked only at Rose. "I mean it," he said and held out a rough brown hand.

Rose stared at it. How easy it would be to stretch out her hand and take his. Then she pictured that brown hand stroking an injured robin she had once taken him. She half smiled, shook her head. If only he had asked out of love rather than pity. She would marry only for love, and she loved Greengarden, not Joff, not really.

"Why do you want to die?" he asked her. "And you—" He turned to Gerald. "How can you? Using her. You should be ashamed!"

The crowd buzzed.

"Move aside, Joff," Gerald said.

"Not unless Rose says so. It's her choice."

She stood, speechless. A man was fighting for her? Risking his job for her?

"I . . . I'm sorry," she said. "Really. But thanks." Joff stood a moment longer, then turned and walked away fast.

"I'll remember this," Gerald called after him. Rose

watched him disappear into the orchard, his blond hair a white flame. She would remember, too.

"Is this going to take all day?" Dorrick asked. Rose walked on with her family until at last the gate in the picket fence swung open.

"Long life!" Mrs. Schill threw a handful of red petals that spattered against Rose's skirt. Rose entered the yard, but when the latch clicked shut behind her, she felt a spasm in her side. Up on the porch stood Mr. Brae and Councilman Dean.

"I welcome a new daughter to this house." Mr. Brae muttered the ritual words and shoved a rose, a Cur King, into her hand. They all went inside.

Maggie's eyes dilated as she glanced toward the staircase. "This heat. I'm worn out." She dropped Rose's arm. "Think I'll wait down here until the ceremony's done."

"I'd better stay with Ma," Dorrick said. He sidled toward the dining room, where Mrs. Schill had arranged the wedding feast on a white linen tablecloth. A stuffed, roasted goose lay on its back.

Mr. Brae started up the stairs, followed by Councilman Dean, then Rose, and last, her father. They crossed the second-floor hallway, watched by the beast-headed sconces with their unlit tapers. When they reached the bottom of the attic stairs—the threshold Mr. Brae had warned her never to cross—Rose stopped. She put one hand on the wall and bent her head.

"Rose?" Gerald touched her shoulder. Everyone stopped.

"Just catching my breath," she said. She hoped to get through the ceremony without having a spell, but her lungs felt frozen again. She crossed her fingers and crossed the threshold.

At the landing halfway up, the stairway turned. Rose glanced into the gloom ahead, then focused on the councilman's shoes; both heels had been burnished to a shine. She willed the stairs to go on forever. She could climb forever—lifting one leg and then the other—she would never tire, never balk like Donney, if only the stairs would go on forever. But, traitorous, heartless, they stopped. There, looming at the end of a short, dark hallway, stood the oak door.

Two padlocks secured it, one near the top and one near the bottom. An iron bar ran across the middle. Above the bar was a square window of iron about six inches wide. Rose's skin prickled, and she cast about in her mind, suddenly lost. How had this happened? How had it all begun? What had brought her here to this door, about to marry a monster?

"Proceed," Mr. Brae said.

Councilman Dean turned to Rose. "Are you certain that no one is forcing you to do this?"

"She is," Mr. Brae and Gerald said together.

"Blighted Earth, I asked her!" The councilman's eyes were crinkled at the corners, perhaps from years of laughing and smiling, but he was not smiling now. "Speak freely," he urged.

"No," Rose whispered. "No. No one's forced me."

The councilman sighed. "As you wish. I think, all things considered, the short ceremony will do. The heat is suffocating, Circel. Isn't there any air up here? Doesn't the creature need fresh air?"

"Its comfort does not interest me." Mr. Brae reached inside his collar and pulled out a golden chain with two keys on the end. While he fumbled with them, Rose glanced around the hall. She smelled mold. Her shoulders hunched; mold could cause a spell. Was it the Thing's stench? Then she saw the black streaks on the walls.

Mr. Brae at last unlocked the iron window. As he swung it sideways, Rose held her breath, expecting some grotesque face to lunge forward, but all she saw was another sheet of iron set a few inches back.

"You!" Mr. Brae called, rapping on the door with his walking stick. "Thing! Come forward."

Something dragged across the attic, thudded and dragged, lumbering closer and closer. Rose pressed against the wall.

"You may begin, Councilman," Mr. Brae said.

"Today we have come together in the bounty and law of the Valley to join in marriage a landowner of Greengarden, Raymont Brae—"

Raymont! Rose blinked. The Thing had a name?

"—and Rose Selene Chandler, a bondwoman of Green-garden, hereafter a landowner. This covenant is witnessed and blessed by the Earth."

Gerald threw a clod of dirt against the door.

"Raymont Brae, raise your right—" Councilman Dean stopped. "That is, raise any . . . hand in sign you swear to the marriage."

Rose watched the window, spellbound. A rasping noise filled the hot, heavy air, as if something slid through a tunnel. A fist thrust in front of the far sheet of iron. It uncurled, blossoming into a white hand with five perfectly shaped, slender fingers. There it hovered, the palm facing forward.

It had no claws or fur, no deformities of any kind—only a red smudge along the middle knuckle of the index finger. And yet Rose backed up until she bumped against her father. The hand looked as if it had been severed at the wrist, a disembodied appendage that was still alive.

Councilman Dean spoke. "Rose Chandler, raise your right hand in sign you swear to the marriage."

She switched the rose to her left hand and raised her right one.

"What on Earth . . ." the councilman said. Both he and Mr. Brae were staring at Rose's hand. She turned her head and saw blood trickling down where the thorns had pierced her palm. Her knees folded . . .

. . . *And she was sliding down a fold of velvet, soft and*

dark and red. She landed with a bump, only to shoot side-
ways down another velvety fold. Bumping, rolling, sliding,
she spiraled inward as the folds tightened and shortened until
she was caught in a whirling funnel. Far below, through a
crack in its black heart, she saw a gleam—a shining wall, a
pool of silver, a green flame, a hand of bone . . .

"Catch her!"

"She's fainting!"

Rose felt a sting against her cheek and opened her eyes. The red haze cleared.

"Circel!" Councilman Dean exclaimed. "There was no need to slap her."

"It woke her, didn't it?" Mr. Brae asked.

Rose blinked. She was still on her feet, but her father was holding her.

"I'm all right," Rose said. "I'm sorry."

"Let's finish this so we all can get some air," Councilman Dean said. "The ring?"

Mr. Brae held out a rusty iron band. "I found this washer on an old broken plow," he said. "It's a good enough ring for a bondwoman." And he flipped the washer to Rose. She caught it. The washer fit her finger perfectly.

In the final part of the ceremony, the bride and groom were supposed to join hands, and Rose knew she could not do it. Not for Greengarden, not for her family's freedom, not for her life itself could she touch that cold, white thing. She bowed her head.

"I . . . I proclaim you married," Councilman Dean said in a rush.

Rose slumped against her father.

"Get back," Mr. Brae said to the Thing—no, to Raymont, her husband. Rose heard the rasping again, then a slam as Mr. Brae shut the iron window.

"Good girl," Gerald said, wiping sweat from his fore-head. "That wasn't so bad, now was it?"

Councilman Dean curled his lip.

Downstairs, Rose collapsed into a chair by the dining table. Her hair straggled over her forehead; heat and sweat had vanquished the false curls.

"Won't you stay and dine?" Mr. Brae asked Councilman Dean after the final papers were signed. Mr. Brae pulled his finely tailored jacket together, but it fell open again, because it had no buttons.

"Thank you, but I have . . . other business." The councilman came over to Rose, looked at her ring, and then pulled on his earlobe. "A washer? Circel, your insults never cease to astonish me."

"Excellent," said Mr. Brae.

Councilman Dean took an envelope from his pocket—the money that Gerald had just paid him.

"This is my wedding gift to you, child," he told Rose. "It is *not* to be given back to your parents." He raised his eyebrows at Gerald, who nodded. Then the councilman left.

While Rose huddled in her chair, clutching the envelope, her family gobbled up the feast. She ate nothing, except for one bite of the fantastic wedding cake to please Mrs. Schill, who had spent hours sculpting the icing roses and larks. Rose, however, saw only a white hand. It haunted the room—in the fingerprints smearing the white frosting, in the clasped hands embroidered on the white tablecloth, even in the streaks of light on the china cabinet doors. It tormented her, reminding her that when darkness fell, she would have to endure its coldness creeping over her skin.

"He didn't skimp on the eats, did he?" Dorrick said, his mouth stuffed with roast goose. "I'm sure glad now Ma made me wait to join the defense force until tomorrow."

"What pretty dishes." Maggie peered through the windows in the china cabinet. "Why weren't they used for the feast?" she asked loudly, looking at Mr. Brae. But Mr. Brae, who was talking to Gerald, ignored her.

"Now that you're mistress, Rose," Maggie said, "you'll decide when to use the best dishes."

When at last the time came for her family to go, Rose clung even to Dorrick.

"I owe you, Rose," he said, to her surprise. Then he let her go. Although she watched until they disappeared into the orchard, not one of them looked back.

Mr. Brae came up behind her.

"I'm tired," Rose said.

There was a silence.

"You will use the small room upstairs," he said. "Take these . . . these sacks of yours and go up to bed." He left.

Her sentence had been lifted—for a night. Rose clutched her sack of candles and stepped out on the porch.

"I'm a landowner," she said, but she felt no different from this morning. A violet light inched over Greengarden, softening the land as the sun dipped down.

"Do you know?" she asked. "Are you glad?"

The white ribbons blew across her face, slapping her over and over, but nothing could wake her now.

PART TWO

8

The Mistress of Filth

When Rose came down to the dining room for breakfast the next morning, she saw Mr. Brae sitting at the head of the table with a book in his hand. On the table lay a cream pitcher, a butter dish, two crystal dishes with shimmering blobs of blackberry and strawberry jam, a silver bell, a blue china cup, a stack of toast cut into triangles, and a platter heaped with bacon and sausage. Only one place was laid, however: his.

"Morning, sir," Rose said, stifling a yawn. She had been too frightened and hungry to sleep well in her strange bed.

Mr. Brae bit the tip off a triangle of toast and then reached for the bell.

"Don't bother to ring, sir," Rose said. "I'll fetch another plate. Mrs. Schill must have forgotten to lay a place for me."

Mr. Brae raised his eyebrows. "You will be taking your meals in the kitchen."

"But . . . I thought, now that I'm one of the family . . ."

"You thought wrong. You have neither education nor

conversation—nothing to grace a table that I can see." Mr. Brae shook the bell, but with a flick of his wrist he clamped his hand over the metal and smothered the ring. Only a dull *clonk* came from the clapper. "I rather enjoy smudging newly polished silver," he said, "even if it is merely plate." He laughed. Fingerprints clouded the once bright bell. "Now go to the kitchen," he ordered.

"But I was wondering about my new duties," Rose said, "now that, now that . . ."

"You're married to a monster?"

She looked away.

"Your duty," he said, "is to breed like a rabbit."

Rose gripped the back of a chair, her fingers sinking into the plush burgundy velvet, and stared over his head at the green dishes in the china cabinet. Propped on their sides and rimmed with silver, the dishes overlapped like the scales on a snake. She counted them: one, two, three—up to fourteen before she finally managed to speak.

"But until I have children—"

"Before, during, and after, you will do what you have always done here, and more. Scrub floors. Wash windows." Mr. Brae waved one hand at the room. "I have sent Verda back to the dairy. From now on, you will do her work as well."

"But I'm not a bondwoman anymore," Rose protested. "I should do the tasks of a mistress and a landowner."

"What, traipse around in silk gowns? Invite ladies to drink tea out of the celadon china that I see you eyeing so covetously?" He pulled on his napkin, his eyes suddenly vague. "I asked my daughter to use the celadon china once when . . ." He stopped and stared up at Rose. "Wear your blue silk when Carlyle comes for dinner tonight, my dear. I want you to make an excellent impression. What did you say?" Mr. Brae rubbed his hands together. "Why, because it's a very advantageous match, naturally—think of the benefit to the land . . . No? Why not? Nonsense! You'll grow accustomed to that . . ."

"What are you talking about?" Rose asked. "I don't care about china and silk dresses. I just want to help with the orchard."

Mr. Brae blinked, picked up his fork, and set it down again. "Oh," he said, "oh, I was thinking of . . . never mind. Go about your business—in the kitchen."

"But I thought you liked my ideas about the orchard. Isn't that one reason why you asked me to be mistress?"

"Mistress!" His head came up sharply. "Listen, for I shall say this only once." He bit the tip off another triangle of toast and then tossed it aside. "I intend to breed your instinct for the land into the Brae bloodline. Nothing more. You are no more *mistress* here than your monstrous husband is master. And you never will be."

"But we agreed that—"

"I said nothing about changing your work. Now, see what's keeping my omelet, then serve me at once." Mr. Brae flipped open his book, then looked up again. "Wait," he ordered. He tossed the silver bell, which chimed with tiny, fluttering rings as it flew toward Rose. She caught it.

"From now on, you will keep that polished," he said. "No matter how many times I smudge it, no one else is to touch it. That's the only way we can be certain the tone stays . . . perfect, now isn't it?"

"All right," Rose said, bewildered. The glint in his eye made her shiver. She started toward the hall, stopped, then turned toward the kitchen and saw Mrs. Schill. Her arm rigid, Mrs. Schill held the swinging kitchen door open and looked with half-shut eyes at the back of Mr. Brae's head. He did not see her. Mrs. Schill nodded at Rose and opened the door wider.

Rose stumbled into the kitchen. Had she married the Thing for nothing? Thrown away her life? Her dreams for

Greengarden seemed further away than ever. Now she under-stood why her mother had insisted that the marriage be legal. Yet, if Mr. Brae refused to treat her like the Mistress of Green-garden, it probably did not matter what the papers said.

*   *   *

With her body halfway inside the oven, Rose chipped at a charred lump that stuck to the back wall. Her mind floated in a daze that had grown each day during the past three weeks of her married life. As footsteps clomped across the kitchen porch, the lump popped free, and her knuckles scraped against the black wall.

"Ouch!" she exclaimed. She backed out and banged her hip against the oven door. "Blast!"

A dirty, bare foot hooked the screen door and pulled it open. Crazy Kalista, a bondwoman in her thirties, sidled in with a basket on each hip, and a red peony behind each ear. She was singing:

> "A bauble for you,
>   Said Tom-a-long,
>   A bauble for you,
>   My pretty young maid."

"Kalista!" Mrs. Schill turned from the counter. "Bite your filthy tongue!" But Kalista sang on:

> "A baby is sweet,
>   Cried Sally May,
>   A baby is sweet,
>   But you'll run away."

One of Kalista's five illegitimate babies had been born with one blue eye and one brown eye, which meant the child would go mad when it grew up. As the law decreed, the babe was taken up into the hills and left for the wildcats and coyotes. Kalista had been half-mad ever since.

"I smell sweet dreams," she said to Mrs. Schill, who stood sipping a cup of laudanum for her raging toothache. The poppy powder dissolved in hot wine made the kitchen smell sickly sweet.

"Here's the master's skin." Kalista put one of the baskets full of pressed, folded clothes down on the table. "They're clean as a cloud, but with nary a button to close him all up."

"Why doesn't Mr. Brae have any buttons on his clothes?" Rose asked.

"He couldn't bind her love with thread," Kalista said. "She snip-snipped! And flew away."

"What nonsense are you babbling now?" Mrs. Schill scolded, and then she turned to Rose. "Amberly collected buttons. All kinds. She made some, too. Whenever His Most Exalted lost a button, she'd sew it right back on with her own hands. Wouldn't let any servant do it." Mrs. Schill squeezed lemon into the egg whites in a bowl. "Her collection's still in the bottom drawer of that folderol chest in your room. Some of the buttons are silver, some gold—"

"And some are bone," Kalista sang softly. "A woman sews her fingers to the bone—sews until her bones turn into buttons. She sews those, too, bone by bone, till nothing's left."

"You're addled," Mrs. Schill said.

"You don't see!" Kalista hissed. "Her eyes in the bony buttons watch over her loved ones!"

Rose brushed soot from her hands. "But why doesn't he have any buttons now?"

"A week after he dragged Amberly back from Middlefield," Mrs. Schill said, "they had a terrible row. He went on a rampage. Said she'd betrayed him. He burned things. Cut every button off his clothes. You can bet it made my teeth chatter—what's left of them. That's when he locked her in the attic."

"He cut his heartstrings," Kalista said. "He holds his drawers up with laces now." She giggled. "And they slip plenty—I seen:

> "Oh, Tom-a-long! Tom-a-long!
> I'll take your bauble now."

"Shut your mouth!" Mrs. Schill exclaimed, glancing sideways at Rose.

"Poor, pretty Amberly," Kalista moaned. "The button's dead; the bones are cold. Amberly lies beneath a stone." She shivered. "The wildcats ate her poor sweet babe."

"Put that other basket down and get out," Mrs. Schill said. "You're making my tooth ache something fierce." Kalista, however, stared at Rose's soot-covered apron and black hands.

"You can't be the new mistress," Kalista said. "You're dirty! Why did I wash these clean?" She raised the basket and dumped out Rose's laundry—all white. Wrinkled drawers, stockings, and shifts fell in a heap on the floor. Petticoats bunched up like overgrown cabbages.

"What did you do that for?" Rose exclaimed.

Kalista hitched her orange skirt, slid one bare leg behind her in a curtsy, and said, "Your clothes must match your station, O Mistress of Filth."

"Look who's talking about filth," Mrs. Schill said. "Sure as a pig roots, you have any more bastards and Mr. Brae will feed them to the Thing."

Kalista sprang up. "Hag! Hag! Mean old hag! Joff's going to marry me tomorrow, just you wait and see. I'll be a bride with white lace dripping from my black, black shroud. I'll be a vision of visions." She danced out.

"Stark-raving." Mrs. Schill began to whisk the egg whites. "He should send her to the mines."

"Mrs. Schill," Rose asked, "would you mind, would you please put my laundry back in the basket? My hands—I don't want to get ashes all over."

Mrs. Schill stopped whisking. She picked up the cup of laudanum, saw it was empty, and then pulled a flask from her apron pocket.

"I'm not paid to tend your laundry," she said at last. She unstoppered the flask and took a swig.

Rose slammed the oven door. She walked toward the sink, yanking off the apron and the scarf over her hair. With three quick pumps of her foot, she brought the water gushing from the spout and then scrubbed the soot from her hands. When she finished, she scooped her laundry into the basket; the clothes felt damp.

"A blight on her peonies," Rose muttered. She carried the basket to the door.

"You get back here," Mrs. Schill ordered. "You haven't cleaned half that oven yet."

"They're still wet!" Rose shouted. She let the door bang behind her and marched down the stairs into the backyard. "Blighted Earth," she swore. "Why can't everyone just leave me alone!"

Everyone had expected her to die, to be eaten by the Thing, but Rose had lived, and some people grew envious of her new status. Then, after they learned that Mr. Brae treated her worse than a bondwoman, they followed his example. No one called her Mrs. Brae. She still crept in and out of the back door. Rose did not care whether people said "Yes, ma'am" and "No, ma'am" to her, but unless they learned to respect her now, she could not help run the orchard later.

At the back of the yard, a clothesline that Mrs. Schill used for dish towels stretched between an oak and a cottonwood.

Rose shook out a petticoat and pinned it up. The only real difference between her new life and her old one, other than living in the Bighouse, was that now Mr. Brae made her work harder and did not pay her a penny. Thank goodness for Councilman Dean's wedding gift—she had used it to pay the balance on the Golden Flames.

"Pretty rags for a fine lady!" a voice called. Rose glanced up. Susa and Opal, each carrying one end of a ladder, walked by the fence.

"Who'd have thought the Mistress of Greengarden would have patches on her underwear?" Susa shouted. The girls laughed.

Rose looked at the petticoat, swaying in some private dance with the wind. Its white cotton had long since yellowed; its bevy of patches and darns stood out like bandages. Maggie had been wrong—Mr. Brae certainly had not dressed Rose in velvets and lace. In spite of all her mending, her few clothes grew more ragged every day from all the heavy housework she did now. She had never cared about clothes, but she did like to look neat.

"Thought you were better than us, didn't you?" Opal yelled.

Rose turned her back and shook out a stocking, but the girls kept jeering until they disappeared into the orchard. A few minutes later, as Rose draped the last shift over the line, someone whistled.

"Has the Thing seen you in that?" Kurt Sowerbee slouched against the fence, his black hair drooping over one eye. "I bet with all those hands, the Thing can really show a girl a good time."

Rose's cheeks burned. She turned her back on him.

"Or maybe it's like I hear," Kurt said. "You're still pure as a daisy."

Rose spun around. How could he have known that? She had not even seen the Thing since the wedding—no summons had come. When she thought of herself as married, she thought of herself as married to that white hand. When she thought of the Thing, she tried to replace the thought with the name Raymont. But Raymont was only a horrible, disembodied hand. At night, she dreamed the hand crept into her room and crawled up the side of her bed, scrabbling for her throat. Her fear of the dark was worse than ever now, and she slept with a chair blocking her door.

Kurt grinned. "Struck close to home, huh? Tell you what. If the Thing needs a little help doing his duty, just give me a whistle anytime. Ugly girls are my specialty."

Rose grabbed the empty basket and ran toward the house.

Mrs. Schill opened the screen door. "Bonded trash," she said, looking out at him.

At four o'clock that afternoon, Rose sorted the dry white laundry on her bed. The clothes smelled fresh now, of sun, mint, and the land. Amberly's red straw hat lay on the pillow. Except for her plain candles arranged on the folderol chest, Rose had kept the room just as it was. She still felt like a guest living in someone else's house. How stupid, how gullible she had been to think that becoming mistress would be easy. The folk would never accept her; neither would Mr. Brae. Instead of saving Greengarden, she would be cleaning ovens for the rest of her life. And Greengarden needed saving more than ever: leafhoppers had infested the Red Cameo apples, and if they spread to the other apples, the crop would be destroyed. Worse yet, there were rumors that Mr. Brae might sell more land.

Rose folded her shifts first, measuring each against the last, arranging them in a neat stack. When she smoothed out the last one, she noticed that the top button was missing. Rose looked at the folderol chest. Was Amberly's button collection still in the bottom drawer? With the shift in her hands, Rose walked over and opened the drawer.

Color exploded out of it—turquoise, red, gold. She saw circles, hundreds of circles, ringed with sparkling stones or beads or ropes of fine metalwork; textures, smooth and mottled, raised and carved; images of faces, ships, flowers, fantastic animals, and enameled insects. Rose knelt. As she reached in toward the buttons, the ceiling creaked.

Thud–drag.

Rose slammed the drawer shut.

Although she heard the thud–drag often now, she had taught herself to ignore it—almost. She stood up. Her white shifts, bloomers, and stockings, all her underwear spread across the whiter quilt.

Has the Thing seen you in that?

Rose ran to the bed, folded the last shift, then picked up the stack to hide them away. When she put the stack on the wardrobe shelf, one shift stuck out a finger's width from the others. She threw them back on her bed and folded the offending shift again, but now it was too narrow.

Thud–drag.

Rose folded the shift once more. The hem rumpled.

Bang!

The third time, her hands folded faster, and the fourth time, faster yet, until finally she yelled and threw the shift down.

Something clanged above, reverberating through the air. Rose grabbed the shift, her head shaking no, her face wet . . . *Has the Thing seen you in that? Has the Thing seen you in that?* . . . and folded the shift again. She slapped it on top of the stack. Now the stack was straight—or was it? Her hands flying, she arranged it over and over . . . *Has the Thing seen . . .* The stack had to be straight; it had to be perfectly straight.

Another clang ripped through the air.

"Stop it!" Rose shouted. "You! Thing up there! Just stop it!" She jumped on the bed and tore into the folded clothes, scattering and whirling them into a jumble of white. "Stop it!" She rolled in the laundry, the empty arms and legs winding round and round her, until exhausted, she lay still. The red straw hat crumpled beneath her hip.

A moment later, her entire body began to shake because the sound from the attic had stopped.

9

Betrayal

At twelve o'clock that same night, Rose dreamed that a bony moon with two horrible eyes chased her through the orchard. White-fingered branches tore at her clothes, her hair, and her streaming breath. Suddenly she teetered on the edge of a well and nearly fell in. She veered, but after a few steps the well popped up in front of her again. She veered again. Behind her, the moon sailed closer and closer until its glow singed her back. She could not escape. Just as the well presented itself a third time, a bang woke her.

"Blighted Earth!" a voice swore.

Rose sat bolt upright in bed. Someone had opened her bedroom door, and it had banged into the overstuffed chair blocking the way. *The Thing!* Rose lunged for the lantern burning low beside her bed and turned it up, only to see Mr. Brae force his head inside her room.

"Remove this ridiculous chair at once!" he said.

Rose threw her shawl over her nightdress, then inched the

chair forward until Mr. Brae managed to fling open the door. It slammed against the wall.

"How dare you?" he said, holding up a candlestick. Gobs of wax flecked the sides like spittle. "You have no right to barricade any door in my house."

Rose said nothing.

"It is time," Mr. Brae said.

"Time?" She blinked, still dazed from sleep.

"I have waited for you to adjust. I have been patient—even foolishly allowed you to burn that lantern all night. But I must have an heir. It is time for you to fulfill your part of the agreement." He walked to the bedside table, and when he lowered the lantern's wick, the light faded.

Rose stepped back until the wrought-iron bars on the bed frame pressed into her calves, her thighs. She looked left, then right, seeking safety in the familiarity of her room. However, in the wisp of light from Mr. Brae's candle, the chintz pattern on the chair changed into oozing blobs of black; the lace curtains swayed like spiderwebs; and, on the folderol chest, her candles huddled like a host of silent specters.

"Come along," Mr. Brae said.

With feet as heavy as stone, Rose followed him. I'm asleep, she told herself, still asleep. It's only a dream, a nightmare.

Instead of turning right toward the attic, Mr. Brae turned left down the hall.

"Where are we going?" she asked.

"Hurry up!" He waved his walking stick. With its mouth frozen wide, the coyote head seemed to howl at the beast-headed sconces on the wall, which howled silently back. Most of the green velvet had worn off Mr. Brae's bathrobe, leaving it mottled with shiny splotches. Rose followed him until he put his hand on his bedroom door, where she stopped dead.

"The Thing's in there?" Rose whispered. "You let it out?"

"Don't be ridiculous." The candlelight lashed across Mr. Brae's face, reddening his eyes. "This pretense of innocence nauseates me." He jabbed his walking stick at her. "Your bed is too small, and because it was my . . . it would be . . . inappropriate. I suggest we go in and get this over with as quickly as possible."

"We?" Rose asked. "Go in there?" Her eyes blurred. The shadow cast by the candle pulsed over the wall, making the beast sconces flash. She remembered odd glances, words, the silver bell; in a flash Rose saw how they had all pointed, not to the attic door, but to this one. The beast was here. Loathing turned her inside out, left her mute and senseless, blind before it, deaf before it. Then rage gave her back her voice.

"No!" she shouted. "Never! Not with you!"

Mr. Brae stared. "What do you mean, *no*? You cannot change your mind about the arrangement now."

"What arrangement?" Rose cried.

"This is absurd."

"What arrangement!"

He sighed. "Your parents said they had explained it to you. Your marriage, though legal, is merely a pretense so that everyone will believe that the Thing is the father of the heir instead of . . . me."

Rose stepped back.

"I cannot marry beneath my rank to secure an heir," he added. "Nor would I allow the Thing to pass its cursed blood to my descendants. Thus the arrangement—and the outrageous price in benefits to your family. Your parents told me you had agreed to all of this."

"I don't believe it." Rose's throat burned. "They knew I would never agree to that. And they wouldn't have either."

"I assure you, they did. Ask them. Your mother would agree to almost anything in exchange for a pretty bauble." He laughed. "I know."

"You're lying!"

Mr. Brae set the candlestick on a chest beside his door. "Am I to understand," he said slowly, "that you married that monster believing you would lie with it?"

"Yes!"

"You were willing to do that . . . for Greengarden?"

Rose nodded, shivering.

He leaned closer. "The love of the land runs deeper in your blood than I suspected. Stronger than fear, stronger than life . . ."

Rose pulled her shawl tighter, dismayed. If he understood that feeling, then he felt the same way, which made him even more formidable than she had thought. And, she suddenly saw, it made her formidable, too.

"Why," he asked slowly, "why couldn't she . . . have been like you?" With three dry fingertips, he touched Rose's cheek. When she shuddered, he jerked his hand back. His lip curled.

"I choose stock well," he said. "Our child will be strong."

"*We* aren't having a child," Rose said. "That wasn't the bargain I made."

Mr. Brae scowled. "Believe me, there will be no pleasure in this—not with someone as ugly as you. It will be business only, mechanical, two creatures in the barnyard."

Rose felt her chest tighten. No. No spell, not now. Please, not now!

"If you touch me again," she said, "I'll scream. I'll shout. I'll smash everything I can reach. Mrs. Schill will hear."

"Mrs. Schill is in Stonewater for the night," Mr. Brae said. "Consider carefully, Rose. The Thing is worse than you can possibly imagine—it has attempted murder. If you come with me, you will not have to lie with a monster. You already have Greengarden. It will not change that." His voice softened. "But if you come with me now, you will never have to go through the attic door and face the horror inside."

Rose clung to the railing. The hall, the house, her mind, all seemed to be disappearing into the darkness. She tried to hold on to her self, to focus on a fixed point, a flickering yellow dot like a candle flame, before it vanished completely. Then, as Mr. Brae began to smile, Rose saw his second chin wobble and sensed the triumph flashing on his hidden face. She remembered that she, too, was formidable.

"I'd rather go through the attic door than yours," she said. "Any other monster in the whole world would be better than you."

"Enough!" He grabbed her arm. "The papers are signed. Your parents agreed!"

"They didn't!" Rose twisted sideways. A button popped off her sleeve and pinged on the floor, where it bounced, wobbled, and then toppled flat. "They wouldn't betray me!" she cried.

Mr. Brae stared down at the button. "Betray?" he asked. One by one, his fingers opened, and he released her. He bent, then picked up the button—a plain wooden button with a straggling white thread—and turned it in his fingers. "Betrayed," he whispered.

Rose held her sleeve together while the expression on his face changed; his eyes looked remote, puzzled.

"Such a simple request, really," he said. "It isn't much to ask, my dear; surely you see that? Surely you agree?"

My dear? Rose watched, wary, as he stroked the wood with his thumb.

"Just one button," Mr. Brae said. "That's all I ask. Even after all that has happened—just sew it here on my blue jacket, and I shall forget everything. I shall forget you betrayed me. I'll forgive you." His hand shaking, he held the button out to Rose. "Take it, my girl, my darling baby girl. One button. Just sew it on. Please. Take it. Just one stitch, that is all I ask. And we will be as we were."

Rose did not move.

His face contorted. He howled and threw the button; it struck her cheekbone. She cried out.

"So be it!" He flung away his walking stick. "You shall have your way!" Mr. Brae grabbed her arm with one hand, and with the other picked up the candlestick. "Keep your loyalty to him." And he dragged Rose toward the attic stairs. "You can rot; you can starve. You can bear your misbegotten babe in a pool of blood!"

Rose staggered after him, slipping on the stairs, banging her knees, but each time she fell, he hauled her up again. At the top of the stairs, he slammed the candlestick on a shelf and shoved her in a corner.

"Stay there!" Mr. Brae ordered. He unlocked both padlocks. When he lifted the bar, Rose tried to run down the stairs, but he swung around and blocked her.

"Back in the corner!" He brandished the bar.

Rose cowered back. Her hands pressed against the moldy wall.

"You, Thing!" Mr. Brae shouted. "Keep away from the door." He kicked the attic door open. It framed a mouth of darkness.

"Get in there," he ordered.

"Give me the candle," Rose begged. "Please!"

"No. After it murders you, I'll marry it to an obedient girl. Now get in there!" Mr. Brae shoved her over the threshold. She fell to her hands and knees on the attic floor.

"The candle! The candle!" Rose crawled toward the doorway and clutched the hem of his robe. "Don't leave me here," she pleaded, "not in the dark." He kicked her in the ribs, and she collapsed. The door swung shut. She beat on it, clawed at the wood, but the bar thudded back into place. With one click, then another, the padlocks snapped shut.

"No!" Rose screamed. "Don't lock me in with it. Earth's Mercy! . . . I can't breathe. Not in the dark!"

Rose scrabbled against the door, looking for a handhold,

a foothold, anything. But she was trapped, trapped in the dark with the Thing. Her breath raged in her throat. She coughed and coughed, trying to spit out the dark while her fists pounded the door.

"That is useless," said a voice.

Rose spun around. The voice had come from the far side of the attic, but it was too dark to see what had spoken.

"Keep away!" she sobbed. "Keep away!" She backed in the opposite direction along the wall until she struck her head on the sloped ceiling. An odd smell—turpentine?—filled the air. Someone was coughing, wheezing. Rose tripped and fell, heard a crash, then a shower of tinkling noises.

She sobbed and put up one hand, groping, and felt the flat top of a table above her. She scooted beneath it, huddling, gasping, making herself smaller and smaller, trying to vanish. Beside her, beneath her—all around her—the blackness itself was wheezing. A hand squeezed all the air from her chest, a gigantic white hand that was the only thing she could see in the dark.

10

The Attic

Rose did not want to wake up. She was too tired, too comfortable. Her head, knees, and ribs throbbed, but they sank into something soft. When she finally opened her eyes, blackness made of speckled, dancing motes quivered before her. She blinked, then raised one hand until it hit a low ceiling. She traced her fingers down the angled slope, her wrist flexing as her hand dropped lower, and then remembered where she was. Her hand pressed against her mouth. She was locked in the attic with the Thing.

But where was it? Beside her? Behind her? That disembodied hand could be scrabbling toward her even now. She fought the fear and tried to think.

She remembered crawling under the table, then suffocating with pain from a spell. She must have fainted. And now? Rose listened, counted to a hundred: once, twice, again, while the attic remained silent. Was it still night outside? Her right hand groped out, exploring the softness that supported her.

After a few inches, the surface angled down and dropped away. A bed. But how did she get to it?

The Thing must have carried her here! It had touched her! Rose curled into a ball. Yet, even as she lay trembling, she realized that the Thing had not harmed her. It had not eaten her; it had not even tried to lie with her. Was the Thing like a cat? Did it play with its prey before it killed?

Again she listened. The silence had life: a submerged hum. A current of air cooled her cheek, and in it Rose sensed a presence. She sat up slowly, bending her neck to avoid the sloping ceiling, and swung her legs over the side of the bed. The springs jangled. She froze. Now the Thing would know she was awake.

On the wall to her right, perhaps twenty feet away, the round attic window glowered, darkly shining, like a muddy moon. The glass was tinted brown, clouding the view of what lay beyond it. That window, so familiar, so feared—was she actually looking at it from the inside? The small hole seemed miles away. The world waited on the other side, if she could only reach it, swim up to the top, and break through into the safety of the light. Even if she could reach it, though, that escape was barred by the black wrought-iron rose, which showed behind the darkly shining glass.

Rose's head spun as though she were floating. When she threw out her arms to catch herself, her elbow hit something hard—a bedpost. The pain brought her back to herself. She grabbed the bedpost and held on, peering into the dark. Although the gloomy light seeping through the window did not help her distinguish one object from another, it did keep the attic from being as black as a closet. Blobs of shadow, some velvet black, some stovepipe black, some the faded black of old broadcloth, blurred in and out of each other. Was that shadow across from her a chair? A pillow? A length of cloth? Or the Thing? Rose stared at one blob after another, desperate to define them and yet dreading to also, because any one of them might be—

"I've been waiting a long time for you to wake up," said a voice.

Rose snapped her head to the right. The voice had come from the direction of the round window, except the window was not round anymore but eclipsed by the dark curve of a head. The remaining crescent of dimly glowing light haloed the head like a crown slipped sideways.

The Thing's head.

> The three-headed monster
> Grabs you while you dream.
> The three-headed monster
> Eats you while you scream.
> Nah! Nah! Nah! Nah!

"You are my wife," the Thing said.

Rose pulled on her fingers, faster and faster, certain it would now crawl forward to lie with her, devour her.

"Rose Selene Chandler Brae," the Thing said.

She rocked back, her mouth open in a silent scream. The sound of the Thing speaking her name reached down and touched the deepest pit of terror inside her. It knew her.

"Rose," the voice said, "tell me, what are the stars like?"

She turned her head and stared at the dark shape, at the crescent of muddy light.

"What?" she whispered. "What did you say?"

"What are the stars like?" it asked again. "I have never seen them."

Rose could not speak.

"And how does it feel to walk in the sunlight?"

She pressed her knuckles against her mouth.

"Rose, tell me! What color is the wind?"

* * *

For what seemed like centuries, Rose could not think. She was shocked by the Thing's intelligence and by the horror that gave to its imprisonment. Outside, raindrops pounded the roof; they fell faster and harder, pelting, then thundering only inches above her head. When the Thing finally spoke again, its voice punctured the swirling dark.

"Talk to me," it said. "I haven't had anyone to talk to since Lee-lee went away. I was dreaming before you came. Do you ever dream? I was swimming in a deep pool edged with stone. A little current spilled in, and I dove into it. Then the current swept me from the pool and swelled into a river." The Thing paused, then added, "I became the river and swept everything before me."

The dancing motes of darkness swirled, and Rose saw the Mirandin River flood the orchard, uprooting trees, toppling cottages, drowning livestock. She saw dead people floating . . . Rose had never learned to swim because her spells had taught her to fear suffocation. More pictures sprang into her mind. She saw Amberly Brae dancing underwater in a silvery-green gown the color of the Appelunes, saw her waltzing with a laughing little girl in a nightdress. Above, on the surface of the pool, a full moon wavered, then splintered into many moons.

"How do you know what a river is," Rose asked, "when you've always been locked up here?"

"So you can say more than two words. I was beginning to wonder if you were an idiot."

If *she* was an idiot!

"My experience of the world," the Thing said, "comes from books. And also from what I imagine."

"You—can read?"

"There is nothing wrong with my brain. You were a bondwoman. Very likely you can't read at all."

Rose clutched the bedpost as pictures erupted from the blackness again, given shape by the dark, dancing motes. This time she saw horrible pictures of the Thing. She moaned, closed her eyes, and pushed the pictures away.

"You're not going to be ill again, are you?" the Thing asked. "Lee-lee was always ill before she . . . went away. But she never made those strange gasping sounds like you did earlier." His voice changed, became eager. "Did you take any laudanum? Lee-lee did."

"I need light," Rose said. "Please, light a candle."

"No! No light."

"But why?" She sobbed. "Why not?" She could not see! Could not breathe! She wanted to punch the blackness, to rip it like a sheet and emerge on the other side, but the blackness had no surface her hands could grasp. Beside her lay the pillow she had slept on. She fluffed it again and again. Then she replaced it, moving it to the left, then back to the right, feeling with her hands until the pillow lay precisely in the center of the bed.

After that, they sat in silence until, after what seemed like another century, footsteps thumped up the attic stairs.

"That will be *him*," the Thing said.

Rose let out a deep breath. She stood up.

"I shall see you tomorrow night," it said.

"Tomorrow?" Rose started. She had not thought beyond this night, had not considered that she would have to endure this again, but of course she would, and worse. Either that or— She heard Mr. Brae reach the landing, and she shuddered.

"I suppose you have to sleep sometime," the Thing said, "but I want to talk to you."

Still Rose hesitated. All that she had believed about the Thing was so different from the truth that she could not adjust her thoughts. He was not insane. He was not an idiot. She did not think he would eat her, but he was still a monster in some way or he would not be locked up. Hadn't Mr Brae said the Thing had attempted murder? If only she could see him, could know the worst.

"Do you think Mr. Brae would let me bring a candle next time?" Rose asked.

"No! I don't want you to see me!"

She paused. "I'll have to ask Mr. Brae how often he wants me to come."

"Oh, very well."

Outside the attic door, keys jingled.

"I shall be counting each moment until you're with me again," the Thing said.

Rose crushed her nightdress in her hands.

"You will bring joy to the hideous Thing in its cage," he added bitterly as the metal bar slid up.

"Did you murder her, too?" Mr. Brae called.

"I'm here," Rose called back. "Here." She held both hands in front of her and crept through the darkness toward the sound of his voice.

* * *

In her own bed the following morning—no, not morning, the sun was too high—Rose examined her arm. Four bruises smeared her skin where Mr. Brae's fingers had grabbed her the night before. She rubbed the bruises, trying to erase his touch. She bent her knees and winced; both were blue-black from being banged on the stairs. On her right side, where he had kicked her, a greenish-brown patch ran like a rumpled carpet over her ribs.

She huddled back in her bed, wanting only to sleep away her aches, but if she did not appear downstairs, Mr. Brae might think he had defeated her. Last night, after he had released her from the attic, he had not spoken one word to her, had not even looked at her. Rose got out of bed, leaned her forehead against the white wardrobe, then dressed and went down to the kitchen. Mrs. Schill was back from Stonewater.

"Is there any lunch left?" Rose asked.

"Lunch!" Mrs. Schill, her hands in pastry dough, glanced up. "There's a bushel of work here with your name on it. That bucket of potatoes needs peeling. The floor needs scrubbing. And His Most Exalted's boots want blacking." She turned the dough and slapped down the rolling pin. "Lunch's over and done. I haven't time to be fixing meals at all hours for a chit who spends her day lollygagging in bed. You'd better hope that Mr. Brae doesn't find out, girl."

"Lollygagging?" Rose's eyes blazed. After the horrible night she'd had? "Well, you'd better hope he doesn't find out how rude you are to his granddaughter-in-law!"

Mrs. Schill laughed. "Fat lot he'd care."

Rose marched into the larder, where she flung open a cupboard and grabbed a loaf of bread. The smell of rosemary drifted from a pie cooling on the shelf. In the wall behind the shelf, the attic dumbwaiter stood with its mouth gaping. Rose piled the bread and a hunk of cheese on top of the pie, then carried them to the kitchen.

"Put that back!" Mrs. Schill cried. "Mr. Brae asked for pork-and-potato pie particularly. He finds out you ate it, you can bet he'll slice you up and have you for supper!"

"Nobody's having me for supper!" Rose shouted. "Nobody!" She started toward the kitchen door, then spun around. She passed an open-mouthed Mrs. Schill, strode into the dining room, through the sitting room, and out the front door. When she reached the gate, she glanced at the attic window, but nothing moved behind the black bars.

She kicked a rock on the orchard path. It rolled, lodged in a clump of grass, and she kicked it again. Rose was sick of people treating her with scorn, sick of it. Mrs. Schill with her orders; Kalista with the laundry; Kurt with his leers and catcalls; Mr. Brae with his evil intentions; and all the other folk with their unending jibes. How could she bear it, and at the same time bear being locked in the dark with the Thing?

A sob burst from her. Although summer heat gripped the land, the wind rippled the leaves and cooled the shade beneath the apple trees arching overhead. Her shoulders rounded over the pie as she trudged slowly, looking down.

Rose knew she did not walk across the land as though she owned it, rejoicing that it was hers. She did not walk briskly, with confidence, with a delighted watchfulness, looking left and right, noting tasks that needed doing—a fence mended, an irrigation ditch patched—or delighting in tasks done well. She did not walk across the land that way because she could not imagine walking that way. The centuries-long subjugation of her ancestors had not prepared her to speak the word that brought the confident stride, to speak the word *mine*. Rose knew she had been born to be a steward, not a landowner. Her marriage had not been enough to give her tongue the power to speak that magic word, because she did not yet truly imagine it. Desire alone did not make something real.

A knoll sloped ahead of her. Soon she could see the Mirandin River twining like a blue curl through the Valley. At the top of the knoll, she tramped around in a small circle until the grass flattened. Then she sat down inside the circle and ate the bread and cheese while looking out at the orchard, the Faredge Wall, and the Valley.

Her pathetic attempt at ownership of the land had been based on a lie. But whose lie? Mr. Brae's or her parents'? Ever since her marriage, her parents had avoided her. Both times she had visited the Guesthouse they had hurried her out. Could Mr. Brae be telling the truth? But Rose distrusted him. He had already lied about the Thing's sanity.

The Thing—It? Raymont?—had not seemed like a monster. Except for his heart-wrenching questions, he had seemed like a spoiled, fourteen-year-old boy. *How does it feel to walk in the sunlight?* Rose put the bread down. What would it be like if she had never felt the sun on her face, or the land beneath her feet, or the wind on her skin? What would it be like to live imprisoned like the Thing? She had been locked in the attic for only a few hours, and that had felt terrible.

Would she have to go back? Or would Mr. Brae repent of his rash decision, made in the heat of his pain and anger last night, and insist that she bear his child? One way or another, she had to have a child. Only through a child could she save this place that she loved and secure her claim to Greengarden. After all, she had known when she had agreed to the marriage she would have to lie with the Thing. She would take a candle to the attic, see the worst, know the truth, and then she could face it.

Better the Thing than Mr. Brae.

Mr. Brae. Rose scowled. She stood up with the pork-and-potato pie cradled in her arms. Although she did not believe that her parents had known about his "arrangement," she intended to find out. Now.

11

Dorrick Comes Home

Why, Rose," Maggie said a few minutes later as she opened the door of the Guesthouse a crack. "Saw you coming from the window. What a nice surprise." She peered out at Rose's old dress—sprigged with daisies, now short, tight, and patched—then slid her tongue over her lips. She did not open the door any wider.

"Are you going to let me in, Ma?" Rose asked.

Maggie hesitated, then moved aside. "Sorry. Don't know where my mind is."

In the sitting room, Rose saw a yellowed piece of lace draped halfway along the curtain rod. The rest puddled on a chair beside the window. Her mother's mind was where it always was—on pretty things.

"These curtains," Maggie said, "they're keeping me up nights." She jabbed a pin into the crescent-shaped pincushion she wore on her wrist. "I can't puff them just so. And puffs are the fashion now, Mrs. Willow says."

"Did you rearrange the furniture again?" Rose asked, uncertain whether the odd groupings of furniture, which looked as though someone had shoved them together for spring cleaning, were supposed to be arrangements or not.

"Nice, isn't it? 'Conversation areas,' Mrs. Willow calls them." Maggie's little eyes gleamed as she looked around. "Wait till Dorrick sees his grand home all fixed up nice. Won't he be proud?" She smoothed the back of an armchair upholstered in blue and purple stripes. The same fabric covered both couches. Behind them, the peach-colored walls stretched upward to the mahogany moldings around the ceiling. The Guesthouse had grown dingy in the years since the Braes' guests had used it, but Maggie had scrubbed, painted, sewn—and puffed—until everything looked fresh, if somehow peculiar.

"Dorrick'll be real proud, Ma." Rose's voice was flat.

Maggie glanced at the pork-and-potato pie. "That smells good."

"It's for you and Pa."

"Won't that be tasty. Bake it yourself?"

"Well—"

"I'm joking!" Maggie chuckled. "Of course Mr. Brae won't let you lift a finger. I'll put this in the kitchen. It's still a wonder—a room just for cooking!" Rose started to follow her, but Maggie waved her hand. "Sit," she said. "That's what a sitting room's for. I'll be right back. Isn't every day I get a visit from the Mistress of Greengarden!"

Rose looked around. None of the furniture looked inviting. A delicate chair with a needlepoint seat seemed crushed between two sprawling, overstuffed chairs. A tiny red doily was draped over the back of an elegant sofa, like a handkerchief on a thoroughbred horse. And the knickknacks! China dolls, inlaid boxes, porcelain cats, and baskets lined up exactly two inches apart along both coffee tables. Rose sat down on a blue chair by the fireplace and realized that her mother had no taste.

Above the mantel hung the cast-off painting from the Big-house. That and the pewter plates on the wall were the only things from the old cottage. The room did not feel like home. It occurred to Rose that she had no home anymore. The Big-house certainly did not feel like home either, not with the Thing and Mr. Brae. How was she going to ask her mother about Mr. Brae's arrangement?

"Did I tell you?" Maggie came back into the room. "I'm in the Sewing Circle with the freewomen now. We're making uniforms for the soldiers."

"How are Egan and Bartla?" Rose asked. They were bondwomen.

"I don't see them much. I quit the dairy. According to Mrs. Willow, the wife of the first-boss doesn't milk cows." Maggie clambered up on the chair by the window and began pinning up the lace. "Life is good. If I could just get these puffs right . . ."

Rose chipped at a crack in the veneer on the oak end table. While her mother had gained everything she had ever dreamed of from the marriage, Rose's own dreams seemed to be over. No one treated her like the Mistress of Greengarden, and without that, she could never save the land. I chose what I did, she reminded herself, chose to marry the Thing of my own free will. But had her parents told her the whole truth before she had made her choice?

Rose wanted to blurt out her question but feared the answer. What if her parents had known that Mr. Brae planned to father the child? What if they had deceived her? What then?

"Rose! Are you asleep, girl?"

"Sorry, Ma. What were you saying?"

"How's this look?" Maggie had coaxed a bunch of lace into the shape of a gigantic yellow pimple.

"Try making the puff smaller."

"Bigger, I'd say. It's work, fixing this house up," Maggie

confessed. "And it's got to be done soon. I'm giving a party when Dorrick gets leave from the war next week." She stuck in a pin. "You talked Mr. Brae into any parties yet? Maybe in that fancy drawing room like in my picture? I'm sure he pampers you something terrible!"

Rose stared at her mother's back. Hadn't she heard the gossip? Didn't she know that Mr. Brae treated Rose like the lowest bondwoman?

"Your pa should be home soon," Maggie said. "There's supposed to be word of Dorrick and our other men today. Imagine, my Dorrick a hero!"

Rose popped a chip off the table. Dorrick again, always Dorrick.

"Ma," she said, "I have to ask you something. It's about the marriage arrangement you and Pa made with Mr. Brae."

The lace fell from Maggie's hands as she almost rolled off the chair. "I forgot to fix any potatoes. And your pa expected any minute!" She hurried toward the kitchen.

"Wait, Ma—"

"Stay there."

But this time Rose followed her through the swinging door to the kitchen. Maggie glanced over her shoulder, then scurried past peeled potatoes soaking in a pot on the stove.

"Stir up the fire," she said. "And pop that pie in." And she ducked into the larder.

Rose sighed. She skipped one finger along the fluted crust around the pie.

"I forgot to ask, Rose honey," Maggie called, "have your spells been bothering you?"

"Some. But, Ma—"

"Did you hear Dorrick's ditched Susa? Says a freeman needs a freewoman for his wife. If he married her, she'd be freed, but he wants somebody better."

"Ma"—Rose tried again—"did you and Pa know that Mr. Brae never planned for the Thing to father—" A rumbling filled the room as Maggie dumped a sack of potatoes into the bin.

"Can't hear a thing," Maggie called over the noise. "Come back later."

Listen! Rose wanted to yell. Why won't you listen! It felt like the dark in the attic. She could not break through.

"Did you know," Rose shouted, "that Mr. Brae planned to father my baby himself? And that my marriage to the Thing was just a sham? So that Mr. Brae wouldn't have to marry beneath him to get an heir? He says you and Pa knew."

"Can't hear you!" Maggie shrieked. "I'm busy—you best go. I got to finish up those puffs."

The back door banged, and Gerald came in. He stared at Rose, his face blank.

"Maggie?" he called.

"That you, Gerald?" She peeked around the corner of the larder, then walked out holding up the corners of her apron, which held enough potatoes to feed a dozen people. "Thank goodness!" she exclaimed. Her eyes blinked rapidly, almost disappearing into her fat cheeks. "Gerald, look who's come for a visit, but she's just leaving."

"I'm glad you're here, Rose." His eyes red-rimmed, Gerald gripped the back of one of the kitchen chairs, then pulled it out and sat down.

"What's wrong?" Rose asked.

He turned his hands over and rested them palm up on his knees. "It's about Dorrick. Word just came."

Maggie flung out her arms; an avalanche of potatoes tumbled down her thighs and rolled across the floor.

"He's hurt!" she cried. "My baby's hurt." Her bulk swelled as though preparing for battle.

Rose picked up a potato from the floor and dug her fingernails into the skin.

"Take me to my boy," Maggie said.

"It's always Dorrick you care about!" Rose shouted.

"Never me! Well, here!" And Rose slammed the potato into the middle of the golden piecrust. Clots of gravy flew out. The potato stood there, leaning, slightly obscene with the broken crust and the bits of pea and pork puddled around it. They all stared at it, even Rose.

"You tell me where he is," Maggie said, breathing hard. "You tell me now."

"Outside. In the wagon," Gerald said.

Maggie hurled herself toward the door.

"Wait, Mag." Gerald turned his hands again and looked at the backs, brown and spotted with age and work. "A Dalriada ambushed him. Shot him in the back. Dorrick is dead."

Rose could not move.

"No." Maggie shook her head. "That can't be. We've got the house now—all these nice things. We're safe now. I'll get the puffs right, I will." She sagged. "He'll be proud, so proud of the house."

"This cursed house!" Gerald shouted. "It's a judgment on us." He looked straight at Rose.

Rose put her hand to her mouth. Her nose filled with the yeasty smell of raw potato and she nearly gagged. Then it was true. It was true . . .

"No." Maggie's arm swung, brushing the dirt on her apron. Again and again her arm swung. "No. No . . ." She began to moan, a low, guttural sound that rose through the kitchen and thundered into a scream that rocked the house, burst through the roof, and rolled its desolation across the orchard and up into the hills.

12

Light in the Leap

In the shade beneath the Appelunes, Rose sat with her
back against the warm stones of the Faredge Wall. A
day had passed—or was it a year? Wherever her body
touched the ancient wall, she sensed it humming, straining to
keep the wilderness from breaking through. It held back the
beasts: wildcats, bears, wolves. It held back the savage lands:
the rising foothills, the furious torrents, the cliffs and caves
and forests of the Red Mountains. Most important, it held
back the cursed magic of the Dalriadas. Rose pressed her
bones against the rocks, helping them withstand the on-
slaught that threatened Greengarden. She had no desire ever
to cross the wall. Dorrick had, and he had died.

So many had died. Of the eight volunteers who had gone
to the war from Greengarden, three were dead and two were
missing. Nineteen men from around Stonewater Vale were
dead. The war was getting worse, and it was coming closer.

A shadow fell across Rose's feet, carving a dark bar in the
sunshine.

"Grief is no excuse to leave my boots dirty," Mr. Brae said. They had not spoken since the horrible night in the upstairs hall. Annoyed, Rose tapped her foot; didn't he understand that she had to concentrate to hold up the wall?

"My condolences on the death of your brother," he said. "In fact, you have my condolences on your entire unfortunate family."

Rose wiped her eyes roughly. Was she supposed to thank him for that?

"It is tragic," he added. "How shall the world survive the loss of one more fool?"

"Fool yourself," she said, not caring.

"Undoubtedly. Speaking of fools, I have just spoken to your parents. They did lie, or at least mislead you, about the marriage arrangement, thereby placing us in this preposterous situation." He spoke coldly, dryly. "So I offer you a choice. You may bear the Thing's child instead of mine. It seems to tolerate you, for now at least. That may prove useful. And I have reconciled myself to having an heir that is half monster and half bondwoman."

"I'm a landowner," Rose said, without conviction.

He laughed. "You may be whatever you imagine. But if we might stay on the subject? Remember, I have warned you that the Thing is violent—that is no lie. If you choose it, I will not be responsible for any harm it does you. And you must agree to this condition: you may never have light in the attic. You will visit the Thing only in darkness."

Rose looked at him then, at his linen jacket patterned with brown-and-white checks, at the line of his tan hat against his forehead.

"Why are you so cruel?" she asked.

"If that does not suit you," Mr. Brae continued as though she had not spoken, "I shall father the heir, no matter how much it disgusts us both." He drew dashes in the dirt with his walking stick. "I have no interest in forcing women. I will not go through another scene like . . ." He stopped. "If I father the heir, you must agree to carry out your choice without—fuss."

Rose put her hand on the trunk of an Appelune. Mr. Brae or the Thing in the dark? What kind of choice was that? She had been prepared to endure the Thing, but not in the dark, not in the suffocating dark.

"Furthermore," Mr. Brae said, "if I discover that you have lit so much as a match in the attic, I will send you to the southern mines. They're in desperate need of workers to mine ore to make weapons for the war. And then you will never see Greengarden again. Now, whom do you choose?"

"I . . . I don't know," Rose said.

"So, I am under consideration, am I? How flattering."

In spite of the heat from the wall, Rose felt cold, cold and still. "I can't think straight now, with Dorrick laid out in the house . . . the burial tomorrow."

"I see. You are upset—death all around you. Yes, that is certainly understandable."

She nodded, relieved.

"Then perhaps you should visit the attic once more before you decide," he said.

"What?"

"Yes, I think that would be wise. You will go tonight." Mr. Brae bent toward her. "When the dead are above ground and ghosts are nearby . . . that's an excellent time to sit in the dark with a monster, wouldn't you agree?"

Rose stared at him.

"Yes, you need another taste of what that choice would be like. After all, I want you to make an informed decision this time."

"No." She pressed hard against the wall—shoulders, head, elbows. "Not tonight, please. After the burial."

"Tonight. Or you will decide now."

* * *

"Tell me about caves," the Thing said from his place by the attic window. Rose huddled on the bed. The heat, which seemed alive, dragged sweaty fingers down her neck.

"I've read about caves, of course," he added, "but books leave out so much. Does the rock feel damp? Does the weight of the earth overhead frighten you? I can almost hear the underground rivers thundering, then swirling into bottomless pools. Are there chasms you must jump over? Bones?" He clicked his tongue. "Imagine dropping a stone into a shaft. You count and wait but never hear it strike the bottom. Maybe if you keep counting, it never would reach bottom. But if you stop counting . . . then?"

Rose did not know how to answer such questions. She felt as if a piece of wet, black wool covered her face, blotting out the air.

"I imagine one cave leads into another," the Thing said, "on and on, deeper and deeper. I unwind a ball of string as I go, to keep from getting lost. But, oh! What if, just when you think you have reached the last cavern—and the end of your ball of string—you see another cave leading in deeper? You hold up a lantern and see jewels sparkling in the stone—the treasure you have been seeking all your life. Tell me, to get it, would you go on without string?"

Rose only stared at the darkness. How long until morning? When would a lark sing the first sweet notes of day?

"It's cruel of you not to answer my questions," the Thing said. "I must know everything!"

"I'm sorry. My brother just died. And I can't think about anything else. He's in . . . His body is laid out in my mother's sitting room—under puffs of lace." Rose paused, then added, "I'm tired. I'm hungry." Something creaked, something shuffled. Was the Thing getting up? She shrank back.

"I didn't do it," the Thing cried. "It wasn't my fault. *He* shouldn't have left Lee-lee here that way. I was starving, I was—but I didn't do it. I never even thought of it! *He* taunted me with it."

"What do you mean?"

"He didn't tell you? Tell everyone? That song, I thought that was why . . ." Something shuffled again. "Never mind," he added.

Rose felt for the bedpost and wrapped her hands around it.

"Does his body smell horrible yet?" he asked.

"Oh, please." Rose shuddered. "Don't." She did not know whether she spoke to the Thing or to the dancing motes of darkness forming a picture in her mind.

She saw a vast, vaulted cave etched with dust. Then she was inside it, her feet stamping and skipping to the beat of reedy music. A skeleton danced toward her, its bones tapping, its burial suit writhing like a mist. Rose stretched out her right hand. The skeleton grabbed it and swung by. She stretched out her left hand; another skeleton grabbed it and again swung by. They kept coming; she kept reaching—right hand, left hand, hand over hand over hand in an endless reel. Two circles of bone dancers interwove, skipping round in opposite directions.

She looked up. High above, a wrought-iron chandelier revolved like a wheel, but only smoke trailed from the seventy-seven black candles encircling the rim. Rose glanced at the bone dancers. Stuffed in each mouth was a potato whose shoots grew into the skull cavern. Leaves waved through the eye sockets. The dancers swayed. Their ribs pulsed. Their breath streamed out and snaked around her throat, her ankles, her waist. Rose could not break away from the dance. She could not stop reaching for each bony white hand, even though her arms grew more numb with every touch.

Faster and faster the circle danced, the music wailing, the

chain of bone dancers linking and breaking and linking again. Rose looked at the walls of the cave as she danced past. Four black archways yawned in the stone, one at each quarter point of the circle. In one of them stood a woman, a living woman wearing a dress that glittered against the blackness behind her. She beckoned to Rose.

"Amberly!" Rose cried. She broke toward her and nearly plunged into an abyss. Water gurgled far below. Then a bone dancer yanked Rose back into the reel. In the next archway, Amberly appeared again, and Rose saw that her dress glittered because it was covered with jewels—rubies and emeralds, diamonds set in gold, sapphires rimmed with silver. Again Rose broke away, only to face the same abyss; it surrounded the circle of bone dancers. She was afraid to jump across. Again and again she ran to the edge, only to be stopped by the abyss and pulled back into the dance.

She could not cross. She could not get away.

"Tell me, how did your brother die?" the Thing asked.

Rose felt her feet grow still, felt her hands grasping the bedpost. The world was solid black again. She fell over onto the bed and drew up her knees. She wanted a candle—one small, miserable, smoky candle—more than she had ever wanted anything, more than Greengarden, more than air. Nothing could be more terrible than this place, even Mr. Brae. Oh, what would she do? How would she choose?

"You're my wife!" the Thing exclaimed. "You're supposed to talk to me! Tell me how your brother died!"

"A barbarian killed him," Rose managed to say. "In the war."

"What war? What barbarians? Tell me."

"Later. I'm too tired."

"You tell me now or I'll—"

"What?" Rose sat up. What had happened to Lee-lee?

"I'll, I'll— Just tell me."

She bowed her head.

She bowed it again the next morning when she stood on the hill beside Dorrick's open grave. His body, covered except for the face, lay across three bales of straw.

"Landowner, freeman, bondman—" Gerald spoke the ritual words—"we are all creatures of the earth. We come from the earth; we return to the earth—body, heart, spirit. The circle is complete; the circle continues." He pressed the heel of his hand first into the pile of dirt and then onto his forehead, where he drew a circle with a horizontal line breaking through it.

A meadowlark trilled and Rose looked up. On the other side of the graveyard, where the edge of the dry hill bit into the sky, the meadowlark swooped over the sage toward its nest. Its yellow breast flickered under its grey wing, as though a leaf flapped in front of a lantern.

"The circle continues," Maggie said as she placed an apple seed on each of Dorrick's closed eyes. She bent, pressed the heel of her hand into the dirt, and, as she paused there, drawing breath to rise, she seemed to balance all her weight on her wrist. Rose thought it might snap. But with a rush of expelled breath, Maggie straightened and traced the symbol on Dorrick's forehead as tenderly as if she were washing his face. "Return to the earth," she said, and then whispered, "My boy, my baby."

After Maggie drew the symbol on her own forehead, Rose scooped up a handful of dirt flecked with broken leaves that would one day enrich the soil. All future growth, all life and sustenance would spring from this dark stuff. Dorrick's body would eventually add to that. Even his bones . . . a wisp of ghostly breath fluttered around a corner in her mind, but she veered away. Death frightened her, yes, but the thought of dying frightened her more: pain, suffocating for air, being entombed in blackness. That was exactly how she felt in the attic—entombed alive.

"Return to the earth," Rose mumbled. When she drew the heel of her hand around her forehead, the moist grit scuffed her skin.

One by one, the mourners stepped forward to perform the ritual. Mrs. Willow, who looked like a black bantam hen in her ruffled black bonnet, frowned at the red hat on Rose's head. So did many others. When Joff Will came forward, he nodded to Rose, but stayed away from Gerald. Even though Dorrick had died defending the Valley and Greengarden, Mr. Brae had not come to the burial. Rose was glad. She felt that her defeat was blazoned across her face, and that he would see it and gloat.

"Here I am, Dorrick!" Kalista elbowed her way through the mourners and strode barefoot into the pile of dirt. A length of muslin circled her head, knotted, then fluttered in two tails down her back. As she smeared the circle and the line on her forehead, she chanted:

> "One side is life,
>   One side is death,
>   Which one is which?
>   Bone in the breath.
>
> Light in the dark,
>   Dark in the light,
>   Which one is which?
>   White midnight.
>
> Keep what you lose,
>   Lose what you keep,
>   What turns the wheel?
>   Life's in the leap."

"See?" Kalista looked at the crowd. When no one spoke, she took five steps backward and cried, "Oh, dullards, see like this!" She flung her arms wide, ran toward the open grave, and leaped. Bangles jingling, scarf flying, she soared up like a strange, exotic bird. For a moment, she hung in the air over the grave with her legs split, her back knee bent. Then, as she was arcing down, her orange skirt flew up and one spongy white buttock flashed in the sun. She landed a hairsbreadth from the edge, then danced away down the hill as the crowd watched, stunned.

"Shameful, shocking," folks muttered.

"Exposing herself like that at a time like this!" Mrs. Willow exclaimed.

Rose stared at the footprint crumbling on the edge and felt her blood throb in her arms.

Just as everyone was looking around to see if this part of the ceremony was over, Susa stepped forward, defiant, swollen-faced. While the old women tsked and clucked behind their handkerchiefs, Susa daubed her forehead. She glared at Rose.

Then Gerald covered Dorrick's head, and four men lowered the body into the grave. After a decent pause, everyone began streaming down the hill.

"We've done all we can for him, Maggie," Gerald said. He put his arm around her; his fingertips barely reached her other shoulder. "Folks will be arriving at the house." Rose watched her mother weep—a burial feast was not the kind of party she had planned for Dorrick. Her parents turned away.

"Wait," Rose said. "Shouldn't we wait until . . ." She nodded at the men shoveling dirt into the hole.

"No!" Maggie sobbed. "I can't watch! Can't bear to see my boy shut up in the dark."

Rose felt her throat filling with hate and she leaned forward, imagining her hands circling her mother's throat, imagining her fingernails digging into those mounds of flesh. Rose wanted to shake her, cut off all her air, and throw her down into the hole. Maggie's bulk would fill the grave, seal it like a slab of stone. Then, frightened by these thoughts, Rose sank back onto her heels. It was hopeless anyway. Her mother would not have budged an inch. She could not be moved, not by Rose.

As her parents walked away, Rose stood vigil. Even though she'd had little love for Dorrick, he was her brother, and she would not abandon him to be buried alone no matter how much it hurt to hear the sound of the dirt falling onto his body below. When the hungry hole was at last filled, the men mounded the dirt and tamped it down with the backs of their shovels.

Rose stumbled away. Those Dalriadas—the cowards! When they shot a man in the back, did they even consider that he might be someone's brother or son or lover? Dorrick would never be first-boss now; his dreams were over. And hers? If only she could have a candle in the attic, a single candle.

Above the graveyard, to the north, a cloud scratched the sky. Rose stopped at the Braes' plot and knelt beside the white picket fence around Amberly's grave. According to the chiseled dates on the headstone, she had lived only twenty-two years. Rose counted. If she died when she was twenty-two, she would have only seven more years to live. Her head jerked up.

She saw all the days that had passed since her marriage, days she had wasted while the orchard withered. With every pot she had scrubbed, with every floor she had washed, her hopes for Greengarden had slipped away until somewhere, at some unmarked hour, Rose had given up without even knowing it. She had abandoned what she loved most. Was it too late to bring those hopes alive again?

Rose touched the gritty dirt circle she had traced on her forehead.

"Return to the earth," she said, and suddenly Rose knew how to choose between Mr. Brae and the Thing in the dark. She, too, had to return to the earth—to base her decision on the land. Which choice would be better for Greengarden?

If she chose the dark, she would be entombed alive, and perhaps die by the Thing's hand. If she chose Mr. Brae, she would be more defeated than she was now. She would live, but lose her last hold on the small yellow dot that was her self, because inside she would die. If she was dead inside, how could she bring life to Greengarden? If she was dead inside, how would she learn to walk across the land with delighted watchfulness? How would she learn to say the word *mine*? Without that, she could not save the orchard. No one would recognize her authority.

Death in the light. Or life, perhaps, in the dark. Only in the attic was there a chance she might land on the other side, a hairsbreadth of hope for what she loved most.

Rose stood up. She pushed Amberly's red straw hat down on her head and chose to leap.

13

Beginning

The padlocks snapped shut behind her.

"There is a chair here," the Thing said. "Come sit beside me."

Rose, leaning back against the oak door, shook her head, and then remembered he could not see her in the dark. This was her fourth visit to the attic—she came every third night. Each time the Thing was waiting in his chair by the window. He had never left it while she was there.

"Please," she said. "I'd rather not." She held her hands out in front of her and counted her steps toward where she thought the bed was. One step, two, three—and a sound like galloping horses pounded through the attic. Rose stopped, ears straining, then recognized the sound of fingernails drumming on wood. Fingernails on the disembodied white hand.

"Oh, never mind," the Thing said. "I know I am hideous."

Her left shin bumped something. Rose groped for the

mattress and sat down, puzzled. On Tuesday, it had taken nine steps to reach the bed. Why only seven this time?

"How are you hideous?" she asked.

"Guess."

"Do you have more than two arms?"

"No."

"More than two legs?"

"No, but the right one drags. I can't walk very well."

Rose nodded. That explained the thud–drag sound.

"Some folks say you've got three heads," she blurted.

The drumming stopped.

"Let me count," the Thing said. "One, two, three, four . . . oh, and there might be a few more that I can't reach."

Bang!

Rose grabbed the bedpost. Had he struck his chair? Stomped his foot?

"Of course I have only one head!" he exclaimed. "Why are you so stupid?"

"I'm sorry. But, well . . . then why do you say you're hideous?"

"*He* says so."

Bile burned Rose's throat. The Thing must be even worse than she had thought. What horror sat across from her? The dancing motes of darkness spun and became an image of the Thing shuffling forward. His gigantic body hunched. His arms, oozing with sores, swung from side to side—long and loose-jointed like a spider. His head was a black blur with one red eye glowing in the middle. A mouth formed. When he opened it to swallow her, his fangs spiked, and a tornado swirled over a yellow spot on his tongue.

Leave me alone! Rose shouted to the darkness. Stop putting terrible pictures in my mind! She scraped her wrist against the crack on the bedpost, back and forth, back and forth until pain masked the picture. Oh, this was useless— useless! How would being here ever help Greengarden? Each time she came to the attic, strange waking dreams seized her, and she could not control them. She left before dawn, exhausted, overwhelmed, and then spent the day doing housework. By evening, she was too tired even to check on her apple trees.

Her wrist throbbed. Rose wrapped her hand around the bedpost, feeling the knobs and rings. By now, she knew them intimately. First she touched the small knob at the top, then the two rings beneath it. Next she traced the long curve where the post narrowed like a woman's waist and then belled out again. At the bottom were three more rings; her index finger checked for the crack on the second one. Rose felt as if her eyes were in her fingertips.

Her hand tightened on the wood. She imagined the bedpost spinning on a lathe, taking shape as the wood shavings flew. She had seen many bedposts. This one she had never seen, yet Rose knew it in a way she knew none of the others. Sometimes it seemed like a bony leg, sometimes a gnarled old tree trunk. Tonight it felt like a woman's body. This piece of wood was the most solid thing she had here, and even it betrayed her by changing into other things.

Think of something else, Rose told herself, think of light, yes, a circle of light. If only she had a candle, if only she could see, then she would be safe. Then the wood would be a bedpost again, a plain ordinary bedpost.

"If I sneak up a candle," she said, "I could tell you if Mr. Brae's right. See if you really are hideous."

"No!" the Thing exclaimed. "He swore he would take you away if you ever see me."

Under Rose's fingers, the bedpost changed into a carved taper. Could she make a candle like that? Maybe, if she used—

"Besides," the Thing added, "I don't want you to see how hideous I am."

Rose sighed. She peeled her damp collar away from her

neck. How could the Thing bear this heat day after day? The relentless August heat, and the dark, and the—

"What's that smell?" she asked. "Is it turpentine? I've noticed it before, but it's stronger tonight." She clapped one hand over her mouth. What if the smell came from the Thing?

"It is turpentine," he said. "I mix it into my paints."

"You—paint?"

"Odd, isn't it? A monster who paints pictures and writes poetry."

"How did you learn?"

"Lee-lee taught me—my mother's old governess."

Rose had heard people talk about Amberly's governess, but they had used a different name—Emily Harsgrove.

"She raised me," the Thing said, "taught me to read and write and draw. But she"—his voice caught—"died when I was eight."

"She must have seen you," Rose said.

"That was different."

"Why?"

The Thing ignored her question. "If I keep quiet, *he* sends up all the paints and books I want. The books never have enough pictures, though. I like to look at things, really look at them. Then sometimes I can see beyond the surface when I paint." He laughed. "Even a painting is only a surface that can lead you to other places—if you can see."

Rose thought of her mother's painting of the Bighouse party and asked, "What kinds of pictures do you paint?"

"Still lifes, with objects Mrs. Schill sends up on the dumbwaiter, and—" He stopped.

Rasp, creak. Rose listened. Was that his feet moving? Or a rat?

"Once I escaped on the dumbwaiter," he added. "I got out!"

Rose did not want to think about him getting out.

"But *he* caught me. Afterward, he changed the mechanism so I could not escape again. I dream about being outside. I also paint landscapes, but I can't see much through the window bars. And the brown tint changes the colors. So I make up fabulous landscapes from my dreams—like that cave I told you about."

"I hate dreams," Rose said.

"Why?"

"They take you to terrible places."

"And beautiful places."

"Greengarden's the only place I want to be."

"It's the only place I *don't* want to be." He sighed. "But I shall never go beyond those bars again."

Rose looked at the dim light coming through the round window.

"I don't want to go out in that hard, bright world," the Thing said, "where people will see me and loathe me."

Rose scrunched a pillow into a ball. If only she had something to do, some work to keep her hands busy so that she would not see the pictures in her mind. She imagined herself holding a brush dripping with yellow paint. With small dabs, Rose lit all seventy-seven candles in her mother's painting. Next she painted the dresses: the shining surfaces of satin and silk, the filigreed surface of lace. The women were landowners, like her, and yet—Rose's fingers crept to the patch on her skirt—not like her.

"Tell me what you are thinking about," the Thing ordered.

"Paintings. Down in the drawing room, there's a little one of your mother when she was a girl."

"I paint her often." After a pause, he added, "*He* hates me because I killed my mother."

"Lots of women die in childbirth. Maybe it wasn't your fault." But Rose crossed her fingers. How could she be certain when she could not see him?

"I dream about her all the time," he said. "I even found a message from her once. A piece of paper wedged between the window molding and the wall."

"What did it say?"

"That someone she trusted had something for me. The rest of the message was ruined—mildew. So I have never known whom to ask." The Thing sighed. "Not that I could have, anyway."

Rose dug her fingernails into the crack in the bedpost. She wished her mother had left a message for her in the dark, but her mother did not even leave messages in the light. There was no one to help her but herself, and she did not even know where to begin.

Again the motes of darkness spun, and a moment later Rose heard the wail of reedy music, then the hollow sound of bone hitting stone.

No! she cried. Not again! She stood in the vaulted cave looking over her shoulder at the bone dancers weaving their endless reel. Above them, the black chandelier turned, grating and groaning while the smoke spiraled upward. But she was standing on the other side of the gurgling abyss, beneath one of the four black archways. How, when had she crossed?

Someone tugged on her hand. Rose turned and saw Amberly. She pulled Rose inside the tunnel, where the walls changed from black to a pale red veined with ruby. Here and there, the walls had been sculpted like an enormous cross-stitch: hundreds of tiny x'es formed pictures of ancient roots, moons, cornucopias, and a woman holding a dying man. Rose's hand brushed the red wall; it felt like a petal. The smell of baking bread hung in the air. A slow beat throbbed through the tunnel, and Rose saw that the ruby veins pulsed and sparkled and wept.

Amberly pulled Rose onward through the spiraling tunnel. She pulled her around fountains shaped like breasts from which milk spurted in glorious streams. She pulled her over gaps in the floor. She pulled her past a three-headed statue—a trinity of girl, woman, crone. Last, Amberly pulled Rose past seven rocking cradles to a place where the tunnel split in two directions. Halfway over each opening hung a tapestry.

Amberly stopped. *Choose,* she said.

Rose hesitated. On the right tapestry, a woman crouched half-hidden behind a door. Her hand reached around to the doorknob, whether to shut or open the door Rose did not know. On the left tapestry, a woman in a sagebrush dress threw her river of blue hair across a meadow. Fish leapt from it. Her arms—made, like her face, of mud and sticks—reached up to the sickle moon that crowned her head.

Rose chose that opening and followed Amberly around the tapestry. After a few yards the tunnel turned, leading toward a grey, pearly light. The roof ended, but the floor led out like a tongue from the tunnel and became the top of the Faredge Wall. Twilight hung over Greengarden.

Bewildered, Rose stopped. Amberly grabbed her other hand, and they began to waltz along the top of the wall. As light shot into her eyes from Amberly's jeweled dress, Rose saw that the jewels were not jewels at all but hundreds of shining buttons. They covered every inch of the dress, as if Amberly had stitched her entire collection onto the fabric. There were round buttons, square buttons, buttons rimmed with jewels, buttons of silver and gold and carved horn that tinkled together as Amberly twirled.

Soon they had completed a circle and returned to the tunnel opening. *But the Faredge Wall is straight,* Rose said. Again they went round, and again, around and around and around. Rose looked down. Along the outside of the wall, spindly sticks grew—the grafted Golden Flame trees. Green leaves sprouted from the tips of the finger-long grafts. Along the inside of the wall, contained within the circle of stone, a black pool churned as though the northwest well had overflowed.

A white claw as big as a house emerged, dripping, from the water. Rose screamed, but Amberly only pulled her along in the waltz. The claw opened, snapped in front of Rose's face, and then sank. Next rose the torsos of two giants locked in combat; black water streamed like oil from their hair. With their hands throttling each other's throats, they, too, fell back and sank. Amberly kept waltzing. Two wistful eyes appeared, one blue and one brown, looking, seeking, until the water climbed higher and drowned them. Soon the Faredge Wall would be unable to contain the rising pool. The wilderness would break through and sweep Greengarden away. And all the while the sky darkened, and then the sky was black. Rose could no longer see the wall. One wrong step and they would fall in.

Light! Rose cried. *I need a candle.*

To light a candle in the dark, said Amberly, *close your eyes. See with your breath, your soul, your heart.*

Rose closed her eyes. She breathed, and when she smelled the sage, fruit, and dust on the hot wind, she saw it was the soul of summer. She heard the roar of pines and saw it was the expression of the Earth's longing to fly. She felt the Faredge Wall scrape her bare feet and saw it was made of the bones of her ancestors, who helped her hold back the wilderness. She heard the slow gurgle of the tree roots and saw they were drinking from the black pool.

Oh! Rose cried as her heart saw the Golden Flames. *Look!* The spindly trunks were tapers, the finger-long grafts were wicks, and the green leaves sprouting from the tips had burst into green flames. Her trees were living candles. Like a ring of emeralds, they circled the dark pool, lighting the wall and the water's edge. The green flame of Greengarden was her light in the dark.

Amberly stopped waltzing and cupped Rose's face in her hands. *To begin,* said Amberly, *leaping the abyss is not enough. To begin—to find strength in love—dive into the well, dive into the terrible and the beautiful.* She smiled, then turned and dove into the black pool.

"No! Amberly!" Rose shouted. She knelt on the shining wall, beside the shining candle-trees, and looked toward the black heart of the pool, but the green light that shimmered around the edges did not stretch that far. She saw no sign of Amberly, only tiny ripples spreading outward.

Rose sobbed. She began to count—one, two, three, four—hoping that if she kept counting, maybe Amberly would never reach the bottom.

Eight, nine . . .

The ripples became waves.

Fourteen, fifteen . . .

The waves divided into streamers. As Rose counted, they grew longer and narrower until the surface of the pool was a mass of black ribbons that rose and fell and rippled. Some were shiny, some were dull, all were beautiful.

Thirty-two, thirty-three . . .

Rose reached into the water, but the ribbons felt dry, soft as velvet, then slick as satin, then rough as lace. Low in the sky hung a golden, horned moon studded with pins.

Forty-nine, fifty . . .

Something bumped her hand. Rose seized it and straightened. In her hand was a black pearl button, rounded on top and circled with glittering emeralds. When Rose rubbed the top with her index finger, blackness enveloped her. No sight, no sound, no smell. All she felt was her fingertip rubbing the button.

Seventy-six, seventy-seven—

Then Rose was back in the attic with her feet pressing the floor and her fingertip rubbing the rounded top of the bedpost. She knew exactly where to begin.

14

Guile

The next morning, after a spell that left her chest feeling raw, Rose walked down the stairs wearing her shabbiest dress, which was made of flour sacking and blistered with patches. Once Susa had seen her wearing it in the vegetable plot and shrieked, "Scarecrow! Rosecrow!" Below her ragged hem, Rose's big toe poked out of a hole in her shoe. She wiggled her toe at herself in one of the full-length mirrors in the front hall and smiled grimly.

"A vision of loveliness," she said, and then added in a deep, arrogant voice, "You are an ugly enough Rose to serve my purposes well." On the grandfather clock, the quarter moon dial was rising.

A moment later, she knocked on Mr. Brae's study door. No answer. She glanced in the sitting room and the dining room, but both were empty. Rose frowned. Naturally, now that she had made a plan and gathered her courage, he would be out. Maybe Mrs. Schill knew where he was.

On her way to the kitchen, Rose noticed the drawing

room door stood open. She went to shut it—one of Mr. Brae's rules—and saw him standing inside the room with his back toward her, mumbling to the three portraits on the wall.

"Oh." Rose stopped. "There you are."

Mr. Brae turned. "Sneaking around as usual? A mouse poking her nose into stale corners looking for crumbs?" His second chin wobbled as he laughed.

"Can I speak to you, sir?"

"Any fool can speak."

"It's about this." Rose held out her arms and turned slowly in a circle. "Folks are talking."

"I do not presume to understand you."

"You don't think I'm a Brae, but the people do. And I hate to see them make fun of you because of my clothes. They say you must not be so rich as you claim." Rose gazed at the floor. "I hope I'm not stepping out of my place, but it isn't respectful to you, sir. I thought you should know."

She held her breath, though her chest still ached from the spell. If she looked like the Mistress of Greengarden, as Amberly had, maybe Mrs. Schill, Susa, Kurt, and everyone else would treat her that way. "Your clothes must match your station," Kalista had said. Rose knew that most people did not see what a person was like on the inside, only what she looked like on the outside. Well then, why not show them what they expected to see in a Mistress of Greengarden? If that meant silk, satin, and lace, then she would stumble about in them, however ridiculous she felt. It was the first step in gaining the people's respect, since Mr. Brae would not let her gain it any other way.

Mr. Brae scowled. On the wall behind him, the three portraits of his ancestors—two old men and, between them, a pinch-nosed woman—stared out at Rose.

Impostor, they seemed to whisper. *We know her lies. We know her tricks.*

Do you see only with your eyes? Rose asked them. *Is there nothing behind you but a wall?*

They hissed, *Upstart! Behind us are generations of the landowners of Greengarden—we who have watched over this land since the Golden Age.*

Without the sweat of my ancestors, Rose told them, *yours wouldn't have had any land to watch over.*

She is not one of us, said the man holding a brace of whistling ducks.

She cannot speak the word, said the pinch-nosed woman. *Mine, mine, mine—*

I'll learn, Rose told them. *Don't you care that the land is dying? Why don't you help me save it?*

They did not answer.

Mr. Brae thumped his walking stick. "Attend! Are you daft, girl? Who has been saying I am not rich?"

"Most everyone." Rose tried not to tremble as he examined her from top to bottom. His glance rested on her big toe, and his right nostril curled.

"You are a disgrace—as usual," he said. "Very well . . ."

Rose smiled—a mistake, because Mr. Brae stopped talking and stared at her. Then, with a great laugh, he tossed his walking stick into the air. He caught it and poised the silver coyote head a foot from his face.

"My friend," he said to it, "I fear my dear granddaughter-in-law is not well practiced in the art of deception. I am disappointed. I had hoped some of our influence might have worn off, but sadly, it is not so. Why should we give her a patch to cover that obscene toe when it would be easier to cut it off?"

Rose looked down at her big toe, which stuck out like a turtle head, and tried to pull it back in.

"There, there," Mr. Brae said. "Your attempt at guile was laudable. Admirable! There may be hope for you yet. Now go away and think of another ruse. If you come up with something amusing, I may even give you a new shoe—but only one, mind you." And he looked back at the portraits.

Disappointed, Rose turned away. She hugged her arms across her aching chest. The red carpet felt soft against her cold toe, and she curled it down into the nap.

"Wait," said Mr. Brae, still looking at the portraits. "Perhaps . . . perhaps you do have a point." He paused, staring at the pinch-nosed woman. "As the mother of the heir of Greengarden, you should at least be respectable—for the sake of her respectability."

Mr. Brae took his key ring from his pocket and drew off a key. "In the room across from yours there are some old clothes. You may make a few over to fit yourself. Nothing fancy—only the very plainest ones. Return this key by four o'clock."

When Rose reached out to take it, his hand snapped shut.

"There is something else," he added. "That slut of a washerwoman says she has seen no sign."

"No sign? Of what?"

"I instructed Kalista to watch the Thing's bed sheets to make certain you have had your"—his eyebrows raised—"barnyard tumble?"

Ha! He has her there, the bearded man said.

Rose turned red. Blast that Kalista!

The pinch-nosed woman sniffed. *Did she think she was different from the rest of us? Think she would not have to pay the price? To be Mistress of the Land, she must embrace the plow.*

"Well?" Mr. Brae demanded.

Rose could not speak.

"I shall take that for a no. If you are unwilling, or if that feeble Thing cannot perform its duty, you know the alternative—the one that disgusts you so much."

In the silence, the dust flittering in the air seemed to come alive, and Rose coughed, sickened.

"I shall give you two more visits," Mr. Brae said. "Next Monday, and then Thursday will be your last chance. I shall inform the Thing as well. One way or another, I want a child from this farce." Mr. Brae threw her the key, then left the room.

Rose sank down on the spinet bench. How she hated him! She raised the sheet over the spinet and picked up the painting of Amberly. Had Amberly hated him, too? The little girl's face glowed, mischievous, joyful, unaware of all that would happen later, as alive as though she could skip right out of the glass and scamper up the old oak tree.

Rose remembered the crossed-out words on the sampler, then the words stitched boldly instead: *If a woman chooses her own path . . . She leaps every mountain between her and her beloved . . . Then, in her midnight hour, Love will be her Light.*

Rose clutched the key; it felt hot, greasy from Mr. Brae's hand. She dropped it in her lap and scrubbed her hand against her skirt.

You will *hang beside me,* said the pinch-nosed woman.

15

Women in Red

An hour later, Rose inserted the brass key into the door of Amberly's old room. The key turned as smoothly as if the lock had just been oiled. When the door swung open, Rose squinted against the light plunging through the paned windows. The room had no furniture, no drapes, not one speck of dust. Why keep an empty room so clean? And why had Mr. Brae kept Amberly's childhood room intact but not this one? Rose stepped inside and shut the door.

On the left wall, a full-length oval mirror shone, surrounded by a gilt frame. On the right wall, three closet doors stood in a row. Rose opened the middle one. Garment bags made of white canvas hung on the hangers like headless ghosts. She hooked one over the closet door, then undid the buttons until the canvas fell away to reveal a dress of chestnut-colored silk. She unbuttoned three more bags and found dresses made of grey-green broadcloth, indigo wool, and, last, ruby-red velvet. When Rose rubbed the sleeve against her cheek, the velvet felt softer than a cat and smelled faintly of jasmine. Sparkling beads edged the neckline, running from shoulder to shoulder in a soft line.

Rose carried the red dress to the mirror and held the velvet against herself. At least five inches puddled on the floor. Amberly must have been tall. Rose turned this way and that, then sighed. If she tried to wear this dress, she would look like a mouse playing the great lady. Instead of respecting her, everyone would laugh. And yet Rose hitched the dress higher: something about the style suited her—the simple, elegant lines perhaps, or the severity of the straight neckline. Maybe without the velvet, without the beads—yes, that might work. She could use the fabrics from the plainer dresses to copy the styles of the fancier ones. That would suit her well and evade Mr. Brae's instructions in such a way that he could not accuse her of disobedience.

Guile again. Would he see through it again?

Thursday will be your last chance. One way or another, I want a child from this farce . . . Rose shivered. She looked at the velvet dress, at the drapes and folds flowing down her body like a river of red. At that moment, light from the window struck the mirror, which gave a thundering flash and then went black. Rose stepped back, watching as the mirror began to ripple like water. When her reflection reappeared—her eyes first, searching, then her face and hands—superimposed upon it was a tall young woman with a shaved head.

The woman held an identical red velvet dress in front of herself, but her bare white shoulders gleamed behind it. High on her left arm were four purple bruises in the shape of fingerprints. Like the little girl's in the portrait downstairs, her brown eyes shone, but their expression was deeper, tinged with love and sorrow.

"Amberly?" Rose whispered.

Amberly held the dress out to Rose, who was too frightened to move. Then Amberly dropped the dress and stood naked, no girl, but a woman whose belly swelled with child. Around her neck hung a white cord with a round white pendant that lay over her heart.

Rose shut her eyes. This had to be a dream, only a dream, like those in the attic. "Think of Donney," she told herself, "think of walking Donney around the well." She heard the plod of the ox's hooves, then smelled his warm, sour breath. Her feet felt like ice, though, and Rose saw that she was wading through black water. It crept to her knees, to her thighs, to her . . . Rose jumped onto Donney's back. When her hands grasped his horns, they changed into a sickle moon that pulled her up into the sky, higher and higher until the stars surrounded her. Then the sickle moon plunged down, dragging her toward a dark field where white hands were throwing grain.

Rose gasped. She opened her eyes—only her pale reflection looked back at her; Amberly had vanished. Rose fled from the mirror, but halfway across the room she tripped over the dress and fell. She lay still, panting, her legs tangled in the red velvet that pooled around her on the floor.

Never before had the visions that seized her in the attic come to her in the day, in the safety of the light. Were they consuming her? What was real? What was not? Paintings spoke to her, dust spoke to her, bedposts and trees and mirrors spoke to her; everything had meaning. Even thinking about Donney, her stalwart Donney, no longer protected her. Was she going mad? Rose scrambled up, ran to the door, grabbed the handle, turned it—

She stopped. Mr. Brae wanted the key back by four. If she left without the dresses, her plan would fail, and it might take months to think of another one. Greengarden could not wait. Rose pressed her hands against the door until the sunlit wood beamed its warmth into her skin. Then she picked up the velvet dress, carried it to the closet, and went to work. She did not look at the mirror again.

* * *

"What's all this?" Gerald asked, opening the door of the Guesthouse later that day. He looked at Rose, then at the three sullen boys holding garment bags who stood behind her on the porch.

"You're home early, Pa," Rose said. "Can we come in?"

"Why not?" He stood back, and the boys followed Rose inside.

"Put those on the sofa," she told them, trying to speak with authority, as Mr. Brae did. The smallest boy dragged one of the garment bags behind him. It swept the floor, gathering dust wads. Rose frowned. Dust wads? In her mother's house?

"Thanks, boys," she said as she looked around the room. "You can go now." Not only did dust wads litter the floor, smudges streaked the woodwork and windows. Hollows dented the yellow lace puffs as though they had been punched. On the tables, the knickknacks were scattered; one glass woman had toppled over, and a crack zigzagged from the base to the foot. Rose straightened it. Something was wrong.

"So what *is* all this?" Gerald asked again, nodding toward the garment bags.

"Something I want to show Ma," Rose said. "Is she out?"

"In bed. She's still mourning for Dorrick. We all do, of course, but hers is something unnatural. I don't mind telling you, I'm a bit worried. I look in on her during the day."

"Why didn't you tell me? I'd have checked on her."

Gerald hesitated, the cords tightening in his neck, then shrugged. "I'll get her." And he went upstairs.

Rose's breath rushed in. Her mother did not want to see her, and Rose knew why. Her parents believed Dorrick's death was their punishment for the marriage arrangement; seeing her would remind them of that.

"Fine," Rose said, "then I don't want to see you either!" She started scooping up the garment bags, wanting to scream because, even dead; Dorrick was more important than she was.

Something thunked overhead. Rose glanced up. She saw the cast-off painting from the Bighouse hanging over the mantel, saw the women dancing in their exquisite dresses under the light of the seventy-seven candles. She hesitated. For her plan to work, she had to look like those women, and for that she needed her mother's help. Besides, didn't her mother owe her that much?

Rose carried the garment bags into the downstairs bedroom, whose walls were lemon yellow. One at a time, she unbuttoned the bags and draped the dresses across the bed and chairs. She had decided to make six dresses, four ordinary ones and—she swallowed—two loose ones to wear while she was with child.

On which night would she finally lie with the Thing, Monday or Thursday? Sweat trickled down her back. The bedroom was hot. Rose opened the window and looked out at the block of apple trees across the yard. Wooden props supported branches laden with Shaulas, early apples harvested in late August. Already their honeysuckle scent dazzled the air. Rose leaned farther out. All this nonsense about clothes when there was so much real work to be done in the orchard. She smiled as a line of quail skittered off the lawn and ran up the hill. Near the top of the hill, a shadow lunged. Although it was only a cleft in the rock fringed with swaying branches, Rose drew back inside.

She pulled on her fingers. Did the Thing have fangs? Fur?

If only she could see his monstrousness, she could bear it better. All she needed was a candle . . .

Rose pictured herself in the rose garden looking up at the round attic window shrouded in night. Someone lit a candle in the attic. Light escaped through the brown glass, splintering out through the black wrought-iron rose. Could she make a candle look like that? Rose imagined a wax pillar, its flame sunk so low inside that the wax gleamed golden brown, sending broken light through the fine black lines on the surface. She would need translucent wax, a mold, black thread . . .

"Rose?" Maggie called.

Rose blinked, then turned and walked toward the door, calling, "Here. In the bedroom."

Maggie, wrapped in a wrinkled blue robe, stopped outside the door. She had lost weight; her round cheeks had sunk, and the skin wrinkled above her upper lip. Her hair hung in a greasy braid.

"Ma?" Rose asked, shocked.

"Your pa says you brought something," Maggie said. "But I'm too tired to visit." She glared at Gerald, who stood beside her. "He woke me from my nap."

"All you do is nap," he said.

"Look, Ma." Rose stepped away from the door. A breeze from the window fluttered the dresses of red and blue, emerald and forest green, charcoal, brown, and yellow, lifting a sleeve here, an emerald collar there; making the room look as if it were filled with butterflies.

Maggie clasped her hands beneath her chin. She took one step into the room, then another.

"These—Amberly's?" Gerald asked.

Rose nodded.

"I've never seen anything so"—Maggie's hands dropped—"pretty."

Gerald reached toward a blue silk dress. "She was wearing this the day she told me about—" He stopped and put his hand behind his back.

"I'm going to make them over," Rose said.

"Who for?" Maggie asked.

"Me."

"You?" Maggie stared. "You're going to wear *these*?"

"Yes, but you know I'm hopeless with a needle. And you're the best seamstress in Stonewater Vale. Will you help? It has to be a secret, though—even from Mrs. Willow."

"I don't know. I'm awful tired—"

"Does Mr. Brae know about this?" Gerald interrupted.

"It was his idea," Rose said.

Maggie looked dumbfounded. "He wants you in pretty clothes?"

"As twisted as my life is," Rose said, "I am the Mistress of Greengarden. Isn't it time I looked it?"

There was a silence.

"Didn't I tell you," Maggie said, casting furtive glances at Rose, "before you were married, didn't I say he'd dress you up fine?"

"You sure did." Gerald nodded.

"We said it would be all right," Maggie added. "Said you'd get used to it."

Rose felt her rage swelling at what neither of them were saying but both were thinking: that she shared Mr. Brae's bed.

"And . . . it is all right," Maggie said, pleading, "isn't it, Rose?"

Rose opened her mouth to shout "No!" then stopped because her mother moved slightly. Maggie slipped her right foot over her left, covering the toes of one foot with the arch of the other. Her huddled feet were so small in their red crocheted slippers that Rose wondered how they could support those massive legs. As she looked, she saw with her breath, her soul, her heart. She understood that at this moment rage would solve nothing, gain nothing, and, strangest of all, offer nothing.

She needed help from this woman who was her mother, this woman who had never liked or wanted her, but who had fed her anyway, tended her when she was sick, sewn ruffles on her flour-sack aprons, and embroidered apple blossoms on her wedding dress. For Maggie, pretty things were a way to make life better, an attempt to find beauty in the world. This, Rose saw, was similar to how she felt about her trees. Then she understood what she needed to say next and knew it was not an attempt at guile, but an offer of redemption.

"No, Ma," she said, "it isn't all right. But it might be, if you help me now. All you have to do is use your needle. You can help put things to rights by doing what you like best—making something pretty."

"No." Maggie's lips trembled. "I know. I've seen." She looked at the floor and said slowly, "Pretty things won't keep you safe."

The words hung in the air. Rose imagined them spreading through the room into the walls, where they shot straight down to the foundation bricks. The house seemed to groan, as if the entire building were about to collapse and sweep away the knickknacks, the lace curtains, and the carved, mahogany moldings, leaving only dust and ashes. Rose realized that pretty things were to her mother as walking Donney was to her: a way to be safe. What happened when you were surrounded by beautiful things and still were not safe? What happened when you walked Donney around the well and still were not safe? What then?

"I don't know," Rose said. "But pretty things make the world nicer, don't they?" And she smiled.

Maggie smiled back.

"I need you," Rose said. "You're the only one who can help me with this. Will you?"

"Sure she'll help." Gerald put his arm around Maggie's shoulders. "Think what fun it will be, Mag. And it'll give you something to do."

"As if I haven't got enough to do," Maggie exclaimed, "taking care of this house and you!"

Gerald's eyes lit up.

Maggie stroked the blue silk dress, then straightened her shoulders and said, "Fetch my pincushion, Rose—the gold satin one."

16

Elixir

On Monday night, while the Thing rambled on about a mountain, Rose sat in the dark crocheting a long chain. She hooked stitch after stitch, concentrating on the feeling of the rough yarn slipping through her fingers. It held her, anchored her, kept her from thinking of the horror ahead.

She did not have to lie with the Thing tonight—Mr. Brae had given her until Thursday. Yes, Thursday, not tonight. Thursday was forever away. She would capture the minutes with her stitches so that this night, this Monday, would last forever, and Thursday would never come.

What if the Thing did not want to wait?

"I can't bear this," Rose said and reached for the bedpost.

"Why did you interrupt!" the Thing exclaimed. "I was nearly there. I could see the cavern where the shining tree rises out of the mountain—" He stopped. "Bear what?"

Rose thought quickly. Mr. Brae must not have spoken to him yet.

"I mean," she stammered, "how can *you* bear this? Being locked up in here? Sitting in the dark all the time?"

"It isn't dark in the daytime, Mouse."

Rose let go of the bedpost and jerked yarn off the ball. She had made the mistake of telling the Thing her nickname. Now he used it all the time even though he knew she hated it.

"I prefer the dark," he added, "because then I can't see my prison walls. My imagination flies free—now more than ever because of all the things you have told me about the world." He paused. "But sometimes, like tonight, the Elixir helps me to bear my wretched life."

"The Elixir?"

"That's what Lee-lee called laudanum. Poppy powder dissolved in wine. The drink that opens the eye of the soul."

"But that's only for toothache or other sickness," Rose said. "Are you sick?"

"Am I sick?" he considered. "I am a monster. Are all monsters, simply by virtue of being monsters, sick?"

How could she answer such questions? Rose looped a stitch around the hook and felt the weight of the crocheted chain gathering in her lap. How long before the chain spilled down her skirt, surrounded her feet, and filled the attic? What would she do when the yarn ran out?

"Every once in a while," the Thing said, "when *he* wants something, he brings me a cup of the Elixir as a bribe. He never sends it up on the dumbwaiter. It's the only thing he gives me with his own hands—through the slot in the door. He brought a cup this morning."

The crotchet hook lay still, a thin, bone stem forgotten in Rose's fingers. So Mr. Brae had spoken to the Thing. But what was the bribe for?

"He only gave me a half-draught," the Thing added. "Barely enough to stir me. He promised to give me more after we—" He stopped.

Rose plunged one hand into the crotcheted chains in her lap. So he did know.

"It's another way he torments me," the Thing said.

"You don't have to drink it."

"Oh, but I do. You should see how well I can paint and write on its wings. I feel I understand everything! But afterward I come crashing down. I suffer and crave and long for it. It's torture. That is what he likes, torturing me."

Rose felt the chain stretch out, linking her to the twisted lives of the landowners of Greengarden, to Amberly, Mr. Brae, the pinch-nosed woman, and all the others, stretching back to the Golden Age.

"Lee-lee began it," the Thing said. "She gave me laudanum to keep me quiet, because if I made a lot of noise, *he* would come up and beat her."

Rose dropped a stitch. "He beat Lee-lee?"

"I tried to stop him once. I hit him with my stick-horse, Minnie . . ." The Thing paused. "But it was useless—like a fly buzzing against a wall. He grabbed Minnie and started beating me with her. That was the first time he hit me instead of Lee-lee."

"But that's horrible! Why on earth did she stay?"

"Because she loved me, of course."

Rose sat back, trying to imagine this.

The Thing sighed. "Drinking the Elixir was the only way she could bear *him*. Remember I told you I escaped on the dumbwaiter? I was eight. He'd beaten her that morning. That night, Lee-lee drank too much of the Elixir. After she fell into a stupor, I stole the dumbwaiter key from her pocket and lowered myself down. When *he* dragged me back to the attic, Lee-lee was dead in her chair."

Rose pulled the yarn tight. Would that happen to her? Would they find her dead on Friday morning, wrapped in a shroud she had crocheted for herself?

Crash!

Rose cringed. What had he thrown this time?

"I know what you're thinking!" the Thing cried. "But I didn't kill her, I didn't! It was the Elixir!" He panted, then his voice changed—it sounded small. "But *he* took away all the candles and lanterns. He left her with me for five days. In summer. With no food. He said, he said that . . . I should eat her."

Rose could not move. She had turned to stone.

The three-headed Thing
Grabs you while you dream,
The three-headed Thing
Eats you while you scream.
Nah! Nah! Nah! Nah!

"After that," he whispered, "there was no one, no one ever to talk to, for years and years—until you came."

Rose shook off the pity she felt for him. Her fingers moved again. She began to count the stitches, one, two, three, fifty, seventy-seven . . .

* * *

. . . ten thousand. Rose felt as if the crocheted chain were wrapping around her as she followed Mr. Brae up the stairs on Thursday night. She crotcheted as the key jangled in the locks, as the iron bar clanked.

"Thing!" Mr. Brae called as he opened the door. "Here's your ugly wife. You will never see her again unless you do your duty. Though I doubt if you could impregnate a rabbit, you're such a sorry excuse for a man."

Mr. Brae raised his hand to push Rose across the threshold, but before he could touch her, Rose stepped inside. He slammed the oak door and locked the padlocks; then his footsteps faded away.

Rose clutched her crochet hook, her yarn, her armful of chain, and blinked at the darkness. Tonight the bed would be only one step away, but that step was enormous, an abyss filled with rattling bone dancers, muttering pinch-nosed women, and gurgling black water. She pushed her back against the door. Wasn't it still Monday? Earth's Mercy, let it still be Monday. It had to be Monday, Monday, Monday—

"He can't take you away," the Thing said. "He musn't!"

Rose heard snuffling from the chair by the round window.

"I would die if I were all alone again," he sobbed. "I'd go mad, I would. But I can't . . . I'm scared, Mouse. I'm frightened."

The rattling stopped, the muttering stopped, the gurgling stopped.

"*You're* frightened?" Rose asked slowly. "Why?"

"Because," he whispered, "I don't want you to touch me."

Rose was so startled she dropped the ball of yarn. She heard it bounce, then felt a tug on the crocheted chain as the ball unwound and rolled off into the dark.

"Why not?" she asked. "Because I'm ugly?"

"No! Because, because when you find out how hideous I am, you'll hate me. I couldn't bear that, no matter how much of the Elixir he promises to bring."

To her surprise, Rose found that she did not hate him already. She feared him, yes, but he was too pathetic to hate.

"I thought of saving some laudanum for you," he said, "so you could bear me, but I'm too weak, too weak! I drank it all—but it was only a quarter-draught."

"That's all right. I don't want to live . . . numbed. That's what I'll be like if I have Mr. Brae's child."

"Then, we will both be worse off if we don't?"

"Yes."

"But I don't know how to . . . what to do," he admitted. "Not really. *He's* right. I am a sorry excuse for a man."

"Earth's Mercy!" Rose exclaimed. "I hope you're a sorry excuse for a monster!"

The Thing laughed. "Yes, that is first, I suppose, isn't it? Just that? May we start with just that? And then see about . . . the other?"

"All right." Rose took one step, not toward the bed, but toward the round window. Tonight the moon shone full, and the window was a ball of molten silver. The curling bars of the black rose outlined the silver petals. As she took another step, the dancing motes of darkness spiraled. The window began to revolve slowly clockwise.

The chair creaked. A thud echoed through the attic, and the floor vibrated, followed by the dragging sound of his bad leg. Then again, thud–drag, and again, closer. In spite of her resolve, Rose pressed her fist to her mouth. The trembling began in her shoulders, then ricocheted through her body until even her heart seemed to shake. Her breath grew shallow; the gurgling black water had risen to her nose.

The Thing stopped an arm's length away, indistinct, amorphous—she could not see even one of his features. If she touched him and learned the truth, no matter how dreadful, wouldn't the worst be over? Then the darkness could no longer play terrible tricks on her mind. Yet Rose could not raise her hand. She saw herself standing frozen in the darkness forever, wound in her crocheted chain as eternities passed outside, as the window-wheel turned and the seasons went round, as the years spun into eons—and all the while the land brooded, waiting for her to move.

To light a candle in the dark, see with your breath, your soul, your heart.

Rose held up her hands.

"Can I touch you?" she asked.

"I . . ." His voice wobbled. "Yes. Only—don't hate me."

Rose pictured that white disembodied hand that she dreaded, then reached out, fumbled in the air, and clasped it.

She was touching the Thing.

Her knees buckled, and she grabbed his other hand to keep from falling. His flesh was warm, not icy cold as it had looked on their wedding day.

"There," he said. "See? Only two hands."

Rose slid her hands up his arms. She felt something coarse; was it . . . yes, rough cotton. At least he wore clothes. His right shoulder sloped lower than his left. The Thing stood about eight inches taller than she did. Her hands recoiled at a sudden change in texture, then she realized she had touched his bare neck. No sores or scabs marred his skin, only the bump of a mole lodged beneath his left ear. The veins in his throat throbbed against her fingertips. And yes, he had only one head.

"Don't hate me," the Thing said, trembling. "Don't, don't, please don't."

Braver now, Rose traced his jaw, then the indentation at his temples. His brow jutted over his eyes; there were only two. When her thumbs pressed his cheeks, whisker stubble prickled back. He shaved? The Thing shaved? Rose brushed her fingers down each side of his nose to his mouth, fearing to feel fangs, but there were none.

"Am I hideous?" he asked. "Am I?"

Confusion and elation collided in her heart. This was the Thing in her hands. She had touched it, and it was not so different from her. His tears dripped against her fingers.

"You are a sorry excuse for a monster," she said and felt his cheeks raise into a smile. She dropped her hands.

"Your fingers are petals, Rose," he whispered. "You are my Elixir now."

"And you," she said, "are Raymont."

He stepped closer, blocking her view of the window—except for a silver slip of light that curved like a sickle moon above his head. Rose stared at it and heard a creaky old voice mutter: *To be Mistress of the Land, she must embrace the plow.* Rose reached toward the sickle moon and saw her fingers silhouetted black against the light, saw the bump of the ring on her finger.

The motes of darkness spun. Rose found herself clinging to the horned moon as it plunged toward a dark field. She landed on the earth with a plop and began to roll. The darkness raked over her body, digging into her flesh, shredding her into pieces that it turned over and over, scattering her across the field, mixing blood, bone, and breath into the land.

All her scattered pieces searched for each other. They wove roots throughout the dark earth, making new pathways toward her self. Her roots dove into the black water—into the beautiful and the terrible—and drank until she grew fertile, bulging, swelling, ripe! She was the land and she was a Rose and she sprouted forth over all that dark field, blossoming beneath the horned moon.

PART THREE

17

The Candles

I've never seen anything like that."

Rose turned, her hands slick with wax, and saw Joff Will staring over the picket fence at the half-finished candle on the stump. She looked at it, too. The blue wax flared around the taper, like a cloak swirling around a woman or a wave caught in a tornado.

"I guess it is kind of strange," Rose said, but she had made so many unusual candles in the last dark month that none of them seemed strange to her anymore.

"Strange in a good way. Makes me wonder what it might be." Now Joff was looking at her. His white-blond hair slanted across his forehead, the tips just touching his left eyebrow.

Rose wiped her own forehead. Sweating in her old muslin dress in the heat from the outdoor oven—and in the heat of early September—she knew she looked nothing like the Mistress of Greengarden. No, surrounded by her pails and paraffin and crazy candles, she undoubtedly looked more like Kalista than Amberly.

"I know," Joff said, grinning. "It's a blue rooster!"

Rose laughed. The yellow-checked curtain flicked at the kitchen window, propped open with a stick. Rose was working at the far end of the backyard, at a table beside the stone oven, but Mrs. Schill had keen ears.

"Sure," Rose said. "Call it a rooster, if that's what you see."

"It's something. How did you make it?" Joff asked.

"Like this." With one hand, Rose picked up the blue candle by the tip; the bottom was attached to a wax disk. With her other hand, she picked up a pail of hot, yellow wax from the top of the oven. Rose poured the wax onto the disk, and then, twirling the candle, she plunged it into the bucket of water. She forgot about Joff. She did not think. She exhaled, and the stream of yellow wax she poured seemed to be her breath, which the water sculpted to hold the light. When the wax hardened, Rose pulled the candle up, dripping, fantastic, with gossamer swirls.

"Like that!" She laughed again.

"It's really something!" Joff exclaimed. The yellow wax had hardened over the blue, but here and there the blue still showed. "Now it looks like a summer day."

"Do you want it?"

Joff looked up, startled, and their eyes held.

For some reason, Rose's new knowledge of what happened between men and women came into her mind. She reddened, then put the candle down on the stump, hoping he would attribute her blush to the heat from the oven fire. She tried to concentrate on wiping her hands against her apron, but she kept wondering what it might be like to lie in his arms. Would he touch her gently, the way his hair just touched his eyebrows? Would it be different from how it was with Raymont?

Even though Rose had discovered nothing monstrous about Raymont's body, she simply did not want him to touch her. She had found no pleasure in the marriage bed, only endurance and sometimes panic. Pushed into the mattress, surrounded by him—his smell of turpentine, his hot skin, his groans—she felt smothered. Once, when the bed had rocked so hard that it thudded against the floor, her panic had triggered a spell. Raymont had been reluctant to stop even though she was wheezing. So she was grateful whenever the visions took her mind away, even if they showed her something terrible.

"I . . . I mean," Rose stammered now, "I have lots of candles—almost fifty. I wouldn't miss this one. If you'd like it, that is."

"I would. But I'm leaving on Thursday—for the war. They need more men. It's not going well. The barbarians are still pushing south."

Her hands stopped moving. "I'd heard you were on the defense force here at the orchard."

"Someone had other ideas."

Pa, Rose thought.

"But that's crazy," she said. "Who'll look after the animals if they get sick? And with harvest coming right up?"

"I suppose the fighting men need their horses looked after, too."

"I'm sorry," she said.

"I'll be all right." Joff stretched an arm behind his head, cradled the back of his neck with his hand, and looked up into the branches of the oak tree. A pair of squirrels chittered and chased, sending leaves drifting lazily down. He caught one.

"I was over by the Faredge Wall yesterday," he said. "The Appelunes are looking fine."

Rose smiled.

"They're loaded," he added. "Best crop on the place. When are you picking?"

"They should ripen up in a few weeks," she said, and then felt embarrassed again by the word "ripen."

"We ought to graft other varieties onto a dwarf root-stock—plant them close together like you did. I don't know—do you think it would work with the Penna pears? It's sure time the old ones came out."

They talked about orcharding for a while. Flattered that someone cared about her opinions, Rose told him about the intermediate graft on the Golden Flames.

"Where do you get all your ideas for things?" Joff asked. "For the orchard and the candles?"

Rose looked down into the bucket—at the bits of floating yellow wax, at a fallen oak leaf sinking into the water, at her reflection on the round silver surface of the water. She knew, a little, where her ideas came from, but she would sound like Kalista if she tried to explain.

"From out of the well," she said.

Joff laughed. "Wherever they come from, we could use a lot more of them around here. Otherwise this place won't be worth saving from the Dalriadas." He rubbed the back of his neck. "I better be going."

"I'll save an Appelune for you. For when you get back from the war."

"Yes, ma'am," he said. "Bye."

Rose nodded and traced one finger around the rim of the bucket, afraid to look at him. Joff turned and walked away. Wood crackled inside the oven, and she could feel heat radiating from the stones.

"Wait!" Rose called. "You forgot your candle." She picked it up, then held it out over the fence.

Joff came back. When he took the candle, his hand touched hers for a moment, only a moment, but long enough to feel—fire. Not a golden fire, like a candle flame, but a red fire, roaring hot. Was it his, or hers? Then she knew it had to be hers, because during the last month in the attic, she had felt nothing like it.

* * *

After dinner, Rose stood in the sitting room of the Guesthouse having the final fitting on one of her new dresses. She sweltered in the dark blue wool that swathed her from throat to ankle. Maggie had gone upstairs to find her thimble. Gerald sat by the open window, beneath the bilious lace puffs, and reviewed the orchard account book.

"Pa," Rose said.

"Hmm?" He turned a page.

"Joff stays here."

Gerald looked up. She could almost see him switching his thoughts around.

"That isn't your concern, Rose," he said.

"It is. Harvest is coming. We need all the stock healthy to pull the wagons. Joff sees . . . I mean, he has a feeling for the land as well as the animals. I'm the Mistress of Greengarden, and he's good for Greengarden. Joff stays."

Gerald shut the account book. "I don't know what you're up to, Rose. But it sounds like trouble. Big trouble."

"What do you mean?"

His index finger tapped the armrest. "You're a married woman now."

"I see." Furious, Rose pulled out a pin jabbing her side. "Since you arranged for me to be with one man who's not my husband, you think it will be a snap for me to lie down with another?"

The color drained from Gerald's face. The lie about her marriage swelled through the room, ballooning the lace puffs and bloating the fake roses in a vase on the end table.

"You must think I'm an 'indecent woman,' " she added.

"Isn't that what you called Amberly?" Without waiting for an answer, Rose turned and looked at the painting hanging over the mantel, where the women danced in their splendid dresses beneath the blaze of seventy-seven candles. Only twenty-six more candles to make, and Rose, too, would have seventy-seven. And then? Rose twirled; her blue wool skirt flared around her like the blue water candle.

"Joff stays," she said.

18

Recriminations

One morning two weeks later, Rose opened her eyes and blinked warily at the folderol chest in her room. She pushed back the covers. Then, moving as carefully as if she balanced an egg on her head, she sat up. A patch of light on the folderol chest rocked like a boat. Her stomach shifted.

"Not again," she moaned. With one hand clapped to her mouth, she sank back down on the bed and closed her eyes. This was the third morning in a row she had felt sick. Downstairs, the grandfather clock tolled eight times. Rose dragged herself up and got dressed. She was tightening the bow on her apron when her stomach lurched. As the room tilted, she grabbed the folderol chest, and her elbow knocked off one of the candles on top. Rose tried to breathe, determined not to throw up, while the candles swam before her eyes.

During the last two weeks she had made twenty more, bringing the total to seventy-one. Candles not only covered the top of the chest but also lined the floor along the walls.

Each one was different, each strange. The two nearest candles she had made after her conversation with Joff. One was shaped like an oak leaf, with real oak leaves visible in the translucent wax—a tip, a stem, a flash of green. Beside it stood a tall stone-white pillar. Rose had carved and molded the wax into overlapping petals, revealing red inside.

At last the room stopped spinning. Rose picked up the candle she had knocked to the floor and smoothed the wick, which was still white. She had not yet lit any of the candles. She put it back on the chest and went downstairs.

By the time she reached the kitchen, Rose felt so nauseous again that she slumped down at the table with her head in her arms.

The kitchen door banged. Mrs. Schill came in carrying a slab of greasy fatback. Rose swallowed hard.

"You're late," Mrs. Schill said. "Third time this week."

Rose glanced at her, barely caring, then dropped her head again. Mrs. Schill tossed the meat onto the wooden counter and turned toward the table.

"What foolishness is this?" she asked.

"I think I'm dying," Rose said. "Everything's spinning. I've been throwing up every morning for three days. It can't be influenza—it goes away in the afternoon."

Mrs. Schill did not move. Then she laughed. Rose had barely enough strength to scowl up at her.

"You're not dying," Mrs. Schill said. "You're with child."

Rose sat up. "I am? How do you know?"

"What do you mean, 'How do you know'? How long since your last moon-time?"

For a moment, even as Rose realized what Mrs. Schill meant, the image of the bright, horned moon gleamed in her mind. "Two months, maybe. What's that got to do with it?"

"Didn't your ma teach you anything, girl?"

Rose opened her mouth, then shut it again fast.

"You've got the morning ails," Mrs. Schill said.

Of course! Rose knew about the sickness that troubled some women during childbearing. Why hadn't she realized?

"It'll pass in two months," Mrs. Schill added. "Maybe three."

"Three months!"

"You'll live." Mrs. Schill put her hands on the table and leaned closer. Rose smelled applejack on her breath.

"Be honest now, girl," Mrs. Schill's voice dropped to a whisper. "I won't give you away. It isn't the Thing's child at all, is it?"

Rose stiffened.

"I bet the old goat's the real father."

Rose slapped her.

Mrs. Schill straightened, a mixture of wonder and bafflement in her bloodshot eyes.

"So the rose has thorns," she said. "I was doubting you'd ever show any gumption. Oh, you've flared once or twice, so I knew you had it in you. But you're sure one to let folks grind you down."

The kitchen seemed to dip, and Rose sank back in her chair.

"So you did lie with it." Mrs. Schill pulled a flask from her apron pocket. "Either you're brainless or you've got more courage than everybody on the place combined. Be warned, though, sure as the sun comes up, more folks than me are going to wonder about the father." She looked sideways at Rose. "So what does the Thing look like?"

"I don't know."

"You don't . . . know?" Mrs. Schill stared.

"Mr. Brae makes me go up in the dark."

"Earth's Mercy." Mrs. Schill tipped up her flask, took a swig, gave it a pat, and then stowed it back in her pocket. She banged around the kitchen, slicing bread and heating milk on the stove. Ten minutes later she set a bowl of bread pudding in front of Rose.

"Get some of that down," Mrs. Schill said. "I know you think you can't, but try anyway. It helped me."

"You had the morning ails?"

Mrs. Schill sat down on the other side of the table and nodded. "When I carried my Adrena."

"My ma never told me anything about women's ways," Rose said.

Mrs. Schill snorted. "Who can fathom the likes of Maggie Chandler? A woman who let her own flesh and blood marry that Thing for a few sticks of furniture and some useless freedom."

Rose nibbled on the pudding. She had not realized her mother's failings were so widely known.

"Once," Mrs. Schill said, "His Most Exalted wanted my Adrena to marry the Thing. She's a freewoman, pretty as a pin, and a fourth cousin, too. Quite a step up from you. He promised I wouldn't have to cook anymore." Mrs. Schill reached into her pocket. "But me, I'd have none of it. I know his tricks, you can bet your life on that. So I sent Adrena away to work at East Dale Ranch, where she'd be safe."

Mrs. Schill unstoppered her flask and stared at it. "Safe. Ha! Turns out the bloody Dalriadas attacked not five miles from Darrowdale." She took a long drink, then wiped her mouth on her shoulder and added, "I haven't heard a word from her since."

"But now that Raymont's married," Rose said, "why can't Adrena come home?"

"Raymont?"

"The—my husband."

Mrs. Schill blinked her red-rimmed eyes. "Mercy. I'd forgot the Thing has a name. It's not a puppy, you know, girl! It's dangerous. It drove Emily Harsgrove to kill herself. And not four years ago, that Thing came as close as this"—she snapped her fingers—"to killing the old goat himself. Laid a trap and damn near throttled him with a wire. Why do you think Brae always wears those neckcloths?"

Rose shook her head.

"To hide the scars."

Rose frowned. She did not know whose stories to believe.

"Brae pays to keep my mouth shut," Mrs. Schill added. "But you got a right to know. Don't let that Thing lure you into thinking you're safe. That's when it will turn on you."

"But Adrena?" Rose asked.

"Brae won't let her come back. The only thing that man holds on to tighter than gold is a grudge." Mrs. Schill spit on a corner of her apron and rubbed at a spot on the table.

"Why don't you go over to East Dale Ranch and see if she's all right?" Rose asked.

"His Most Exalted won't give me leave."

"But you're free! You can do what you want."

"Free!" Mrs. Schill scoffed. "Not when he can take away my job. A freewoman my age, I'm too old for fieldwork. Too drunk for a mercantile. Too proud for a boardinghouse kitchen. Other jobs are scarce."

"Wouldn't a baker or another Bighouse hire you to make your pastry concoctions?" Rose asked, thinking of the way Mrs. Schill's coarse hands created fanciful wonders from sugar, egg whites, whipped cream, and bits of pastry.

"Those are for me," Mrs. Schill said. "They're mine. I don't do them on command for no one."

Rose scooped up another spoonful of bread pudding. How easily Mrs. Schill had said the word *mine*.

"When I'm truly mistress here," Rose said, "I'm going to free everyone."

"You poor little fool. I don't care if you have forty children, I'd bet my life that old goat will never let you be mistress here."

Rose said nothing. She ate three more bites of the bread

pudding and tasted a hint of cinnamon and sugar that she had not noticed before.

"My stomach feels a bit better," she said. "Thank you."

For the first time, Mrs. Schill looked almost kind. "I hope your babe's not a Thing," she said.

* * *

"And *he* didn't think I could father a child," Raymont said that night. "I guess he knows I'm a man now. What did he say when you told him?"

Rose sat in a chair beside his, listening to the rain ping against the round window behind her. It seemed odd, disconcerting, to be unable to see the window with its curving wrought-iron rose. She looked instead at its intricate shadow, which fell like a shadowy rose carpet across the floor at her feet.

"I haven't told him yet," she said. "I thought you should know first."

"It's wonderful—wonderful!"

Rose agreed, though sadly, because hers were not the usual reasons why one rejoiced over a baby. This baby was wonderful because now she would be safe from Mr. Brae, would be firmly established as Mistress of Greengarden, and would no longer have to lie with Raymont.

"My son," said Raymont, "will be free."

"Or daughter." Annoyed, Rose looked at the shadowy rose carpet and heard her mother say, "Imagine, my Dorrick a freeman. Imagine, my son a hero." Why hadn't her mother said, "Imagine, tricking my Rose into a horrible marriage so my Dorrick can be a freeman"? Or "Imagine, my daughter a hero for sacrificing herself for her family"? Why not speak the truth, even if it was terrible? Especially if it was terrible.

Rose followed the spiraling path of the petals with her eyes until she reached the center of the shadowy rose. She imagined her baby growing there, in the center of herself. Rose already almost loved her baby, and she already feared for it, feared it might be growing into a Thing inside her. Would her baby inherit Raymont's monstrous defect? But what was his defect? Why was he locked up? What was the truth? She thought of the candles waiting in her room.

"Mouse," said Raymont suddenly, "you told me once that you married me—when you thought I was a monster—because you loved Greengarden. You wanted to save it."

"Yes."

"What a sweet little dream. And you were brave to marry me to get it—particularly since you believed I was really a monster. I have been thinking about that, about all that you've told me about the world, and about the baby coming, and I think, I think . . . there is something I want to be brave enough to do."

"What?"

"My dreams are becoming strange and powerful," he said slowly, "even though I haven't had a drop of laudanum for weeks. Something is calling me. I see apples streaked with gold. Glaciers snaking down mountains. And that tree I told you about, the one growing out of the cavern? I see it, too." Raymont paused. "Sometimes I wake with my head filled with the pounding hooves of horses. They're so vivid I can still see the colors."

"And?"

"You were brave enough to come into the attic," Raymont said. "I think I am brave enough to . . . leave it."

Rose clutched her skirt. "What?"

"I want to go outside."

The Thing outside? Loose? The darkness seemed to wrap around Rose's chest, crushing her ribs. Her breath grew shallow.

"I thought," she said, "that you were afraid to have people see you? Because they would loathe you?"

"I was, until you said I do not seem like a monster. There is nothing really wrong with me except for my bad leg."

"Then why won't you let me see you in the light?" Her voice rose. "And why won't Mr. Brae? There must be a reason why you're locked up!"

"But what if there isn't!" Raymont cried. "What if I'm not a monster at all? What if *he* simply hates me?"

Rose tried to take a deep breath. This was all her fault.

"Help me," Raymont whispered. "Rose, my elixir, help me escape."

The dancing motes of darkness leapt, and Rose saw a white, disembodied hand swing an ax against an apple tree. When the blade bit into the trunk, wood chips flew. The wound turned into a mouth that cried, *Don't let it out!*

"Say that you'll help me," he pleaded.

Rose did not answer.

"Earth's Mercy!" Raymont hit the sloping ceiling. Rose cringed. His chair screeched as he pushed it back and stood up, a dark shadow above her.

"You have told me so much about the world outside," he said. "You're my guide, my elixir! Don't let me die without ever feeling the sun. Don't let me die without ever seeing the stars. Or without seeing a bird fly overhead. You are not that cruel, Mouse, you're not."

Outside, something wailed. It sounded like a ghost, or— Rose pressed a hand to her stomach—a baby. The wail spun out like a thread, then faded into the rain.

"I don't know," she whispered.

"There is some other life for me than this!" Raymont said. "I would rather die tomorrow trying to escape than live like this for a hundred years."

Rose bowed her head. A current of air swept past, and Raymont's black shape knelt in the center of the shadowy rose carpet at her feet.

"Perhaps I was a monster once," Raymont said, feeling

for her hands, "but I'm not anymore, now that I have you. You have changed me." He paused. "So my sweet Mouse, will you help me escape?"

Rose was silent. "Let me see you in the light."

"I will."

"Then get a candle." She started to rise.

"No." He pulled her back down. "Not yet."

"When?" she exclaimed.

"Soon, very soon."

"If you escape, you won't see your child grow up."

"Of course I will," Raymont said, surprised. "You are coming with me. We will travel up to the North Valley."

"Me? Leave . . . Greengarden?" She spoke with a gasp, as though someone had punched her in the stomach. "You want me to leave Greengarden? And let it die? When you know how much I love it?"

After a silence, he said coldly, "Surely you love me more."

Love him? Although Raymont was her husband and the father of her child, Rose did not love him and doubted she ever would.

"Your dream about Greengarden is sweet," Raymont said, laughing. "But surely, Mouse, aren't I more important than a clod of dirt?" His grip tightened on her hands.

"Aren't I?" he asked.

She did not speak.

"Aren't I!"

Rose felt her knucklebones crushing together. She silently watched his black shape, kneeling in the center of the shadowy rose carpet where she had imagined her baby growing. A flash of pain shot from her hands to her shoulders.

"Anyone," he said, "who loves a clod of dirt more than a human being is a Thing. A monster."

19

The Mistress
of Greengarden

At noon the next day, Rose pushed open the kitchen door and went into the dining room, where she set a plate of veal pinwheels in front of Mr. Brae. Already on the table was a bowl of green salad, a basket of peaches, a plate of buttermilk rolls, and, as always, the silver bell he used to summon her, the silver bell she polished every morning. Instead of returning to the kitchen, Rose pulled out a chair and sat down.

"Are you unable to remember the simplest instructions?" Mr. Brae asked as he peeled a peach with a paring knife. He skinned it from the top down, leaving delicate shreds of skin dangling from the bottom. "I have made it quite clear that you dine in the kitchen."

"I have something to tell you," Rose said. "I'll have a baby in the spring."

His knife stopped. Then, for a few moments, he stared at the slippery, half-naked peach. "So," he said at last, "there it is, then. My descendants will be . . ." He looked at her and then started peeling again. "That was quick—once you came to the point. Of course, most bondwomen are excellent breeders."

Rose stiffened.

"As of now," he added, "your visits to the attic are over."

She stared—she had not expected this—and felt the tension ebb from her shoulders. No more endless hours in the dark. No more visions. No more enduring the touch of a man she did not love, and who after last night—Rose rubbed her sore hand—she had begun to fear again. After Raymont had finally released her, he had spent the rest of the night brooding in silence.

"He'll be lonely," Rose said to Mr. Brae, surprising herself.

"Lonely?" Mr. Brae laughed. "Come now. The Thing is incapable of any emotions except hatred and rage. Surely you don't feel affection for that monster?"

"I'm not sure that he is a monster."

"Then it has deceived you—hardly surprising. It is a master of manipulation. I assure you, the Thing is a monster and more dreadful than you can possibly imagine."

"What's so monstrous about him?" Rose asked. "He isn't misshapen. And he isn't an idiot or a lunatic. Kalista's crazier than he is."

"Have you never considered, my dear granddaughter-in-law, that monstrousness can be a quality of the soul?"

"The soul?" Rose pulled on her fingers and thought of the words that had haunted her all morning: *Anyone who loves a clod of dirt more than a human being is a Thing. A monster.*

"But you can't see a soul," she said slowly. "There must be something wrong with him that can be seen. Otherwise, you wouldn't care about the light."

"This is irrelevant. Your visits are over—you should be grateful to have survived this long." Mr. Brae sliced the peach into a bowl. "The Thing can be horrendously violent—even murderous."

Rose looked at the white neckcloth around his throat. What violence did it hide?

"I am leaving presently," Mr. Brae added, "for two days—on business about the war. When I return, I shall inform the Thing that you will no longer be visiting the attic." He wiped his hands on his napkin. "Now get out."

Rose stood. As Mr. Brae reached toward the plate of pinwheels, she snatched the one he was about to take and shoved it in her mouth. He scowled. Rose went back to the kitchen, where, feeling ridiculous, she swallowed her small rebellion.

* * *

The following morning, the twenty-fifth of September, dawned bright and hot. After breakfast, Rose stood near the stone oven in the backyard priming wicks. She dipped a length into the melted wax, counted to thirty, and then fished it out with an old fork. Now and then, a wave of nausea from the morning ails made her groan. Behind her, Mrs. Schill hung dish towels on the clothesline. Rose had just laid a wick out to cool and stiffen when she heard a shout.

"Mrs. Schill! Oh, Mrs. Schill!" Opal came running up, her apron covered with blood and straw. "An emergency meeting," she panted, hopping from one leg to the other, wiping tears with the corner of her apron. "At noon—down in the old oak field. Mr. Chandler—he's called all hands from harvest."

"Stopped harvest!" Rose exclaimed.

"What's going on?" asked Mrs. Schill.

"Don't know," Opal said; then she sobbed.

"What a state you're in, girl," Mr. Schill said. "Why are you carrying on so?"

"Had to kill poor Tillie's pups," Opal sobbed. "Poor little things came out all twisted. Joff couldn't do nothing to help. Poor Tillie's beside herself."

Mrs. Schill snorted. "Get a grip, girl."

"I got to go—spread the word," said Opal, still sobbing. "Poor Tilleeee . . ."

Rose watched her run off down the road, trailing straw. "What could be so important that Pa would stop harvest?" she asked.

Mrs. Schill snapped a wet dish towel. "My bet's on the bloody Dalriadas."

* * *

The grandfather clock struck eleven as Rose opened the wardrobe in her room and laid one of her new dresses on the bed. She and her mother had removed yards of ruffles from the dark green silk—in spite of Maggie's protests—but they had kept the honey-colored piping that edged the neckline, the hem, and the long, straight sleeves.

Rose wondered if she dared wear it to the meeting. With Mr. Brae away, she could appear before everyone dressed as the Mistress of Greengarden without the possibility that he might publicly scorn her. She might not have another chance for weeks. Besides—she smiled—soon the dress would no longer fit.

Rose took off her old calico and slipped the green silk over her head, hoping Mrs. Schill was wrong about the reason for the meeting. If the Dalriadas did come, Rose would fight for Greengarden. She would show them no more mercy than they had shown Dorrick.

The ceiling creaked. Rose stopped with half her buttons done up and looked at the floor. Around her, circling the edges of her room, seventy-six fantastic candles stood guard. Only one more to make and she would have seventy-seven—

she did not count the one she had given Joff. She watched the candles as Raymont limped across the attic above her: thud–drag, thud–drag. *The Thing can be horrendously violent, even murderous.* Until the other night, Rose would not have believed it, but now . . . She flexed her bruised hand and finished buttoning the dress. Now that her visits to the attic were over, she would not have to consider whether or not to help him escape. She felt relieved, and yet, as the thudding stopped, she felt guilty, too. Raymont would be lonely.

After she finished dressing, Rose pinned up her hair in an elaborate braid. Then she left her room and tried to glide as gracefully down the stairs as Amberly might have. In the front hall, where the two full-length mirrors faced each other on opposite walls, Rose looked at herself. The green silk coaxed a sheen from her skin. The crowning braid made her neck look slender and her face more mature and, best of all, made her lashless, froggy eyes look like huge, bottomless pools of brown. No longer did she look like a bondgirl or even a freewoman; she looked like a landowner.

Rose could also see her reflection in the mirror on the wall behind her, could see her self repeated endlessly between the two mirrors as though she were moving backward in time, as though she were all the mistresses of Greengarden stretching back to the Golden Age. She breathed; all of her reflections breathed, too, and suddenly each had a different face. Directly behind her was Amberly; further back, the pinch-nosed woman.

"This has to work," Rose told them all. "Greengarden needs me—us."

However, when she reached the old oak field a few minutes later, her courage faded. Over two hundred people sat on the ground with their backs toward her, warding off the sun beneath a sea of straw hats, bonnets, muslin sheets, and, on one man's head, a pot that flashed each time he moved. In front of the crowd, beneath the ancient oak tree, her father stood talking on an overturned crate. In the shade near him, were a few stools, but they were all taken. She was late.

Rose had wanted to sit in front, to take her rightful place as mistress. Now, unless she stood in back or sat on the ground—neither of which would make the impression she desired—she would have to skulk away.

Her father saw her. He stopped talking and put his hand on the oak as if to steady himself. Everyone turned around to see what he was looking at so intently.

"Who's that?" a few voices asked. "Who's she?" Then murmurs rippled through the field like wind through grass as everyone realized who she was and how she was dressed.

Rose nearly panicked. Then something—maybe a whisper from the pinch-nosed woman, or maybe the creak of the old oak—urged her to start walking toward the front of the crowd. She did. With her head high, Rose again imagined she was Amberly. Each time the wind fluttered her sleeves, the silk felt like butterfly wings brushing her skin.

"Would you look at Mistress Mouse," Susa said to Opal. "How fitting—a beast married to a beast."

"I say she stole that dress," Mrs. Willow said as Rose passed her.

"Who from?" Bartla asked. "It fits her like a glove."

Kalista popped up, crying, "She'll unbind the dark, a flame in the heart—"

"Quiet, you!" A man yanked her down.

"My daughter . . ." Maggie's voice piped from somewhere in the middle.

Rose passed Joff, who sat staring at the ground with his knees drawn up. Then she reached the front.

"Good afternoon, Mr. Chandler," she said in a strong, clear voice. "I've come to attend the meeting."

"Uh . . ." Her father blinked. "Uh . . . Mrs. Brae," he said loudly and tipped his hat.

A gasp swelled through the crowd. Rose realized that no

one had ever actually thought of her as Mrs. Brae. She turned toward the man on the nearest stool, and her heart sank: It was Kurt Sowerbee. By all rights and custom, he should have offered her his seat. Instead, he hooked both thumbs in his belt loops and smirked.

"I'd appreciate the use of that stool, Sowerbee," Rose said.

"I just bet you would," he said. "It's sure comfortable. Yes sir, it surely is."

"Sowerbee," began Gerald, "you heard Mrs.—"

"That I did," Sowerbee said. "But what I want to know is this. Just whose Mrs. Brae are you?" He grinned. "The master's or the Thing's?"

A hiss went through the crowd.

"Or are you two Mrs. Braes for the price of one?" Sowerbee added. He laughed so hard that he doubled over and went limp.

Rose slammed her foot on the bottom rung of the stool and shoved him off.

"Hey!" he yelled, sprawled on the ground.

Everybody roared with laughter. Rose climbed onto the stool and smoothed her skirt over her shaking knees. Sowerbee jumped up. He glowered down at her with his fists clenched. Then Joff was beside her.

"Why don't you sit down, Sowerbee?" he suggested. "We got enough trouble with the barbarians. We don't need to fight among ourselves as well."

"You tell him, Joff!" Mrs. Schill yelled.

"Yeah—sit down already!"

"Let's get this blasted meeting over with," Jord shouted, "before we fry."

"We need to get back to harvest!"

"That's right!"

"Let her be!"

As more voices rose against him, Sowerbee stormed off.

Joff glanced at Rose, then walked away and sat down again—to a chorus of whispers.

"Please go on, Pa," Rose said, so amazed that the folks had supported her that she forgot to call him Mr. Chandler.

Gerald nodded. "As I was saying, we just got word about the latest raids up north. It isn't good, folks. Fifteen farms destroyed. Hundreds dead. Crops, houses, and barns burned to the ground."

The crowd muttered angrily.

"And women raped," Gerald said. "You know what that means."

A silence followed, and then Rose heard the whispers swelling through the field, "Abominations, abominations." She shuddered, sickened by the thought of half-blooded children.

"It gets worse," Gerald said. "The Dalriadas are getting closer. A patrol found traces of a camp just three miles up the Mirandin."

Three miles? Rose's back grew rigid.

"We think it was a scouting party sent to plan attacks on the farms in Stonewater," Gerald added.

Shrieks and mutterings came from the crowd.

"Earth's Mercy!"

"Flee!"

"They killed my Dorrick!"

"Bloody barbarians!"

"Sure as the sun rises, they'll kill us all!"

People held each other and sobbed.

Gerald held up his hands. "Now, calm down, folks, there's no reason to panic. Mr. Brae's gone to talk with the other landowners and the Village Council. Meanwhile, we've got to take new precautions. And everybody's got to work harder than ever so we can protect ourselves and still get the harvest in."

After the meeting, Rose changed back into her old calico

dress and trudged through the orchard. She was still in shock from her father's news. All she really wanted to do was hide from the barbarians, not fight them.

"Some mistress," she muttered. Her thoughts swirled, and she saw barbarians breaking down the Faredge Wall. "No!" she cried. Then she started running as fast as she could—down through the Penna pears, across the ditch, between the rows of Cameos, around the last bend by the stack of crates . . . and there was the Faredge Wall, still standing, still solid, its rocks pearly grey in the sunlight. Rose stopped.

"It's all right," she said, panting. "All right." But she began to cough and wheeze, then doubled over as the invisible hand seemed to squeeze her chest, and a spell seized her. She pulled air into her lungs and forced it out again, in and out; fortunately, the spell was neither deep nor long and soon released her. She straightened, her hands pressing the small of her back.

When her breathing calmed, Rose walked slowly along the three-foot-high Golden Flames, thick now with leaves and branches. Would she see them bloom next spring? Would there even be a Greengarden next spring?

She stopped by a dead tree. A few leaves had sprouted from the top. Now, though, they were as black as a burnt-out wick. The dead tree left an unprotected gap along the wall. She moved into the gap and put her sore hand on the rocks. Heat shot into her skin. She could feel the wall humming, fighting to hold back the northern wilderness and the Dalriadas, but she could feel cracks of strain, too.

"Hold strong," she whispered—to the wall, to the land, to the pinch-nosed woman, to the bones of her ancestors. Rose stared up at the eight-foot wall. There could be a Dalriada on the other side, and she would not even know—unless she looked. She hesitated. Then she hitched her skirt, found toeholds and handholds in the rock, and climbed up. She got to her knees, to her feet, then straightened, turning so that she faced Greengarden. On either side of her, the wall stretched out long and straight, a two-foot-wide path of stone running northwest.

Rose found that she could not turn and look north. Although her back prickled in fear of a Dalriada arrow, her feet would not move, her neck would not turn. She could not look.

Up here, the Mirandin sounded louder. Across the river, the green trees of Einley's Orchard sloped up and then surrendered to the upswept, golden-brown hills—dry at summer's end. To the east, Rose saw red apples glimmering like jewels on the trees stretching down to the freefolk's cottages. Here and there, a silver glint flashed from the irrigation ditches that veined the land. Not far to the west, Rose could just see Donney, visible briefly on one arc of his circle around the northwest well.

As the heat of the sun burned down on her head, and the heat of the rock burned up through her feet, Rose felt she might burst into flame. She flung her arms wide, fierce in her desire to see the trees bloom year after year; to watch the fruit ripen; to know that the cycle would continue endlessly, and that she would participate. She saw the future when she would be striding across Greengarden, able to speak the word *mine*. Her child would be skipping along beside her. Her child . . . Rose's arms fell.

Would her child's father still be locked in the attic? After Mr. Brae died, she would be Raymont's jailer. Even as the absurdity of this struck her, the old frightened voice inside whispered, *Don't let it out!* But it would be monstrous—in either the future or the present—to imprison Raymont if nothing was wrong with him.

Southward, a slice of red roof shone between the maples—the Bighouse. The attic. But she would not help Raymont escape now even if there was nothing wrong with him, because she feared him, and because he would try to make her leave Greengarden. She would not leave, now or ever. With the Dalriadas near, Greengarden needed her even more. Raymont could wait. After the war, she would light a candle in the attic and learn the truth. Then she could decide what to do.

A barn swallow skimmed over the wall and helped itself to water in the irrigation ditch, which needed repair. It seemed unbearable to Rose that just when the people had almost accepted her, just when she was in a position to begin helping the place she loved, barbarians might destroy it.

Hooves beat on the lane. Startled, Rose looked east and saw a man on horseback patrolling the Faredge Wall. When his blue neckerchief fluttered, Rose recognized Jord, a middle-aged freeman with the expression of a stunned jay. He saw her, then rode over and stopped. Jord took both reins in his right hand and squinted up at her, puzzled, rubbing the palm of his left hand against his thigh.

High on the wall, with one hand resting on her stomach, Rose looked back at him. Her trees stretched out beneath her; the hills rose up behind her—the same honey-gold as her old dress; and the larks, singing and swooping from branch to branch, glorified the air around her.

Jord stared for another minute, then lifted his hat and said, "Fine day, Mistress."

20

A Candle for the Dark

The next night, a scream shattered Rose's sleep. She opened her eyes and lay frozen. Had the Dalriadas come? Were they creeping down the hall to her door? She stared at a golden spot shining on the brass doorknob—the reflection from the lantern burning low beside her. Was the spot turning?

Another scream—from the attic. Had the Dalriadas skipped her room and gone straight to Raymont? But the locks, the key, how?

The scream changed into a keening that wailed up and down, louder and then softer—a flood of agony, grief, rage. Rose pulled her knees to her chin as the sound went on and on, knocking like a fist at a door in her mind: knocking, knocking, knocking.

"Stop," she whispered. "Stop. Keep out." Rose bit down on her hand, but the fist was pounding now, the door splitting . . . She jumped out of bed and grabbed the lantern. In the attic, metal crashed on metal. Raymont shouted torrents of gibberish. Maybe the Dalriadas were not attacking. Maybe the house was on fire, and Raymont was trapped. Rose ran into the hall.

Mr. Brae lurched out of his room, thrusting one arm into his green robe. On the chain around his neck, two keys clanked.

"Is it the Dalriadas?" Rose asked. "Fire?"

He stared, incredulous. "No, it's not fire! It's that cursed Thing!" Mr. Brae lifted his walking stick, rapped the coyote head on the ceiling, and shouted, "I demand that you stop this commotion!" But the screams grew louder, shrieking and whistling.

"What's the matter with him?" Rose asked.

"Foul to the root!" Mr. Brae said.

A circle of light bobbed on the ceiling as Mrs. Schill, lantern in hand, came up the stairs. She wore a pink robe that had white frills billowing around her neck. On the next to last step, she stopped, looked at Rose, and mouthed the words, "I told you so." Mr. Brae continued to rap on the ceiling, to no effect because the screams went on.

Rose breathed too fast. Why didn't Raymont stop? Why didn't somebody make him stop? She set the lantern on a chest and was about to plug her ears, when someone pounded on the front door.

"Answer that," Mr. Brae told Mrs. Schill. "But do not let anyone inside yet. Tell them to get Chandler."

Rose coughed. Her father? But he could not help. A long, ragged howl from the attic rammed through her mind and at last broke down the door in her memory.

The screams turned the night inside out, and she rocked in bed and banged her headboard against the wall and hunched over baby Hildy; and she was screaming back—no, hush! It would hear and the hand would creep and the moons

would come, and she bit off Hildy's button eyes to keep from
making a sound.

> *The wild Thing screams,*
> *Eats you if you're mad.*
> *The wild Thing screams,*
> *Chokes you if you're bad.*
> *Yah! Yah! Yah! Yah!*

"I can't do anything about it," her father said. "So stop
crying. You'll make yourself sick. Do you want a spell?"
"Stop crying!" her mother shouted.
Rose cried harder and her chest collapsed. Hildy squashed,
Hildy killed. She screamed.
Her mother's slap. "Little monster! You're as bad as it!
This'll stop you."
Water sloshed on her head and her back and her coughs,
and kept coming forever: cold, cold, cold.
"ROOOOSE!"
"Don't let it out!" Rose cried. The memory snapped. She
was back in the Bighouse, crouched in a corner of the upstairs hall while Raymont screamed her name.
"ROOOOSE!"
"Misbegotten bastard!" Mr. Brae yelled. He climbed
the attic steps, leaving Rose alone in the hall. She stood
up and leaned on the banister around the hall stairway. Raymont was a monster, insane, savage, just as she had been
warned.
Mrs. Schill came back up the stairs and lit a candle in one
of the beast-headed sconces. Light lapped the wall. It shone
down on the beast's spiny forehead, but left the face below in
shadow—until a draft joggled the flame. Then the shadow
slipped and slid. An eye sprang out, then a snout, a fang, a
forked ear. When Mrs. Schill had lit all the candles, it seemed

to Rose that the hall writhed with shadowy faces dancing against their pools of light.

"ROOOOSE!"

Mr. Brae returned. "I'll not have this madness begin again."

"Then make him stop!" Rose said.

Something crashed in the attic. Mr. Brae turned up the collar on his robe and clutched it around his neck.

"You will go up," he said, "and you will calm it."

Rose's mouth opened. "Me? Now? With him—it—like this?"

"You can't send the girl up there in her condition," Mrs. Schill said.

"She's right," Rose said. "Think of the baby. He might hurt us!"

"Doubtful." Mr. Brae yanked a hairpin from Rose's hair, ignoring her "Ouch," and slid the pin over his collar to hold it closed. "The Thing is angry because I stopped your visits," he said. "It wants you. When it gets what it wants, it will calm down."

"I don't want to go," Rose said.

"You will do as I say."

"No." Rose shook her head. "Not anymore."

Mr. Brae's face turned red. He stepped toward her and raised his walking stick, but Rose did not flinch. Directly above them, a shriek stabbed the air, then a second, a third, a fourth.

"Stop it!" Rose shouted. "Stop it! Stop it!"

Mr. Brae eyed her like a crow. He let the walking stick slide slowly through his fingers until it tapped the floor. His thumb rubbed the silver coyote head.

"The Thing can continue ranting for hours," he said, "sometimes days. You remember that, don't you?"

Rose shuddered.

"You want it to stop, don't you?"

She nodded.

"But the Thing will go on and on," Mr. Brae said, "screaming, shouting your name. Consider all the frightened children who are listening, who are wondering why their mistress does not help them."

Rose pulled on her fingers.

"Poor, terrified little girls," he said. "Mandy Pertin. Teretha Hill. Alyce Smythe . . ." As he spoke each name, Rose pictured the girl's frightened face inside an oval frame similar to the one that held Amberly's portrait.

"Of course," Mr. Brae added, "we mustn't forget little Sally Oxdon, whose family lives in your old house—so near by. Perhaps she's weeping in your old bedroom this very minute." He twirled his stick. The candlelight licked the coyote head and turned the silver a sickly yellow. "Unless you stop this madness, they will have years of nightmares. A true Mistress of Greengarden would help them!"

His last words held the passion of conviction. As Rose looked at him in his mottled velvet robe, protecting the old wound on his throat, she saw that he really did not know what to do. This man with his power and his money and his land and his silver-headed stick was helpless before the Thing.

"ROOOOSE!"

If only the screaming would stop! If only the beastly shadow heads would hold still, then she could think. How could she let the children suffer? But she could not possibly go up there—Raymont was too angry. If only he were calm, then the children could sleep, then they all could sleep . . .

Sleep. That was the answer.

"I'll go up," she said slowly, "if I can take him the Elixir."

Mr. Brae and Mrs. Schill looked at each other, then at her.

"Laudanum," Rose explained. "It would make him sleep. And he'd be so happy to get it he wouldn't be mad at me. You know he loves it."

"I refuse to reward a tantrum," Mr. Brae said.

"Then I won't go."

A scream spilled over them like falling water. Mr. Brae snapped his fingers. "Quick, Schill, prepare a cup."

"But we're low on powder," Mrs. Schill said. "I bet there's scarce enough for half a draught."

"Then add more wine, you fool. Go! And if Chandler's arrived, send him and only him up. I shall need him for Minnie."

"Minnie?" Rose asked. "Raymont's stick-horse?" Mrs. Schill only pressed her lips together and went downstairs.

Thunder boomed as though hammers beat on the attic door. The sconces jumped on the walls; the shadowy faces careened; and the candles, standing like black pillars against their pools of light, flickered. Don't go out, Rose told them. She thought of the darkness awaiting her.

"I . . . I need my pillow," she said to Mr. Brae. "I'll sleep better, and I need my sleep—with the baby."

"Then get it," he said.

Rose darted into her room and kicked the door half-shut behind her. After she grabbed her pillow, she paced beside the fantastic candles lined up along the walls. She could not go back into the darkness without a candle. But which one should she take? None of them seemed right. In front of her was an empty spot along the wall that looked vulnerable—a gap in the guarding ring of candles where something might break through. She had left it open for the final candle, the seventy-seventh candle that she had not made yet. Oh, why hadn't she made it? She needed that one. She had to have that one!

"ROOOOSE!"

"Hurry up!" Mr. Brae shouted.

Rose grabbed a small round candle, stuffed it into the pillowcase, and threw in three matches. With the pillow pressed against her chest, she ran back into the hall, where her father stood beside Mr. Brae. Gerald held a club with a spiked metal ball on the top.

"That's—Minnie?" Rose asked, horrified. "I thought Minnie was a stick-horse."

"Used to be," said Mrs. Schill, holding a steaming cup. "Somebody's idea of humor." She gave the cup to Rose. A protective warmth flowed into her fingertips.

"Come," Mr. Brae said.

"I can handle this without Rose, sir," Gerald said.

"She is going up to calm it," Mr. Brae said.

Gerald stared. "You're sending Rose into the attic? With the Thing?"

"You were well compensated for her, Chandler. She is no longer your concern."

His face stunned, Gerald turned to Rose. She knew he had never expected she would see the Thing at all.

"MOOUSSSSSE!"

"You can't let her go up there, sir," he said. "Please."

"Keep your place, or I'll find a new first-boss."

"Don't worry, Pa," Rose said quickly. "I've been up lots of times. And I've got the laudanum."

"Lots of times?" Gerald stared at Mr. Brae. "You've been sending Rose up there? By herself? You've got me here to protect you with Minnie, but you'll send a girl up with nothing but a cup of poppy wine?" Gerald lowered Minnie until the spiked ball rested on the carpet. "I never agreed to that! That wasn't—"

"It's all right, Pa," Rose interrupted.

"No, it isn't. The marriage arrangement was supposed to protect you! Oh, I know we didn't tell you everything, but we meant to make your life better. But not this." He looked toward the attic. "Not that horror . . ."

"That horror," Mr. Brae said, "is the father of your grandchild."

Gerald looked at Rose, who nodded. She flinched at the revulsion on his face.

"You want to go up there?" Gerald asked her.

"No. Yes—for the children who are scared."

Gerald dropped Minnie's wooden handle, which thunked onto the carpet. "I was wrong before, that arrangement I made, sir. This is worse. Even though Rose is willing, I won't help deliver her into the clutches of that Thing. I'll use Minnie on you first."

"You're fired," Mr. Brae said. "Be off my land in forty-eight hours."

"No!" Rose cried.

"It's all right," Gerald told her. "I won't live a life built on your suffering." Then he turned to Mr. Brae. "I've always thought Amberly was wrong, sir—what she did. But I see why she ran from you."

"Get out!" Mr. Brae exclaimed.

Gerald put his hand on Rose's shoulder. "Why not come with me and your ma? We're free—we can go anywhere. What do you say?"

Rose pushed the pillow against her stomach. "I . . . I'm sorry. I can't leave Greengarden, Pa." Her chin dropped. For the second time, she had chosen a bit of dirt over a person. Was Raymont right? Was she monstrous?

He sighed. "I know." He touched her arm, then walked down the stairs.

"ROOOOSE!"

"Schill," Mr. Brae said. "Take Minnie."

"That's not my job, and I . . ." Mrs. Schill began, but then she squinted. "Why not?" She picked up the club and cradled the spiked head in her fuzzy pink arms. One white frill on her collar curled over the metal. As the three of them walked up the attic stairs, Rose smelled the fruity, sugary vapors swirling from the warm cup in her fingers.

"Wait here on the landing, Schill," Mr. Brae said. "If it gets by us—kill it."

Mrs. Schill nodded. Rose followed Mr. Brae up the rest of the stairs and down the moldy hall.

"ROOOOSE!" Raymont threw himself against the door.

"Rose is here," Mr. Brae called. "But you must move to the end of the attic. No light, no tricks. We have many men—and Minnie."

"Is it you, Rose?" Raymont cried.

"Yes," she said, "and I've brought you the Elixir." In the sudden silence, the stairs creaked behind them.

"Truly?" Raymont asked. "You really truly have the Elixir?"

"If you go over to the window, I'll bring it in." As Raymont moved away, Rose heard another creak on the stairs. Why was Mrs. Schill creeping toward the attic hall?

Mr. Brae lifted the iron bar. He unlocked the padlocks with one of the keys on the chain around his neck and opened the door.

"Now!" he said.

Rose ran through. Hot wine splashed from the cup onto her hand. The door slammed behind her, and the bar banged into place.

"Schill!" Rose heard Mr. Brae exclaim. "I told you to wait down on the landing!" First the upper padlock clicked, then the lower. Wheezing slightly, Rose stood in the blackness with her pillow clutched against her chest.

"Rose?" Raymont croaked.

"Yes," she gasped and leaned forward, trying to exhale slowly, trying to avoid a spell that might harm the baby.

"Bring me the Elixir," he said, his voice raw. "Now. I need it."

I don't care what you need! she wanted to shout. She wanted to dash the laudanum onto the floor.

"Where are you?" she asked.

"On the bed."

Rose wondered how many steps it would take to reach the bed tonight. After two, she tripped over debris on the floor—something he'd thrown during his tantrum. After two more steps, Rose bumped into the bed.

"Hold out your hand." She found it and gave him the glass. He gulped the laudanum as if he were dying of thirst.

"Oh," he sighed. "That soothes. That is much better." He drank again. "Now, do you see my power over *him*? It's the only power I have ever had. When I was little, I thought that if I could only scream long enough, he would let me out. But either my voice would fail or he would come and beat me." Raymont coughed. "But I'm too big for him now."

"Haven't you ever thought that your tantrums might hurt other people?" Rose asked.

"Tantrums!"

"You give children nightmares! Do you know what my ma and pa used to say to me? 'If you don't be a good girl, the Thing that screams in the night will come and eat you up.'"

Raymont moaned.

"All the children hear that from their parents. And after tonight—"

"Don't, Rose, don't! I didn't know—I didn't! First my mother left me, then Lee-lee, and then you. I could not bear being trapped here all alone again. You can't blame me, Rose. But children—nightmares! How horrible. I'm loathsome, I'm hideous, despicable . . ."

Rose sighed. "I know you didn't have much choice," she said at last, "not when you were small, anyway. We'll talk about it later."

"But, Rose . . ."

"Don't talk. You've hurt your voice."

"I'm tired."

"I don't wonder."

"Now that you are here, I can sleep. I have both my Elixirs. I would have died if you had not come. Sweet Mouse, promise you'll never leave me."

"Go to sleep," she said.

* * *

During the hour that passed while Raymont slept, Rose turned her chair to face the round window, and she sat with her back toward him. The attic smelled sour—of sweat and wine. Only this morning she had thought she would never sit here in darkness again. She put her hand on the glass and traced the wrought-iron rose on the other side, following its spirals, its curlicues, its lapping petals, but never quite finding the path to the center. The window seemed to breathe: a diaphragm expanding and contracting with the rhythm of her own breath.

Cupped in Rose's other hand was the small, round candle.

She had thought about many things while Raymont slept: her father defying Mr. Brae, her parents leaving, Amberly and Lee-lee dying in the attic, but most of all she had thought about lighting the candle. Three times the dancing motes of darkness had shown Rose a picture of herself with a flame in her hands. Three times she had ignored it.

Rose slid her thumbs across the wax until they felt an inlaid button—one of the strangest buttons from Amberly's collection. It had a silver border on the outside and on the inside a miniature painting of an eye. When Rose had made the candle, she had fancied the eye was Amberly's. Was it watching over her now?

"What should I do?" Rose whispered. For months, she had longed for this moment, but now that it was here, she feared the revelations of the light more than she feared the dark. If she discovered that Raymont was not a monster, then she would have to help him escape. Leaving him imprisoned until after the war would be . . . monstrous. She might have to fight him to remain at Greengarden herself. If Raymont was a monster, though, then her baby might be one also. The light would reveal the truth, and the truth could be terrible. Its light could burn. If only she held the seventy-seventh candle, she would not hesitate to light that one. Why did she want it so much? She had never even imagined how it might look.

The swirling motes of darkness spun, they danced, they teased—snatching her skirt, her hair, spinning around her head, dashing down to her toes, and spiraling up again, tormenting, dazzling, whispering, "Imagine Rose a flame! a flame!"

She took a deep breath. She found the matches in the pillowcase and pushed two behind her ear. With the candle in one hand and a match in the other, Rose eased her weight from foot to foot and crossed the attic. A board groaned beside the bed, but Raymont did not stir. When she raised the match to strike it against the ceiling, the invisible hand squeezed her ribs. Rose lowered her arm, shaking, lost.

The rose window hummed. Was it turning? Rose felt something coming. She felt it deep—gurgling, then surging up through the dark earth, up through the rock foundation of the house, up though the walls; coming up through the floor through her feet through her bones came a voice that roared:

Look!

Rose raised the match again, then dropped it. She reached for the second match, twirling it in her fingers, and threw it away. A faint ping echoed.

Look!

She grabbed the last match and, before she could think, dragged it against the ceiling. The match hissed. The flame snared the wick. A glow blossomed, spreading over her hands, her white sleeves, then the orange and blue ceiling; and at last in the attic shone a wondrous, dangerous light.

Rose held the candle toward Raymont, who lay on his back. The candle flame cast a pool of light over his shadowy face. She bent closer, then cried out.

Raymont opened his eyes.

"Rose? What . . . ?" He rolled up on his elbow.

She screamed and backed away.

21

Revelations of the Light

Don't look at me, Rose!" Raymont covered his forehead and cowered on the bed. "Don't look at it! Put
out the light!"

The candle trembled in Rose's hand. She swung it in an
arc, searching the room. The sweep of yellow light fell across
an easel, and she grabbed a butter knife lying on the rim.
When Raymont turned toward her with his long red hair
swinging out, Rose held up the knife.

"Keep away," she said.

"Now you hate me. I knew you would—I knew it! You've
betrayed me." He moaned. "Please, please put out the candle.
I'm too hideous."

"Hideous!" she cried. "You're a Dalriada!"

"A—? What's that?"

"What you are! A barbarian from the Red Mountains.
You eat human flesh. You bring blight and barrenness to the
land."

"A barbarian? The same ones who are attacking the Valley? You never called them Dalriadas before." Raymont stared at her from beneath his hands, which were still clamped on his forehead. "Then there are others like me? With . . . this?" Slowly, he opened his hands.

Across his forehead lay the biggest, ugliest birthmark that Rose had ever seen. The orange-brown marks began at the corner of each eyebrow, near his nose, then swept up, curved, and branched across his forehead to form reverse images of each other.

"When I was fourteen," Raymont said, "*he* showed it to me in a mirror. Told me it was a mark of evil. He said, 'Your dark soul is eating though your skin and revealing the loath-some beast inside.' " Raymont shuddered. "He told me he had to keep me locked up for my own protection. If anyone ever saw me, I would be reviled, then killed. I have never looked at myself since."

"They would kill you," Rose said. "But not because of the birthmark, because you're a Dalriada!"

"But . . . isn't it the birthmark that makes me one?"

"No!"

"Then what does?" he asked.

"You have blue eyes. And your hair's red. You must know that Valley folk don't have red hair, and that we all have brown or black eyes."

"Everyone?" Raymont glanced at the round window. "Through the tinted glass, everyone and everything looks brown. I thought it was only the tint."

Rose swayed, overwhelmed by the color of him, by the lurid color zinging out everywhere the candlelight played. This room she had never seen before had an orange and blue ceiling, a puce-splattered wall, mustard starbursts on the floor, and a green bed—or was it purple? More colors showed dimly beyond the candle's reach.

"I don't believe you didn't know," she said.

"*He* never told me—neither did Lee-lee."

"But all those books you read—I know it's forbidden to write about the barbarians, but you must have found some hint."

Raymont shook his head. "My books always have pages torn out. Perhaps because they hinted of these . . . Dalriadas. *He* must have done it to keep me from knowing. But why?"

In spite of her fear, Rose stared at him: his eyes shone as blue as the deep, treacherous pools in the river; his bare chest was spindly, hairless, a pasty white above brown trousers; and his chin drooped like a knob coming loose. He looked younger than seventeen. As Rose watched the candlelight prowl over him, a pain in her side made the attic contract. Had all this uproar harmed the baby? Suddenly Rose felt so exhausted that she sat down on one of the starbursts on the floor. She put the candle beside her but kept hold of the butter knife, which was crusted with dried paint.

"What are you doing here?" she asked. "How did you get here? And where's Amberly's child?" Rose looked at his curving cheekbones and wide mouth; his face seemed familiar. She glanced at the candle, at the eye watching her on the embedded button, and then pictured Amberly's portrait on the spinet. He looked like her. The butter knife clattered to the floor.

"Earth's Mercy," Rose whispered. "You're an abomination." Amberly's lover must have been a barbarian. They had produced a thing that was half Valley and half Dalriada. *He is a monster and more dreadful than you can possibly imagine.* Amberly had broken one of the greatest taboos of the Valley: She had sinned against the land itself.

"Why?" Rose cried. "Oh, Amberly, how could you? I admired you! I wanted to be like you!" Then Rose sat straight up, her back rigid, her eyes staring. What had Mr. Brae done to her? What had he done! Rose slammed her hand over the candle flame. It burned her palm, but she dug her fingers into the wax and banged the round candle against the floor again and again. She wanted to kill him. The pain in her hand burned to the bone, to the heart, to the truth no darkness could hide: She, like Amberly, was a Mistress of Greengarden who would give birth to an abomination.

*　*　*

At eleven o'clock the next morning, when the September sun shone on the peeling wallpaper in Rose's room, and the harvest wagons creaked by on the road below, Mrs. Schill came up to ask Rose if she was sick.

"Just tired," Rose said, "from all the commotion. I'm worried about the baby." And that was no lie, she thought, whacking her pillow into shape after Mrs. Schill left. Rose was worried about the—abomination, though not about miscarrying it. That would be a blessing because as soon as it was born, the baby would die anyway—of exposure in the hills. Rose really wanted to stay in bed because she needed time to think, but her mind felt as grey as ashes.

Before daybreak, when Mr. Brae had let her out of the attic, Rose had not spoken one word to him. She had known that if she opened her mouth at all, if even one sound escaped, all her fury would burst out and she would attack him. So she had hidden the truth in her burnt hand and closed her fist over it. The truth—Rose whacked the pillow again. She had been so desperate to know the truth. Fool. She sobbed and threw the pillow at the candles on the chest. If only she had never lit the wretched candle in the attic.

After the grandfather clock struck twelve, Mrs. Schill brought up Rose's lunch on a silver tray laid with the best china—the celadon plates with silver rims. A white chrysan-themum perched beside the impeccably pressed and folded napkin. Rose glanced at her in surprise.

"Don't expect me to start waiting on you hand and foot," Mrs. Schill said. "Or sure as night follows day, you're in for a shock. In case you want to know, His Most Exalted won't be back until tomorrow night."

* * *

After breakfast the next day, Rose walked out of the Guesthouse with a rolled-up apron under her arm and a bandage around her palm. She had just told her parents they could stay at Greengarden, though she had not explained why. In front of her, an irrigation ditch led south, and she followed it through the block of Penna pears. Her despair over what she had learned had changed. It still roared on the inside, but outside it had baked as hard as the dirt edging the ditch, no, harder—rock-hard, bone-hard. Tonight, when Mr. Brae came home, she would confront him. She would neither scream nor shout, but act deliberately. She would use what she had learned to strengthen her position as Mistress of Greengarden. Meanwhile, she was on her way to the packing shed to help with harvest.

A cold wind blew. With every step Rose took, the branches lifted away from her, the water shrank in the ditch, the sparrows fled, even the grass that brushed her skirt seemed to flinch, shunning her. The monster she carried was a curse upon the land. Rose could bear having people despise her, but she could not bear the thought that Greengarden despised her. How would she ever learn to speak the word *mine*?

She came to a rise, shaded her eyes, and looked out at Guther's Way, the main road through the valley, which wound along beside the Mirandin River. A long line of carts lumbered north, filled with men, food, weapons, and supplies for the army. The people were fighting so hard to beat the Dalriadas. Little did they know there had been a Dalriada right here among them for seventeen years.

Rose went on, following the irrigation ditch until it turned left and the lane turned right. Across the lane, the red door of the packing shed stood open. Inside, a dozen women talked and laughed around the tables while their hands flew through the Cheldys, sorting the green-pink apples for size and quality, and then packing them in straw-lined crates. The women saw Rose in the doorway and fell silent.

"Who needs help?" Rose shook out her apron, but no one spoke. "Is something wrong?" she asked. The women glanced at each other.

"We all know," said Mrs. Willow.

Rose looked at them, terrified. "You . . . do?"

The women nodded.

"Mrs. Schill told us," Bartla said. Big-boned, with a jaw like a horseshoe, Bartla had often looked after Rose when she was a baby. "Schill told us how it was you who went up to calm the Thing from its rage."

"When Mr. Brae feared to do it himself." Mrs. Dale sniffed.

"Schill said you did it so the children wouldn't have nightmares," Mrs. Willow said.

"Not just the children," added Egan.

"Think of it," said Verda, who held two full crates stacked in her huge arms. "And her bearing her own babe, too." They all stared at Rose's stomach. During the silence that followed, the sunlight beaming through the cracks in the walls gleamed on the straw dust hanging in the air. Rose knew, because Mrs. Schill told her every scrap of gossip, that a debate raged over whether she carried a bastard or a monster.

"Well." Mrs. Willow pinched the hem of the work glove

on her left hand and, with several delicate tugs, pulled it tighter, as though it were fine kid. "We all want to thank you for what you did, Mrs. Brae." The others nodded in agreement while Rose stood thunderstruck.

"Here, ma'am," said Bartla. "We'll set you up a place to work near Verda. We can't have you lifting anything heavy now—in your condition."

Rose joined them.

22

An Oath and a Curse

That night, Rose redid her hair, pinning her braid in the elegant style that she always wore now. Next she buttoned up the chestnut wool dress she had copied from Amberly's red velvet. Amberly! Rose slammed the wardrobe door. How could she ever have admired that horrible woman?

Rose took Amberly's sampler out of the folderol chest, crushed the linen into a ball, and took it down to the kitchen. Once she was certain that Mrs. Schill was out, Rose opened the oven door. The embers glowed. She tossed in the balled-up sampler, which opened as it flew and then splayed across the embers. A spark caught the linen. A ripple of light curled along the edge, and the border of oak leaves burst into flame.

Rose shut the oven door and stood plucking the bandage on her burnt hand. It hurt. After four deep breaths, she walked down the hall and knocked on the study door.

"Yes?" Mr. Brae called. When Rose stepped in, he glanced up from his desk, glanced down, and looked up again sharply, half rising from his chair. His face lit up. "Amberly?"

"It's Rose," she said.

Mr. Brae closed his eyes, then opened them. "I told you to make your clothes plain!" He sat down again.

"It is plain." Rose held out the skirt. "There aren't any ruffles or ribbons, no puffs or lace or trim. And it's all one dark color."

He frowned, puzzled. "Well . . . that is expensive fabric; you will ruin it scrubbing floors."

"I won't be scrubbing floors anymore. It's not the proper work for the Mistress of Greengarden or"—Rose looked him in the eye—"for the wife of an abomination."

Mr. Brae's face turned red.

"What!" He gripped the edge of his desk. "I forbade light! Forbade it!"

"Your grandson is half Dalriada," Rose said.

"I forbade it!"

"And your great-grandchild," she added, "your precious heir, will be one-quarter Dalriada. Another abomination."

Mr. Brae sank back into his chair, the leather creaking beneath him, and closed his eyes. The silver coyote head on the walking stick leaned its muzzle on the desk—like a pet dog.

"Damn you." Rose uncurled her burnt fist. "I hate you." Out in the hall, the grandfather clock struck nine.

Mr. Brae sighed. "And thus I am rewarded for my mercy."

"Mercy! Why didn't you ever tell Raymont the truth?"

"You heard it screaming last night. Consider what it might have revealed if it knew the truth." Mr. Brae opened his eyes. "You did not tell it?"

"Oh . . . I didn't think of that. I was startled."

"Idiot!" He slammed the desk. A black porcelain bowl clattered on the corner. "Now Greengarden is doomed."

"Raymont isn't stupid," Rose said. "He knows he'll be killed if anyone finds out. But why is he here? Why wasn't he taken to the hills to die?"

"As I have explained before, I needed an heir. I concealed the father's identity, hoping the baby would have brown eyes."

"He'd still be an abomination."

"But who would have known?"

The land, Rose thought. But she said, "Raymont would have known. Amberly would have told him about his father."

Mr. Brae pulled the porcelain bowl toward him. "I am not 'stupid' either. If the baby had been born brown-eyed, I intended to . . . to send Amberly where she could never talk to anyone again. However, after that Thing was born, she lay dying—saving me a great deal of trouble." Mr. Brae pushed one finger through the buttonhole on his jacket.

"However," he added, "she insisted I take an oath—swear on the land that I would send the Thing to the barbarians. If I did not, she would curse Greengarden with her dying breath."

"Curse Greengarden?" Rose could not believe it. "Amberly?"

Mr. Brae turned and lifted the blue curtain. Outside, the night flattened against the glass. "My daughter lived a privileged, cultured life. She was a landowner, heir to one of the finest orchards in the South Valley. In those years, this land lived up to its name. It was indeed a garden, a luscious green garden where the fruit hung so heavily that branches broke from the trees . . . It was a bounteous land. We were happy. She was loved . . ." He stopped, then spit on the window. "She traded it all for a rank barbarian."

"Why didn't you take the oath?" Rose asked.

Mr. Brae dropped the curtain. "I did take it."

"But—?" Rose thought of the land that was no longer a garden, of the fruit that dwindled each year, of the weeds and water sprouts and skeleton trees that littered the orchard. At last she knew why the land she loved was failing. Everything terrible always came back to this man with his face like a rotting squash.

"You broke your oath!" she shouted. "Maybe you don't care about this place anymore, but other people do!"

"Lower your voice," he said. "I did not break it. She never said when to send the Thing. In one year? Five? Twenty? At first, I was too much in shock, the baby too sickly. Later—it's not easy to smuggle a blue-eyed toddler so far. A child is too stupid to know when a cry or a laugh may imperil you both." Mr. Brae twirled the lid on the black bowl. "And how does one contact the barbarians without being killed first? I could not speak their foul language. I could trust only Emily Harsgrove—Lee-lee—but she would have been a liability on such a journey."

"You should have found a way!" Rose said.

"Perhaps." He shrugged. "However, by the time the Thing was five, I suspected I might fail to remarry and secure a pure-blooded heir. The rumors I had circulated about the Thing's monstrousness proved my own undoing." He stroked the silver coyote head. "Ironic, isn't it? No landowning woman of childbearing age would marry me for fear the defect would pass to her own child. Then I knew I would need the Thing to masquerade as a father."

"If I had known the truth," Rose said. "I wouldn't have married Raymont, not even for Greengarden."

Mr. Brae looked at her. "If you reveal the truth, the High Council in Middlefield will revoke your marriage—and your freedom."

"I'll tell anyway, unless you agree to certain things. And if I tell, the council will take away your land for harboring a

Dalriada. You'll be bonded or sent to the southern mines. The Brae name will be disgraced. So will all those fine ancestors of yours on the drawing room walls."

Again Mr. Brae twirled the lid on the bowl. "What are these . . . conditions?"

"My father keeps his job. You'll treat me like the Mistress of Greengarden. I'll do the tasks a Mistress should, but no others—unless I choose. And you'll let me try some of my ideas about improving the orchard."

"I see. Anything else?"

"I need a little money of my own, too."

"As your dear father would say, 'Why not?'"

"And," Rose added, "I'll see Raymont any time, night or day."

"You cannot have the key."

She hesitated, then agreed. "I don't want him to get out either."

"Very well." Mr. Brae pulled on his double chin. "Be wary of Mrs. Schill, however. She is eager to learn the truth and use it against us."

Rose nodded.

He stared at her. "One reason I chose you from all the other riffraff was that you were the most timid, spineless girl on the place and would do whatever you were told."

"I was timid, but I've had to learn to be . . . braver."

"Here is what bravery may get you." Mr. Brae lifted the lid off the porcelain bowl; a stink filled the room. Inside was a fibrous brown wad crusted with black clumps, some big, some small like charred raindrops.

"What's that?" Rose asked.

"Burnt hair. After I brought my daughter back here, we had a . . . disagreement. She had told me her barbarian loved her hair, so I shaved it off and burned it."

Rose thought of Amberly's sampler burning in the oven and felt sick.

"Is that supposed to scare me?" she asked. "I've faced worse. You can cut off my hair any time you like, what there is of it."

Mr. Brae slammed down the lid. "I hope you remember your bravery when your baby arrives. You will have neither a midwife nor any other attendant."

"But . . . why not?"

"For the same reason my daughter did not. If the baby looks like a barbarian, we wouldn't want anyone to see it, now would we?"

The pain in Rose's blistered palm burned so much she feared it might set her on fire.

"Make no mistake," he said. "I want a child, a child I can raise to love Greengarden and understand her duty. I know where I went wrong before. This time I shall raise her better." Mr. Brae added. "However, I shall endure no more monsters in my attic. If your baby is born with blue eyes, I will follow the law and take it up into the hills to die."

23

Fear of Fire

"Kill the baby!" Raymont exclaimed the next night from his chair near the round window. "Tell me, Mouse, who is the monster now?"

In the chair beside him, Rose turned slightly away.

"We must escape," he added. "Soon."

Rose sighed. She'd had another spell that afternoon, a bad one, and she was tired. She reached over and turned up the lantern glowing on the table between them; a second lantern burned beside the bed. In the sconces on Raymont's easel, four candles cast their flickering light over an unfinished portrait of Rose.

"You must get the key," he said.

"But I've told you before, he eats with it on, sleeps with it on, and probably bathes with it on, too. He takes it off only to unlock your door."

"I know you," Raymont said. "If you really want something, you can find a way to get it."

Rose felt him looking at her, but she could not bear to look back. Part of her longed for the nights when she did not know the darkness hid a Dalriada, or—she glanced at the ceiling—the mind-boggling colors of a laudanum dream.

The first rafter was painted blue, the one behind orange, the next green, then magenta, yellow, pink—the colors marching down the attic like a deranged rainbow. In between the rafters, the ceiling bristled with painted scrawls: yellow splattered with pink dots; purple fractured with lightning bolts; and red licked with golden tongues outlined in black. Every other surface—floor, walls, chimneys—was covered with painted pictures. Stacks of canvases leaned against the walls.

"I have an idea," Raymont said. "Why not give him wine until he falls into a stupor?"

"Mrs. Schill says he doesn't drink. I think he's afraid of what he might let slip." A hot ache throbbed behind Rose's eyes. She dabbled her fingers in a bucket of water an arm's length away. Beside it sat another bucket, and beside that another, and then another. All around the edge of the attic, where the sloped ceiling met the floor, stood a row of buckets filled with water. Rose had not realized the extent of Raymont's fear of fire.

He stamped his foot. "I refuse to stay caged while he murders my child."

Rose dabbed the water on her eyes. Everything she had been taught compelled her to believe that blue-eyed babies should be killed, but a fluttering of her pulse whispered that half the baby was she, was Valley.

"The baby might have brown eyes," Rose said.

"Once we find out for certain, it will be too late! *He* will have the baby in his power. Our only chance is the Red Mountains."

Rose shuddered. She could not imagine living away from

the Valley or living with murdering barbarians. And if she let Raymont out, would he, too, begin killing people?

"But you're only half Dalriada," she said. "Are you sure you want to live with them? You're civilized. The Dalriadas are barbarians. They don't have books, they—"

"If I don't go to my people, I will die! I need color—life." Raymont slammed his fist against the window. "Can't you understand? Everything through there is brown—everything! Until you came, I had almost grown resigned to this prison, but not anymore. No more!"

"Mr. Brae should never have kept you here," Rose said, thinking of Amberly's curse. Regardless of that, however, Rose knew it was wrong to keep Raymont imprisoned, helpless against fire and Minnie and Mr. Brae's whims.

"My people will welcome us," Raymont said.

"But what if they hate abominations? Besides, you can barely walk, and you couldn't ride much faster. We wouldn't get half a mile before someone caught us."

"*He* won't send anyone after us."

"Mr. Brae really wants this baby."

"Use your brain, Mouse. He can't risk having anyone discover I'm a Dalriada."

"But he'd come himself," Rose said. "And the Valley's full of soldiers looking for barbarians. If we get caught, everything would get worse."

"Worse for whom? You have your precious land and your precious freedom. We must leave!"

Rose plucked at the bandage on her burnt hand. Leave Greengarden for a child she did not want and a husband she did not love? She walked over to Raymont's easel and looked at the unfinished portrait of herself. The nose blended into cheeks as pink as cherry blossoms; the full lips, with the upper lighter than the lower, curved in a sweet smile; and the eyelashes swept halfway to the brows. Only in the expression of the close-set eyes, timid and startled, shying away from the viewer, did Rose recognize something of herself. Perhaps Raymont captured her timidity correctly because it was the quality that he, like his grandfather, liked best in her.

"We will be happy in the Red Mountains," Raymont said. "Gloriously, deliriously, ecstatically happy! I shall paint you a picture of the life we will lead." He paused. "Now, tell me you will get the key."

Rose dipped her finger into the green paint on Raymont's palette. She did not know what to do. And she would heed no more unearthly advice from Amberly Brae. If Amberly had not run off with the barbarian, Rose would not be faced with leaving Greengarden and with freeing one abomination while giving birth to another. She would not have spent a single hour in the dark attic. For Greengarden would be a garden still, and Rose would never have needed to become mistress in order to save it. Mr. Brae might believe that he had kept his oath, but Rose believed the land would keep declining until Raymont joined the barbarians. Only then would Greengarden be free of Amberly's curse—and the blighting presence of a Dalriada.

"You know this is the ethical thing to do," Raymont said.

"Yes," Rose said, but added silently, "partly." She looked at the false portrait again, at the waves of hair rippling past the waist—so different from the lank stuff she coiled up every day—and thought of the burnt hair in the porcelain bowl.

"If Mr. Brae catches me trying to get the key," Rose said, "he might hurt me, baby or not."

Raymont shrugged. "Then don't let him catch you."

* * *

On Monday night, after the grandfather clock struck two, Rose crept to Mr. Brae's door and listened to his guttural snores rasp through the air. She turned the knob, shielded the candle's light, and went inside.

In the middle of the room was the biggest bed Rose had ever seen. Mighty slabs of oak—the headboard and footboard—soared halfway to the ceiling, like majestic hills flanking a plain. Tossed over the headboard was Mr. Brae's robe, which hung down in green folds. Mr. Brae himself slept on his side beneath a brown blanket. The walking stick rested against the nightstand, its silver head hooked over the top, its coyote eyes watching her, its coyote tongue gibbering *guile, guile, guile*.

Rose could not move. She was thinking of what had almost happened to her in that bed. She imagined herself grabbing the walking stick and bashing the coyote head against Mr. Brae's skull as he lay helpless. Then she imagined the sound of a skull cracking and felt sick.

The key, Rose told herself, just get the key; that was the first step. As she inched forward, she reviewed the rest of her plan. Under her bed were saddlebags packed with food and clothing for Raymont. After they stole a horse from the north pasture, she would lead Raymont a mile into the hills, where she would leave him to find his people. That should be easy enough—the hills were probably crawling with Dalriadas. Raymont would be furious, but Rose hoped his sense of self-preservation would prevent him from following her back. She knew her plan was mad or at least ridiculous. They could easily be caught at any point by either side.

The stale air in the bedroom pressed close—did Mr. Brae never open his windows? Rose stopped beside the bed and raised the candle. Something flashed on the far side of the pillow—two brass keys. Rose walked around to the other side of the bed, where she leaned forward and then wrinkled her nose; Mr. Brae's breath smelled like mutton.

Although the chain was still around his neck, it had swung out from his chest and lay near the edge of the bed.

The two keys—one for the padlocks and one for the door slot—were fastened to a ring on the chain. The links looked too strong to break with her hands. Could she slip the chain over his head without waking him? Impossible. Should she remove the ring? Rose had watched Mr. Brae unhook it many times, but in the dim light, she could not see how the clasp worked.

She had to try anyway. She put the candlestick on the bedside table. Her fingers reached toward the key, but the moment she touched it, Mr. Brae woke.

"Barbarians!" he cried. "They've attacked!" He rolled away and seized a knife from under his pillow.

"Wait!" Rose cried. "It's me!"

Mr. Brae blinked at her. "You! What are you doing?"

"I—"

"Is the house on fire?"

"I'm sick." She cradled her stomach. "I'm afraid something's wrong—with the baby."

A line deepened between his brows, but he lowered the knife.

"I need Mrs. Schill," Rose added, "but I'm worried about all those steps. If you could just get her, sir, she'll know what to do." Rose grimaced in pain.

Guile! Guile! Guile! the coyote gibbered.

Mr. Brae shoved the knife back beneath his pillow, lit his lantern with her candle, then looked at her face.

"I see," he said slowly, "very well."

Back in her own room, Rose curled up in bed, her heart racing. It would be easy to convince Mrs. Schill that she was sick.

* * *

"You woke him on purpose," Raymont said on Wednesday afternoon. Rose, who was standing beside the painting he had just finished on the south wall, turned and looked at him lying exhausted in bed, propped up by pillows.

"How can you say that!" she exclaimed.

"Easily. Because I know you do not want to leave your precious Greengarden."

Rose sighed. That much was true. And she did not want to venture even a mile into the hills, where the barbarians might be lurking. Even if she had stolen the key, when the moment came to use it, Rose doubted whether she would have been able to let Raymont out. His blue eyes stared at her, accusing.

"I didn't wake him on purpose," she said and turned back to the painting, which covered half the wall. Red-haired people danced around a bonfire with logs arranged like the spokes on a wheel. Their eyes glowed a luminous blue; their mouths were open; and their breath, which glowed the same luminous blue, floated up to embrace the stars. In a meadow on the left, horses galloped and plunged. The pine trees framing the meadow tipped, pointing every which way. Behind them reared cock-eyed cliffs with the snarling faces of bears, cougars, and wild things.

"You see?" Raymont asked. "That will be our glorious life in the Red Mountains."

"Hmm," Rose said. In the entire painting, there was not one house, not one garden. "You dreamed all this?" she asked.

"Yes. Since you told me I am a Dalriada, my dreams come waking and sleeping. They're more vivid. Colorful."

Rose turned to the opposite wall. The painting showed a maze inside a mountain where caverns opened one into the other. The flights of stone stairs connecting them careened over abysses, or looped into dead ends, or simply ended in midair. Rose had seen this painting before; he once mentioned he had been working on it for years. In a dozen places, Raymont appeared, creeping through the caverns, searching for something.

"What are you looking for?" she asked him.

"An apple, a red apple striped with gold. It grows on a tree whose leaves gleam like emeralds. If I could only find that apple and eat it, all would be well. But I can never find it." Raymont thumped one of his pillows. "Tell me, how do you like the painting on the end wall? I began it the night before last—while you were *not* getting the key."

Rose stepped reluctantly toward the triangular-shaped wall opposite the round window. A red mountain gleamed white with ice and crimson with flame. On the left flank, a river of blood surged into the green valley below, washing away fields and houses and people. Swollen in the heart of the mountain was a deer skull whose antlers formed a skeleton tree that burst out of the mountain, towered above it, and then arched over the valley.

Rose shuddered.

Raymont laughed. "Is something wrong, Mouse? Don't you like it?" She walked toward him and clasped the bedpost.

"That mountain," she said. "I've seen it from the sagebrush flat. It's the tallest of the Red Mountains. How could you have painted it exactly when you've never seen it?"

"I told you—dreams." His pupils enlarged until the blue iris barely contained the black. "Visions. Imagination."

Rose could not imagine such horrors—no, her thumb rubbed the bedpost—she could imagine them, she had imagined them: the cavern where the bone dancers wove their eternal reel, the black well where the giants struggled, and the dark field where the sickle moon plowed her flesh.

"How do we escape now, Mouse?" Raymont asked. "You had better think of something—quickly."

Rose walked as far as she could from the terrible mountain and pressed her hands against the cold window. She could see the Penna pears outside, but, distorted by the thick, brown glass and fragmented by the black bars, the trees looked like a madman's orchard. The rows crashed together or leaned awry. The branches spiked like mangled forks. In the garden below, some of the roses looked dwarfed, some gigantic. The picket fence twisted around them, its points aslant. Every single thing flattened into a dun shade of brown. This was all Raymont had ever seen of the world. Paint-smudged fingerprints showed on the molding around the window. Hadn't Raymont mentioned finding a note from Amberly behind the molding?

"I found a message from her," he had said. "She wrote that someone she trusted had hidden something for me from her." Rose remembered wishing her own mother had left her a message. Now, for the first time, she realized that Amberly was her mother, too—her mother-in-law.

No. Rose pressed the window harder. No, she claimed no kinship with Amberly Brae. A moment later, Rose's fingers began to tingle. The glass grew warm. Hands pressed back against hers, and then the distorted face of Amberly Brae appeared in the window. Her face and shaven head skewed into jagged planes.

Rose of the garden, Amberly said. Her eyes glittered with pain.

"Go away," Rose said, but she could not move her hands from Amberly's. "You betrayed the land!"

Rose of the land—the well overflows, the waters break. Amberly's head drooped, then lifted again. *The child comes, and I am alone. In my hour of greatest darkness.*

"I don't care!" Rose cried, but she did, oh, she did, and hated that she did.

I burn, but I am not consumed, for love is my light. Help my son find the pouch that will set you both free.

"I'm not like you! I won't be like you!"

Amberly nodded. *Be your own mistress.* Then her hands fell from the glass, and she doubled as though punched. She cried, *Candle—Rose! Be a woman of fire!*

"Mouse?" Raymont shook her.

"Wait!" Rose cried.

"Why are you talking to yourself?"

"It's Amberly—"

"What?"

"Your mother—in the window."

"Mother!" He dragged himself to the window and pushed Rose aside. "Mother? Where? I don't see her!"

Rose peered over his shoulder: The glass had turned blood red.

"I . . . I don't see her anymore," she said.

Raymont pounded the window, sobbing. "Mother, come back, come back! Don't leave me here!" He slid slowly down the wall, and as he did, his bad leg knocked over one of the water buckets. He sank into the rush of water that spilled across the floor.

Rose collapsed in her own chair. Her left hand still tingled, so she unwound the bandage. The painful, oozing burn had healed into a clean scar.

"What did my mother say?" Raymont asked.

"Nothing much." Rose opened and closed her hand. She did not want to find anything that would set her free from Greengarden.

"Tell me—or I will have another fit. I'll scream and pound and make such awful noises that the sweet little children will be terrified for weeks. And it will be all your fault."

When Rose did not answer, Raymont pulled himself up. With water streaming from his trousers, he picked up a block of wood, half-carved with moons and stars, then raised it high to strike the rafters. His chest, his shoulders, his stomach—his whole body—seemed to fill with air as he prepared to scream. Rose wondered if a luminous blue cloud would billow from his mouth.

"Amberly asked me to find a pouch," Rose said.

"A pouch?" His breath whooshed out. "That must be the

thing she mentioned in her note. Why would she tell you and not me?"

"I don't know. I can't read a ghost's mind."

"Maybe she told you because you can leave the attic to look for it." Raymont lowered the block of wood. "The pouch must contain something that will help us escape."

"And maybe I only imagined I saw her." But as Rose flexed her healed hand, she knew this was not true.

"My mother didn't leave me," he said. "She's only been waiting until I needed her most."

The hour of greatest darkness, Rose thought.

"So do as she says, Mouse! Find the pouch."

"But I wouldn't know where to start."

"My mother gave it to someone she trusted. You know everyone on Greengarden. Think. Whom would she have trusted?"

Rose shrugged.

"You have three choices," Raymont said. "Find the pouch; try to steal the key again; or nightmares for the children." He smacked the wood against his hand. "Choose."

"All right!" Rose grabbed the wood from his hands. "I'll look for the pouch. We'll never get the key from Mr. Brae."

"No," Raymont said, and he looked out the window at the madman's orchard. "Not unless we kill him."

24

Harvesting Secrets

Pa," Rose said the next afternoon when she found him leaning over the back of a wagon in the east block of the orchard, "can I talk to you?"

"Just a minute," said Gerald, without looking up. He was checking the crates of Redheart apples in the wagon bed. "Brell," he called to a man wearing a picker's bag. "Your crew's snapping off too many stems. And if you see Sowerbee, tell him I want those extra ladders now, not next week." The man nodded and walked down the orchard row, where voices fluttered as the pickers called to one another.

"I don't know why we're bothering to pick these," Gerald said to Rose. "Would you look at that?" He held up a Redheart. "I've seen grapes bigger than that." And he threw it down in the grass.

Rose shrugged her shoulders, which ached from a long morning's work in the packing shed.

"Sure they're small," she said. "They weren't thinned, or pruned either." She watched a picker fight through a knot of water sprouts to reach the fruit. Then Opal trudged up and dropped another full crate into the wagon—now a lumpy sea of red apples.

"Easy with those," Gerald told her. "This load's ready. Drive it up to the packing shed and then get right back."

Opal shifted her weight from foot to foot. "I don't know, Mr. Chandler. I've never driven a load of apples before."

"And your pa's never fought the barbarians before," Gerald said. "Everybody's doing anything that needs doing."

Opal clambered into the wagon and picked up the reins between her thumb and forefinger.

"Maybe I'll race." Opal cast a sly glance at Gerald.

"Maybe you'll get whipped," he said.

Opal stuck out her tongue. "Rose, you hear about Susa?"

"What about her?" Rose asked.

"You can gossip when harvest is over," Gerald said. "Now get."

"Guess you'll find out later." Opal giggled, then clicked to the horse, and the wagon creaked away up the lane.

"Pa," Rose began, "I need to talk—"

"Can't it wait, Rose?" he asked. "We're behindhand here. Harvest is going slow as snails, what with so many on guard duty or away at the war. And I don't like the look of those clouds." Gerald squinted at the sky. "Could be hail coming."

Rose thought for a moment and then said, "No, it can't wait."

He threw up his hands. "What is it, then?"

A woman passed by, wearing a yoke with a bucket hanging from each side: water for the crew.

"This needs to be—private," Rose said. "Let's walk into the field a ways."

"Why not?" Gerald sighed. He barked out a few more instructions, then followed Rose across the lane and up a rise into the fallow field. Fifty yards into it, Rose stopped.

"This is far enough," she said. They turned and looked

back at the orchard in time to see Opal's wagon, still creeping up Coyote Lane, lurch sideways. The wagon bed tilted, and crate after crate of Redhearts slid out and slammed into the ground. A fountain of apples shot up, busy and bobbling, and then rolled over the dirt in a bouncing red stream.

"Blasted Earth!" Gerald swore. "What next? How'm I supposed to run this place with lousy equipment, no money, and a slipshod crew who thinks the place is cursed?"

Rose planted her feet. "All this is going to change, Pa, and soon. Listen—I know you need to get back, so I'll make this quick. Did Amberly ever give you something to hide? Something secret? That she didn't want anyone else to know about?"

Gerald stared at her. "Now, why would she have done that?"

"I thought she might have left something for her baby—a locket or a picture, something like that. In case she died in childbirth." Rose chose each word carefully. "Amberly must have known Mr. Brae wouldn't pass anything on."

"This is more than a good guess," Gerald said. "How did you know?" When she didn't answer, he added, "Why not let it be, Rose? Haven't we all been through enough?"

For a moment, Rose pictured Minnie's spiked head cradled in his arms.

"Remember," she said, "how you always used to tell me that you can't change the way of things—"

"And I should've followed my own advice!" Gerald exclaimed. "Look what happened when I did try to change things—with your marriage." His voice dropped. "I should have tried when I was younger, when it really mattered."

"I have to try and change things, Pa. Things that aren't right or that could be better—or I might as well be dead. If Amberly left something for her son, I need to know. You can trust me." The word *trust* seemed to swell in the air between them until it became as grotesque as one of Maggie's curtain puffs.

He sighed, watching folks gather around the broken wagon. Opal skittered here and there, as frantic as one of her pet chickens. Just when she had collected a bunch of apples in her apron, she threw it over her head to cry, and dropped them all again.

"Oh, why not?" Gerald scratched the stubble on his chin. "About a month before Amberly gave birth, Emily sneaked me up to the attic. Back then, the door had a real window. It had bars, but you could see into the attic." His hands curled into fists. "Amberly was all still and quiet, her pretty hair all cut off. There was something about her, something—I don't know, terrible maybe, or fierce, or bright. That's it. Bright—too bright." He shook his head. "She asked me, in the name of our old friendship, to hide a pouch."

Rose took a deep breath.

"I was to give it to her child when he turned twelve," Gerald added. "She asked me to swear not to look inside or tell anyone about it."

"And?" Rose prompted.

He shrugged. "I didn't want any trouble with Mr. Brae, so I said I couldn't help her. Besides, I was angry at her for the shame she'd brought on herself."

"You loved her," Rose snapped. "You were jealous. Call things what they are, Pa."

He turned white. In the silence, ladders creaked painfully as the pickers climbed up and down. Rose watched her father look across the fallow field, across the orchard, across time, at the Redhearts lying in the dirt of the lane.

"The day after I saw her," he said, so softly that Rose could barely hear him, "I thought, Why not help her? Hiding that pouch was all I could do for her. The only way I could show her . . . So I took the oath and hid the pouch."

"Where?" Rose asked.

But her father pivoted on his heel, turning his back on the orchard, and faced the fallow field. "Why shouldn't I have been jealous?" he cried. "Damn you, Amberly! Damn you! If you had to run off with someone, why couldn't it have been me?"

*　*　*

Ten minutes later, her mind in turmoil, Rose passed the cornfield, where the dried skeleton stalks rattled against the wind. When she turned down the lane toward the old oak field, she heard a rustle and a clop. Joff Will, leading a lame horse, walked out of the block of Shaula apples. He stopped when he saw her, then nodded and said, "Mrs. Brae."

"Hello," Rose said. "What happened to Lucy?"

"Stepped in a mole hole. Nice sprain she's got. And tomorrow she was all set to go over to Sunny Hollow Orchard. Mr. Brae wants her bred to . . . that is . . ." Joff glanced at Rose's stomach, rubbed the back of his neck, and then adjusted Lucy's halter.

Rose felt her cheeks grow hot. Was he, too, wondering whether she carried a bastard or a monster? She swallowed hard, imagining his shock, and her fate, if he or anyone else ever learned what kind of monster grew inside her. And yet the child would be three-quarters Valley, more Valley than Dalriada. In the eyes of the law, though, one speck of barbarian blood tainted the child. What about in *her* eyes?

"It's not true, you know," Joff blurted.

"What isn't?" Rose asked.

"Susa's—stories."

"What stories?"

"Oh . . . nothing." Joff reached under Lucy's neck and

patted her far cheek. "Guess I better get her back to the barn. Get this sprain wrapped up."

"Sure," Rose said.

As Joff led the horse past her, he stared at the ground. Rose scrunched her skirt in her hand and walked on, suddenly and unaccountably miserable because he was so unfriendly.

"Hey, Rose!"

She turned. Joff had stopped and was looking back at her.

"That candle you gave me," he said. "It burns real nice."

"Thanks." Rose smiled. "Thank you."

"I only burn it a few minutes every night—so it'll last."

"I can always make you another one," she said, though she had not made any since the night she had lit the candle in the attic.

"No," Joff said. "I only want that one." He looked at her and she looked at him, and the air danced in her lungs and a swallow—streaking out from the Shaulas—traced golden rings in the sky. Then Lucy snorted.

Rose blinked. Joff simply nodded and went on down the lane as Rose watched, transfixed. She longed to tell him about her terrible dilemma, to have him listen and stroke her neck as he was stroking Lucy's neck this very minute. What would have happened if she had taken his hand on her wedding day? What would have happened if her father had told Amberly how he felt about her? When Joff finally disappeared around the cornfield, Rose walked on.

After she crossed the south irrigation ditch, Rose hopped over a rail fence and waded through the grass toward the old, solitary oak that nudged the sky. Ten feet from the ground, the massive trunk branched like the arms on a candelabrum. Near the top of the tallest arm, the branches stopped. The trunk then soared for five more feet before branches burst forth again and towered into a crown of green at the top.

When Rose touched the bark, she sensed the roots probing down, drinking deep; the sap hummed an ancient tune of the land. She studied the branches, trying to trace her route from her father's instructions, but the tree had changed in seventeen years. The wind cackled through the dry leaves, which were dying in red and orange and lingering splotches of silvery green. Over half of them lay on the ground.

Rose stepped on the crate left behind after the last meeting, found a foothold, and started climbing. At the first fork she went right, as her father had told her, and at the next, left, then twice more to the right. "Climb high," he had said. When she grasped a dead bough, she thought of the horrible dead tree in Raymont's painting.

Had Raymont meant what he said last night about killing Mr. Brae? Rose had been too stunned to ask, but she suspected that Raymont was no different from the other murdering Dalriadas. "Unless *we* kill him," Raymont had said. Did he honestly believe she would help, that she would not try to stop him? As her hands moved from branch to branch, Rose remembered that she had twice wanted to kill Mr. Brae herself: once when she had learned her baby would be an abomination, and again when she had tried to steal the key. Yet those were only wild thoughts inspired by bursts of rage, not real intentions. Raymont had talked of killing as though discussing which hat to wear.

If she found the pouch, Rose might have the means to let him out into the world, where he would be free to cause any harm he liked. She thought of his painting again, of the river of blood engulfing the Valley, and she stopped climbing. If she did not let him out, though, Greengarden would wither under Amberly's curse. And regardless of whether or not she let Raymont out, her baby would still be a blight on the land.

Rose kicked the tree. Every thought tangled in her mind;

every path seemed blocked. If only she were the same meek, little bondgirl she had been five months ago, she could find a hole in the trunk, hide inside like a squirrel, and mull over her biggest problem—having nuts enough to last the winter.

She climbed higher. Green lichen broke under her hands and pattered onto the boughs below. Three-quarters of the way up, she began to search in the crooks of branches. She rested again, knowing she should go no higher. Then suddenly she did not care if she fell, she did not care about anything, and with a heart bitter and reckless and angry, she climbed on.

Above one fork, where three limbs branched, the bark crinkled into ridges and rills. Rose groped beneath the edges. Nothing. She felt as if the oak were laughing at her, refusing to surrender a single secret captured in its ringed history. In all these years, her father had never checked on the pouch. He had seen no point in giving it to an insane, deformed Thing.

The boughs thinned, then shrank to leafless spikes. Rose was high up now, on a bare trunk below the crown. From here, she could see all that she loved: Greengarden, stretching from the Faredge Wall to the northwest, the Mirandin to the east, and to the south, Rattlesnake Cliff that sloped down from the canyon and bordered the old oak field fifty yards away. From up here, it almost seemed possible to speak the word *mine*.

But how tiny the Faredge Wall looked, how arbitrary and tenuous a boundary. Rose wished she had enough candles to surround Greengarden with a wall of fire. But Greengarden was part of the Valley after all, and if the Dalriadas unleashed their river of blood, Greengarden was no island to stand alone while the rest of the Valley fell. If only she could become one of the clouds overhead and stretch herself over all the Valley to protect it from harm.

Rose clutched the oak. On top of Rattlesnake Cliff, something was moving between the boulders. A deer? Too small. A
coyote? She shaded her eyes. No, two coyotes—no, it turned,
and she saw the profile of a man. Who would be lying flat on
the cliff looking down on— She clapped her hand to her
mouth. A Dalriada! Spying on Greengarden! She clutched the
oak tighter and tried to take a deep breath. Maybe the man
was only a guard from the orchard patrol. He crawled closer
to the edge of the cliff, keeping in shadow so that no one on
the ground would see him. Why would one of the patrol hide
from those below?

Rose had to find out if he was a Dalriada. Before she
could weigh the risk, she stood up on the branch, clutched a
spike above, and, leaning out, waved to the man.

"Hello!" she shouted. "Hello up there! Is that you, Jord?
Sowerbee? Hello!" Even as she shouted, she realized she was
doing a stupid thing. Arrows could reach the tree.

The man scooted back and vanished.

Rose scrambled down into the thicker branches that
shielded her from the cliff—and any arrows. She pressed
her cheek against the bark and felt the old oak mustering
its strength, drawing power from the land until its sap
thrummed of danger: Fire! Ax! Flood!

Her right hand, seeking a better grip, slipped into a hollow in the wood. She felt a soft bulge, closed her fingers
around it, and drew out something crusted with dirt, broken
leaves, and bits of acorn shells. Rose brushed them away. In
her hand was a leather pouch worked with two intertwined
initials: an *A* and a *J*. She wanted to cry, laugh, run—throw
the pouch away and hug it close. She slumped against the
oak, overwhelmed, feeling like a speck about to be swallowed
by all the different forces tightening around her. She wanted
to crawl into a hole and hide or, better yet, rush into Joff
Will's arms and hide.

But Greengarden was in danger! She had to alert the others. Rose straightened, looped the pouch strings around her wrist, climbed down the tree, and then ran as fast as she could toward the Bighouse to raise the alarm. As she passed the cornfield, she remembered how brightly Joff's blond hair had shone against the rattling cornstalks.

25

The Letter

In the attic that night, Raymont pulled a piece of folded yellow paper from the leather pouch while Rose paced in front of his chair. For hours now, she had resisted the temptation to look inside the pouch. It belonged to Raymont after all, not to her. But she knew that the letter would affect her also, and she wished he would hurry.

"I've been waiting all my life for this letter, Mouse," he said, laying the pouch on the table. "And now I find myself afraid to read it. What if it doesn't help us escape? What if it reveals something terrible? Or what if my mother hated me? Or—"

"You won't know unless you read it," Rose said. She walked to the middle of the attic, where she looked at her still-unfinished portrait gleaming in the light of a single candle.

"Sit down," Raymont said. "You're distracting me."

Rose went back and sat in her chair, which faced the triangular wall at the far end of the attic. The river of blood flowing from the mountain seemed to be a tongue sticking out at her, jeering, so she scooted her chair across the floor until she faced the round window instead.

"Go on," she told him, "read it."

Carefully, smoothing each crease with his thumb and forefinger, Raymont unfolded the paper. He read silently.

"It is from my mother," he said at last. "And she did love me."

Rose picked up the pouch and twisted the strings until her fingers grew numb.

" 'My beloved child,' " Raymont read, " 'If you are reading this letter, it sadly means that I have not had the privilege of helping you grow up. I am sorry that you have had to struggle alone. You are twelve now, old enough and brave enough to hear important facts about who you are—facts your grandfather will certainly have kept from you.

" 'First, I shall tell you about your father, whom I loved more than breath itself. His name was Jaahdin Genhar. Yes, it is an unusual name, though beautiful, is it not? Now, my child, if you were born brown-eyed, then you have certainly been raised with Valley prejudice, therefore the revelation of your true paternity may shock and pain you. But you must know. Your father was a noble Dalriada, a peacemaker who loved music, fishing, and a delicate, white, five-petaled flower called the pinnea that grows only near Kalivi Mountain—the tallest of the Red Mountains, the Dalriada's holy mountain of vision.' "

With its naming, the horrible mountain on the wall behind Rose seemed to increase in power; a tickly shudder rippled down her spine, as though the red tongue had licked her back.

" 'Never, never for one second believe you are an abomination! You were born of a glorious love, and you, too, are glorious—like the hills of the Valley and the mountains of your father's homeland. Heed no Valley lies: the Dalriadas are not barbarians, indeed, they are truly honorable—a highly civilized people.

" 'If you were born with blue eyes and yet live and somehow remain at Greengarden, you are in mortal danger, my child, and must flee. Now that you are becoming an adult, another Dalriada feature will soon appear upon your forehead—your true identity will be exposed.' "

Rose looked at Raymont. "Then it's more than a birthmark."

"Yes, and *he* knew that all along." Raymont touched the sprawling mark on his forehead. "When he told me the mark was a sign of evil, he knew. What malice! Do you remember what I told you he said? 'Your dark soul is eating through your skin and revealing the loathsome beast inside.' My doting grandfather made me hate myself. And how he enjoyed it." Raymont breathed quickly. "I swear, Rose, he will pay—"

"Read the rest of it," she interrupted.

He held up the letter. " 'Never trust your grandfather, even if he appears to care for you—for his is a selfish love that seeks only to bind others to his will. I shall die of it. Indeed, in his jealous rage, he killed your father, for which act I shall hate your grandfather until my bones are dust—and then my dust itself will be a curse upon all that he loves. At least, with a sharp knife, I managed to somewhat lame him before he dragged me, bound in ropes, back to Greengarden. He will use a cane until he dies—to my great satisfaction.' "

"Amberly lamed him?" Rose thought of the night in the upstairs hall when Mr. Brae, confusing her with Amberly, had offered to forgive her everything if she sewed one button on his jacket. That offer was even greater than Rose had realized, for it must have included laming him as well as running away with a Dalriada, and yet the offer was ludicrous. Mr. Brae's crimes were far worse. Rather than offering forgiveness, he should have been begging for it himself.

"I am glad she did it," Raymont said, "but I wish she had

killed him." And he read on. " 'You may trust Lee-lee—who knows EVERYTHING and has sworn to guard you with her life. I regret to say, however, that she fears your grandfather too much to take you to the Dalriadas herself. (Always remember that your own fear can destroy your life—this happens slowly.) But now you are old enough to find your father's people on your own. Although they bear some prejudice against the Valley folk, they will accept those with mixed blood.' " Raymont looked up. "I told you," he said.

Rose sighed. "Go on."

" 'The enclosed map shows the route to a secret camp that the Dalriadas use on their scouting trips. It is twenty miles from Greengarden.' "

Rose released the pouch strings, and blood pulsed back into her fingertips. Raymont could never travel twenty miles, though he would undoubtedly find his people much closer to Greengarden than that—possibly spying from the cliff or creeping toward the Bighouse at this very moment. When Rose had alerted the orchard patrol, they had found only one blurry boot print on the rattlesnake cliff, but below, in the canyon, fresh horse tracks led west.

" 'Find the camp, my beloved,' " Raymont read on, " 'and may you *sol faringen*—come returning to your people with great joy. However, if you are brown-eyed and wish to remain at Greengarden, then do so. Always choose your own path. Keep your heritage secret, but be proud of it, and work to change the terrible prejudices of the Valley folk.

" 'There is more, so much more! that I should like to tell you. Fight for the life you wish to lead and do not be afraid to leap headfirst into life—to take a risk in order to live fully. When I fell in love with your father, I made such a leap, and though difficult and even terrible at times, it was the best thing that I have ever done. I hope that one day you will find someone to love as much as I loved your father. Love sees with the eyes of the heart: it allows you to soar beyond the prejudices that blind others. And know that love does not perish with death—I watch over you still, forever. Think of me whenever you climb the old oak tree. Yours in love and light, Mother.' "

Raymont dropped the letter in his lap and covered his face with his hands. To give him privacy, Rose stared at the dark, round window, at the black wrought-iron bars of the rose looping on the other side of the glass. Her hands kneaded the pouch, and she looked down when she felt something inside it.

"There's more," she said. When she turned the pouch upside down on the table, three things clattered out.

Raymont picked up a loop of white cord. "Look, there's a button on the end—bone, I think, though it is a bit yellow. Rather crude, isn't it? I wonder why she wanted me to have it?" He wrinkled his nose, put the necklace back down on the table, and then picked up a tarnished silver brooch fashioned in the shape of a five-petaled flower. "Now, this! This is an heirloom, a piece of art. The pinnea, perhaps? What intricate workmanship. I wonder if it is Dalriada? And here, look at this gold locket—"

Rose, however, had picked up the leather cord and was watching the button swing back and forth. Although she had seen this necklace before, hanging around Amberly's neck, Rose had not realized that the pendant was a bone button or that the carved design was a sickle moon. Her eyes dimmed with tears. As they did, the hate she felt for Amberly dimmed, too, and then, grown old and bitter and weary, the hate crumbled.

"What do you make of this map?" Raymont asked.

Rose laid the necklace down in her lap, took the letter, and studied the lines, drawn in ink faded to the same sienna color as Raymont's birthmark.

"The camp's in the hills west of Darrowdale," she said; "that's about seven miles north. From there, the route goes west into the hills another thirteen miles or so." Rose shook her head. "That's awfully deep in the Wildcat Hills. And you can't go on horseback. The area around Darrowdale is crawling with Valley soldiers—they'd catch you for sure. You might go skulking on foot, but with your bad leg, you can't creep and hide—not for twenty miles."

"But you can," Raymont said. "You will go and find my people."

"Me?" Rose laughed. "Find the Dalriadas? Alone?"

"This is exactly the opportunity we hoped for."

"You want me to travel alone in the wilderness in the middle of a war? Risk my life and the baby's? And I'd have to travel by night, in the dark."

"We have no other choice." Raymont stood up. With his right hand he grasped a purple beam on the sloped ceiling, and with his left hand, a yellow beam. "I wish I could break this roof in two!" he cried. "Tear this prison down. I want out, out! Why doesn't someone let me out!" His head lolled between his outstretched arms. "I am dying in here. I shall die in here just like my mother did—and Lee-lee."

Rose felt her heart fill with pity.

"I'm sorry," she said, "but even if I survived the journey, it would be useless. The Dalriadas would shoot me before I could explain anything. They speak a different language."

"The moment you see them you could shout my father's name, or say *sol faringen*, and wave a hank of my hair. How much threat could they see in a lone woman?"

"It's too dangerous," Rose said. "Besides, it wouldn't help you any. You'd still be trapped in here."

"Not for long. Because after you find my people, you will lead them back here so they can set me free."

"I won't bring barbarians to Greengarden! They raid farms. Burn houses and barns—murder people. They'd destroy Greengarden."

"Not if you help them rescue me. I imagine they would be

grateful—" Raymont's head straightened. His arms dropped to his sides. "So grateful," he added thoughtfully, "that they might promise to spare your precious Greengarden from a raid."

Rose stared at him.

"Think, Mouse," Raymont said, his voice spinning out as long and soft as a spider's sticky thread. "You have always dreamed of saving Greengarden, haven't you? That idea has been behind every decision you've made. Well, now you can save it. Then, after my people rescue me, they will take us to the Red Mountains, where our child will be safe." He paused. "Isn't it a small price to pay to make your dream come true? Don't you see? If you leave Greengarden, you can save Greengarden!"

Rose sat still, utterly and completely still, more still than she had ever sat in her life. The bars on the wrought-iron rose began to contract. A dark, desolate hole opened in the round window, and if she moved one inch, took one breath, she would fall in and be lost forever. She heard Raymont speak again as though from an immense distance.

"Of course, maybe you didn't really mean it." Raymont shrugged, but his eyes never left her face. "Now that it comes to the test, you will not sacrifice your own happiness for the land you claim to love. You would rather let Greengarden be destroyed."

All this time, Rose's hands had been clenched together in her lap. Now, ever so slightly, almost imperceptibly, her right index finger touched her wedding ring—the plow band.

"But there's no way to be sure," she said, her voice flat. "To know if they really would spare Greengarden."

"Make them take an oath."

"What's to stop them from breaking it?"

"My mother said they are honorable." Raymont stepped closer.

Rose shook her head.

"Don't do this for me," he said; "do this for Greengarden."

"No."

Raymont touched her shoulder. "Please."

"No!" Rose slid out from under his grasp, and as she stood up, the necklace fell to the floor.

"I never dreamed you could be this selfish," he said.

Rose shrank back. She looked at her unfinished portrait on the easel, at the candlelight slipping and sliding over her face, and for a moment she thought she saw a monster.

"You never think of anyone but yourself," Raymont said. "You refuse to help me because you don't want to leave. You love this disgusting clod of dirt that has done me such harm more than you love me."

But I don't love you, Rose wanted to cry. I've never loved you.

Raymont dragged himself to the easel. He squeezed black paint onto his palette, then threw the tube across the attic, where it struck the painting on the west wall; a black worm squirted over the luminous blue breath streaming from the Dalriadas. Then he picked up a wide brush and with quick slaps worked paint into the bristles.

"You are nothing," Raymont said. He slashed one bold, black stroke across her portrait, then angled a second stroke over the first, crossing out her face. Faster and faster he slapped on the black paint while Rose watched, gripping the back of her chair.

Her neck disappeared first, her hair and chin next, and then, after a quick upward stroke, her right eye. For some time, her left eye remained, although it became increasingly isolated and seemed to float forlornly, wistfully, an island in a black sea, until at last it was the only thing left of her. With a final, savage swipe, Raymont annihilated that, too. Then he threw down his brush. One spot remained, however, a mere speck, a tiny yellow dot.

"You have one day to change your mind," he said. "Then, unless you agree to find my people, I shall have another fit."

"The children will be scared," Rose said, staring at the dot, "but they'll live through it."

Raymont laughed. "Oh, I intend to do far more than merely frighten children. I shall scream out that I am a Dalriada."

"What?" Rose looked at him. "You'll what?"

"I shall scream out the truth. And you will lose Greengarden." He smiled.

"You can't! Raymont—they'd kill you!"

"If I stay locked in this prison, I shall die anyway. So you see, my dear Mouse, one way or another, I am afraid you are going to lose your precious Greengarden. If you do things my way, at least you may save it from destruction. The choice is yours."

Raymont turned back to the easel. He pressed his white hand into the black paint, lifted it, and then pressed it down a few inches to the left. He did this again and again, slowly covering the black canvas with black handprints. Rose tensed as his hand approached the yellow dot. Either he did not notice it or did not think the dot worthy of his notice, and so it survived, huddled miserably in the V-shaped blackness between the prints of his thumb and forefinger.

26

Desolation

arly in the afternoon the next day, beneath a sky that threatened rain, Rose walked toward the Bighouse after picking most of the Appelunes. She was hot, she was thirsty, she was tired, and she knew that she could not do what Raymont demanded. Rose had gone round and round the arguments in her mind, weighing them, railing against them, but always ran into the same problem: She was afraid. Afraid of traveling alone in the dark, in the wilderness. Afraid of running into soldiers. Afraid of Raymont revealing the truth. Afraid of the Dalriadas, and of bringing them to Greengarden. Most of all, she was afraid of leaving Greengarden forever.

Even as she thought it, Rose grasped the gate in the picket fence around the Bighouse. From the sudden shattering in her heart and her bones—as though a wagon were rolling over her chest—Rose knew that until now she had never really imagined leaving. It was a desolation, a diminishment. It was the last yellow dot on her portrait extinguished. She could not leave, not even to save Greengarden.

Rose straightened and looked up at the round window. The black wrought-iron rose looked monstrous. What had Amberly written in her letter? Fear destroys your life—slowly. Rose saw that her fear might destroy Greengarden, and that was monstrous. But she could not leave.

She opened the gate, then the creaking front door, and walked through the house to the kitchen.

"You missed breakfast—and lunch," Mrs. Schill said. On the counter in front of her, a frosted cake stood on a lazy Susan. Her big-boned hands squeezed icing out of a pastry bag, piping delicate green garlands along the side of the cake.

"I was picking the Appelunes," Rose said.

"That's no excuse. You keep missing meals and, sure as night follows day, you'll lose that baby."

Rose stood still for a moment, then walked to the sink.

"I kept a bowl of stew hot," Mrs. Schill said, "on the warming shelf."

"Thanks." Rose pumped herself a glass of water. Mrs. Schill flicked the lazy Susan, and the cake turned as she piped a border around the bottom.

"So, how do you feel about being an aunt?" Mrs. Schill asked.

"What?"

"Don't tell me nobody's spilled the beans about Susa?"

"Opal tried to tell me something the other day," Rose said, "but there wasn't time."

"Well! It seems Susa's having a baby, too. She tried to pin it on Joff—the nerve of that girl! But he denies it. Besides, she's going on five months, and that puts it back in your brother's time. My bet is the two of them went off gathering wild honey in the hills more than once."

Rose set the glass of water, untouched, down on the

counter. Now she understood what Joff had said in the lane the other day.

"Susa kept it pretty well hid, until she fainted picking the Shaulas." Mrs. Schill picked up another pastry bag and swirled sugary red roses onto the cake.

"I think I'd like being an aunt," Rose said slowly, wanting to cry.

Someone knocked on the back door. The hinges creaked, and Gerald stepped inside.

"Where's Mr. Brae?" he asked.

Mrs. Schill jerked her head. "His study."

"Word just came," Gerald said. "The Dalriadas raided again last night."

"Where?" Rose asked.

He hesitated, glancing at Mrs. Schill. "East of Darrowdale."

"Which place?" Mrs. Schill spun the lazy Susan harder than before. The cake turned so fast that the petals she piped out squiggled all over the top. "Which place?" she asked again, louder. When Gerald did not answer, Mrs. Schill stopped making petals but spun the cake until the grotesque roses were a wheeling blur of red. "Answer me!" She turned, clenching the pastry bag. Icing shot across the kitchen in a red arc and snaked onto Rose's skirt. "Gerald!" Mrs. Schill cried. "You know my Adrena works up at East Dale Ranch!"

Gerald looked at the backs of his hands as the lazy Susan creaked to a halt.

"I'm sorry," he said.

Mrs. Schill's face crumpled.

"There may be survivors, or captives, Gwen," he said softly. "The messenger didn't know any details."

Rose stood dumbly for a moment, looking down at her red-streaked skirt while her father led Mrs. Schill to a chair.

"I'm guessing you scared them away yesterday, Rose," he said. "Otherwise it could have been us instead of—"

Mrs. Schill sobbed.

"Now, Gwen," Gerald said, "don't let your imagination run away with you. Why not hope for the best? I'd better go tell Mr. Brae." And he left the kitchen. Rose put her arm around Mrs. Schill.

"Barbarians," Mrs. Schill sobbed. "Bloodthirsty barbarians. Adrena, my Adrena! What if they ate her?"

Ten minutes later, Gerald came back.

"Don't you two worry," he said. "They'll not bother us here. We're doubling the guard."

But Rose remembered what he had said when she was little: "If you're not a good girl, the monster will come. The Thing will get out and gobble you up." Now, if she did not let one monster out, another monster would come. No matter what she did, a monster would be loose, but one way, Greengarden might survive.

After Rose persuaded Mrs. Schill—well fortified with applejack—to lie down for a nap, Rose decided to have one, too. She grew tired easily now. How could she journey twenty miles through the wilderness on foot? Not only Dalriadas but also bears and wolves lurked in the Wildcat Hills. Rose left the kitchen and walked down the hall toward the front stairs, where a voice drifted out from the drawing room.

"I swear," Mr. Brae was saying, "to purge our land of this pollution."

Rose stopped, then peered around the doorway. Mr. Brae stood alone in the drawing room with his back to her, staring up at the three portraits on the wall.

The upstart comes snooping again, said the bearded man.

She bears my great-great-grandchild, an abomination, said the man with the whistling ducks.

If she were not a coward, said the pinch-nosed woman, *she could save us all and be gone—ridding the family of her low birth and ridding the land of two monsters at once. But no, the upstart still cannot speak the word.*

"I swear, Father," Mr. Brae said, "after the heir is born and if he looks like us, I shall kill the monster who has desecrated this land for seventeen years. Greengarden will thrive again, be a garden again. This time, I shall raise the child properly—"

He had his chance with Amberly, said the bearded man, *and he failed.*

He has abused the word, said the man with the whistling ducks. *He let the land go to ruin. I blame Uncle Morley.*

Blame yourself! The pinch-nosed woman snorted. *Always away hunting instead of whipping the boy.*

"The days will be long," Mr. Brae went on. "And the fruit will be so bountiful again that the limbs on the trees will groan. There will be dancing in this room again and music, too. I shall tear the shrouds from the chandeliers and there will be dancing and singing and light again! Happiness—"

He dares speak to us of shrouds, said the man with the whistling ducks.

Rose flattened against the wall and began to back toward the kitchen.

"So please, I beg you, Father—"

She froze. Mr. Brae begging?

"—save the land from the barbarians. Do not punish me by letting them destroy Greengarden!"

Our bones speak to the land, said the bearded man. *What other power does he think we have?*

We will perish in flames, said the man with the whistling ducks.

No, said the pinch-nosed woman. *Flame will save us.*

What do you foresee, old woman? asked the bearded man.

Trim your beard and mind your manners, she snapped.

I can't see anything. The upstart has not dusted us in weeks.

Rose took one step after another backward, terrified Mr. Brae would hear, until she finally reached the kitchen. She went through the swinging door into the dining room and then crossed the sitting room to reach the stairs.

Up in her room, a vase of golden dahlias stood on the bedside table; Mrs. Schill must have put them there. Rose bent toward the blossoms, then sat on her bed and looked at the fantastic candles. She had brought back the one she had taken to the attic, so she now had seventy-six. They were dusty, standing in a row around her walls. Why had she ever believed they would protect her? Would everything have turned out differently if she had made the seventy-seventh candle?

When the familiar thud–drag creaked across the ceiling, Rose's chest tightened, and she curled up on the white quilt. Mr. Brae wanted to kill Raymont, and Raymont wanted to kill Mr. Brae. She began to cough. Again the ceiling creaked. There was a monster above her, a monster below her, a monster inside her, and hundreds more creeping toward her from beyond the Faredge Wall—and all of them seemed to smell as sickly-sweet as the red icing crusted on her skirt. A scream began to corkscrew in her throat. The invisible hand gripped her chest, signaling a spell. Rose wheezed and wheezed through a tunnel whose walls were iced the color of fear.

When the spell ended, she lay spent, with her eyes closed. She put her hand on her stomach and thought of Dorrick's baby. If there had been no war, she might have invited Susa to live here in the Bighouse. Maybe they would have become sisters, though it was odd to think of Susa, of all people, as a sister. They could have raised their children together. Rose had thought about her duty to save Greengarden for her ancestors, but now she thought about her duty to save it for her descendants. Perhaps the ability to speak the word *mine* came not from how you felt about the land but from what you were willing to do for the land.

Later, when dusk fell, Rose went back to the Faredge Wall. She picked an Appelune, feeling for the fruit with her fingers, cupping the apple in her hand, then twisting her wrist and snapping the stem from the tree. Rose threw the apple against the wall, where she had once danced on the bones of her ancestors. Bones would not help Greengarden now. It needed living flesh, a sacrifice: hers.

One by one, in the darkness, Rose threw the apples against the stone wall—to hear them smash, to smell their sweetness, to feel their weight in her hand, and to remember all these things with her heart so that Greengarden would remember her.

PART FOUR

27

Into Wilderness

Three days after Rose left Greengarden, she plodded along a broad, wooded ridge in the Wildcat Hills. If the map was right, she was only five miles from the Dalriada camp. The sun forked low through the pines, making a spectacle of light, but she kept her head down. If she looked only at the ground, she could keep her panic at bay. The trail faded in and out, however, so she had to glance up often, as now, when faced by a gigantic fallen tree. Rose skirted it until the trunk narrowed enough that she could climb on top. As she stood there, looking ahead to find the trail, she saw a heart-stopping view of the northern foothills.

Range after range of wooded hills sloped back one after the other, the near ones green, the distant ones fading into a misty blue that seemed to roll on forever. Rose grabbed a branch to steady herself, sickened by the knowledge that the wilderness had swallowed her. She felt the same vertigo as she had in the attic when the dancing motes of darkness wove their visions. She closed her eyes and clung to the branch as though it were the bedpost. Maybe she really was in the attic; maybe this was only another terrible vision; maybe when she opened her eyes, the branch would change back into the bedpost.

It did not. After Rose started down the trail again, she kept her eyes on the ground, trying to find comfort in the limited certainties of moss, stone, twig, and leaf. She tried to think of home, but Greengarden seemed faint and far away.

When Rose had left it, she had crouched on the edge of the wheat flat, risking a last look—though if all went as planned, it was not quite her last look. Not yet. On that evening, however, fog had hidden Greengarden. She had tried to find the Faredge Wall, but it had vanished.

Now Rose shifted her pack and heard the water bottle gurgle inside. She thought of the remaining apple fritter wrapped in a napkin beside it—Mrs. Schill had given her six as a parting gift. How puzzled she had looked when Rose had asked for her help.

"Let me see if I've got this straight," Mrs. Schill had said, her eyes red from weeping over Adrena. No word of her had come, and Mr. Brae claimed it was too dangerous for Mrs. Schill to travel to Darrowdale. "You want to go away for a few days," Mrs. Schill said, "but you won't tell me where. I'm to say you're under the weather from the baby—nothing serious—and you're resting in your room and don't want to be bothered."

Rose nodded. "It shouldn't be much trouble for you without me. Verda does most of my old work now anyway."

Mrs. Schill sucked in her lower lip. "What if the Thing throws another fit for you?"

"He knows I'm going," Rose said. During one of Mrs. Schill's naps, Rose had sent a note up on the dumbwaiter; she was afraid to be locked in with Raymont again. Soon the dumbwaiter had come creaking back with a bundle containing the map, the silver pinnea brooch, a large hank of his hair, and a note that mixed threats of tantrums with declarations of undying love. Rose had burned the note.

Mrs. Schill squinted. "So it knows, does it?" She was still itching to find out the truth about the Thing. "I bet I can guess what you're up to. You're going off to gather wild honey in the hills with Joff Will, aren't you?" She winked.

"That's it," Rose said. "You've found me out."

Mrs. Schill snorted. "Dreamer! What if His Most Exalted finds out you're gone, and I lose my job?"

"Mr. Brae's too busy with the war effort to bother about me," Rose said. "He's meeting with the leaders of the Stonewater Defense Force every day now. Besides, I'm mistress; I run the household. When I come back, you'll get your job back. And you can go to East Dale Ranch and see what happened to Adrena."

"My dear," said Mrs. Schill, peering at her, "you're looking peaked. I bet a rest would do you good."

Before Rose had left, she had dusted the paintings in the drawing room. "I'm going to save you old gossips," she told them. "I'll show you I can speak the word." They had maintained a dignified silence, even when she tickled the old woman's pinched nose with the feather duster. Theirs were the last faces at Greengarden that Rose had seen.

Now, as she climbed a staircase of root and rock, Rose wondered why she had seen no barbarians when they were said to be massed around Trickle Creek a few miles north. Perhaps they had seen her, but had ignored a solitary woman traveling unarmed. Whatever the reason, the lack of people was fortunate, because Rose had found she had to travel during the day; in the forest, she could not see to travel by night.

After a quarter mile along the ridge, it curved downward. A cold wind funneled in from clouds to the west, but at least the rain held off. Rose followed the trail into a canyon crowded with aspens whose leaves had turned gold. They flittered and flapped in the wind. She stopped to look, then wanted to crouch into a ball and sob.

Although the aspens were not so different from those at Greengarden, these did not speak to her. This entire land did not speak to her. These hills had no names, no meaning, no associations—except fear. The wilderness did not know her.

Then, as the setting sun splashed the leaves with light, it seemed as if the trees wore gowns twig-stitched with brilliant gold buttons. Rose thought of Amberly's jewel-like dress. Had its buttons tinkled together during the dance on the Faredge Wall? Rose could not remember.

Near the bottom of the canyon, the aspens thinned, and the land widened into a meadow ringed with scrubby pines. Rose had just decided to stop there for the night when she heard the thump of horse's hooves. She dropped behind a holly bush as a group on horseback rode into the meadow. If they were Dalriadas, she had to find the courage to stand and shout—Jaahdin Genhar! I seek Jaahdin Genhar!

The ground shook. Her heart pounded. The horses galloped by one at a time, making the green leaves in front of her flash from dark to light, dark to light. None of the riders had red hair; they were a Valley patrol. Rose sagged with relief even though, if they discovered her, they might ask hard questions, might think her a spy. Why else would a Valley woman roam this far into the Wildcat Hills alone? How would she explain the map, or the pinnea brooch pinned to her cloak, or, if it was discovered, the red hair in a secret pocket in her skirt? Then Rose realized that she was a spy. After all, she was planning to lead barbarians to Greengarden.

The patrol sped away. The fading hoofbeats gave way to a chorus of crickets and, somewhere, a frog croaking *runback! run-back!* Not until darkness hid the meadow's edge did Rose stand up. She had to go on: the patrol might return or spot her tracks. She skittered from tree to boulder to bush as the trail edged higher.

Her fear of the dark thickened; it swelled into a malignancy between her shoulder and ear. Three-quarters full, the hated moon drifted like a vagrant over the eastern ridge. Rose pulled her hood forward to hide from the glare.

The wind came up. A nighthawk cried, swooping like a rip in the night, and Rose tripped. Pain exploded in her knee. She lay half-dazed, smelling an odor of rotting potatoes from the plant that prickled her cheek. What was the use of going on? The barbarians would only kill her. All this was pointless, hopeless. Why had she ever believed that she was strong enough to save Greengarden? Rose pounded her fist on the alien ground. "Help me!" she cried. "Why don't you help me!"

The wilderness did not hear her. She wanted to set it on fire, burn it to white cinders, burn out the monstrous trees and the everlasting hills and the savage barbarians. Maybe then the wilderness would wake up and notice her.

When her rage was spent, Rose sat up. She wiggled her ankle, bent her leg, winced, and then eased to her feet; everything worked, if painfully. Rose limped down the trail, trying to see ahead in the dark. It seemed to her that all she had done the last few months was try to see in the dark.

After perhaps a quarter mile, Rose found a dry, rocky riverbed at the top of a gorge that, according to the map, ended only two miles from the Dalriada camp. From here on, there would be no trail. Step by step, stone by stone, Rose picked her way along the riverbed, which spilled, faintly gleaming in the moonlight, like the tongue of a giant.

When she reached the bottom of the gorge, the smell hit her first, the smell of running, of never waking, the sour, rusty smell of nightmare sweat. Her left leg sank calf-deep into mud. A pool by the river had withered to a swamp. It was as black as the darkness in the attic, but as Rose stared into it, nothing whirled, nothing moved. It showed nothing but a raw, dumb hunger to devour. Her leg sank deeper.

"No," she said. "You can't have me!" Rose pulled, and with a long reluctant slurp, the swamp released her. She limped away. On firmer ground nearby, she rolled up in her blanket and slept.

The sun was high when Rose woke, her lungs congested, her knee swollen. She drank some water. Then, dizzy and shaking, she went on.

Sometime past noon—long past caring—Rose stopped and stared. In front of her, a long-handled silver pot hung in midair, twisting and turning in a wind dance. It was empty; the bottom solid black, the sides scorched with black tongues left by the fire. Then she saw the rope that ran from the pot's handle to a branch overhead. She froze.

Rose had walked unhindered into the Dalriada camp. Because the tents, mats, and clothes—in dark green, chestnut, and gray—matched the colors of the woods, she had reached the middle of the camp before she realized where she was. A few barbarians glanced at her, but no one shouted. No one drew a knife or a bow.

Rose opened her mouth. There was something she was supposed to shout—what was it?

An old man approached her. He wore deerskin leggings and a long deerskin tunic. A silver brooch shaped like a star hung over his heart. Across his forehead sprawled a birthmark similar to Raymont's, but where Raymont's was smooth, this man's birthmark followed the contours of thick bony ridges. It looked as though he had antlers embedded in his skull. His left eye shone bluer than a jay's wing. Over his right eye was a black patch decorated with the iridescent eye of a peacock feather. It seemed to watch her.

"I am Kitorl," he said. "We have been waiting for you."

28

The Council of Seven

Rose woke surrounded by a soft, many-colored glow—of blue, gold, and red. A few yards above her, two sloped walls painted with sweeps of color met in a peak. For a moment, Rose thought she was back in the attic, but these colors were beautiful, suffused with light. One blended into another, rippling, sometimes pulsing, much different from the black-edged shapes and jangling contrasts that Raymont had painted on the attic ceiling. She sighed deeply, contentedly, and the breath that came out of her seemed to have color, too.

When Rose woke a little more, she touched one of the walls. It was the inside of a tent—a Dalriada tent.

Wide-awake now, she rolled up on one elbow. She was alone. The tent flap was closed. The sunlight hitting the tent came through the painted walls, making everything inside, including her, take on their glowing color. One gold-tinted bear skin lay beneath her, another lay on top of her. Where was her cloak? Rose looked around but saw only her pack, still fastened with her own knot. If the barbarians had her cloak, then they also had the silver brooch and the map.

Rose tried to remember what had happened. After the barbarian Kitorl had spoken, she had felt sick; she must have fainted. That grotesque forehead would have made anyone faint. Rose lay back on the bear skin, her chest rising and falling too fast, her sore knee throbbing, her stomach growling. At least the Dalriadas had not killed her—yet. Kitorl had said they had been waiting for her, as though they had known she was coming. How could that be?

Outside the tent, quail chirped. Trees creaked in the wind, and water gurgled—a stream perhaps? But Rose heard no voices, no footsteps, no snap of a campfire. Inch by inch, as quietly as possible, she crept forward. She slid one fingertip between the tent flap and the wall, peered out, and found herself looking straight into the terrible blue eye of a Dalriada. Rose scrambled back.

The flap, flung wide, smacked against the tent. The man beckoned her, but Rose shook her head.

"Ergah Didorieth," the man grumbled. His red hair twisted in spikes. He tied the flap open and then left her alone.

For the next half hour, Rose watched a sunbeam glide toward a pinecone that lay outside the tent door. Sometimes now she heard voices, and once, the sound of laughter. When at last the beam struck the pinecone, each overlapping fan shone distinctly, separated by thin, black shadows from all the others. If she had not given up making candles, Rose might have tried to make one that looked like that.

"Maybe someday," she said, feeling as bleak as if she were staring into the black swamp again. Rose could not see what her future days would look like because from now on they would all be spent with the Dalriadas. Then she thought of Amberly's sampler: "If a woman loves with her soul's dance, she leaps every mountain between her and her beloved." Rose crawled to the tent door and looked out at her future.

Scattered beneath a cluster of pines were perhaps a dozen tents mottled with shades of grey, green, and brown—the colors of the woods. The barbarians understood camouflage well. Over each door hung a piece of antler tied with dried herbs and flowers. Rose saw a ring of rocks containing the charred remains of a fire and, straddling it, a three-legged iron pot stand. To the left, a woman stacked wood into a neat pile. Several more barbarians worked alone or in groups: a man slid an oiled red cloth along one of the bows propped against a tree trunk; another man twirled a sheet of dough in the air; a group of men and women sat in a circle, talking while they poked needles in and out of harnesses and saddles; and a few yards from Rose, a young woman with a bandage wrapped around her head repaired a stack of arrows. She glanced up and saw Rose watching her.

With one swift, graceful motion, the woman stood up, her seven red braids swinging out and then falling back again. A black-handled knife showed in a sheath at her hip. She approached slowly, making no sudden movements, as if Rose were a wild animal with unpredictable behavior. Rose, hoping she understood the woman's gestures correctly, limped after her into the woods to a kind of outhouse. On the way back, they passed a waterfall in a grotto of stone and moss, the source of the gurgling stream, and Rose splashed her face and hands until they turned red with cold. Then she drank.

When they returned to the camp, the woman pointed to a mat near the fire ring; someone had started a small fire that snapped cheerfully. Rose sat down and stretched her sore leg straight out in front of her. The man with the spiked hair appeared with her cloak, now clean and dry, but missing the silver pinnea brooch.

"Thanks," Rose said. She wrapped the cloak around herself. The October afternoon was fair but cool here in the foothills. The young woman thrust a strip of dried meat into Rose's hand, but Rose dropped it as though she held a stinging nettle. The woman snatched it up, exclaiming angrily, pulling on three of her braids.

"I can't eat that," Rose said. "It might be . . ." She shuddered, thinking of Adrena. She tried not to look at the big pot swinging on its rope or the flames dancing around the iron stand.

A few minutes later, hoofbeats drummed in the distance, growing louder and louder until seven barbarians on horseback swept into the camp. Kitorl led them. All the horses— blacks, blood-bays, a silver, a chestnut with yellow mane and tail—were magnificent. Rose knew that Joff would have given his right arm to see them. When the barbarians dismounted, they made no thud, rattled no stone, only stirred clouds of dust that swirled around their ankles and then drifted away.

The newcomers walked toward her. Their deerskin tunics and leggings flowed against them like a second skin, dyed in splotches of sage-green and gold, brown and grey. Though obviously meant to act as camouflage, the colors looked too vivid for these woods. Rose squinted. Then her heart beat fast as she realized they were Valley colors, designed to camouflage the barbarians during their raids. She scowled.

The barbarians—Kitorl, two other men, and four women—sat in a half circle on the other side of the fire ring and studied Rose in silence. She felt as if she sat before a gathering of stags, each independent, proud, intelligent. All of the barbarians had the raised antler mark, yet no two were the same. Kitorl's had thick ridges. The woman beside him had thinner ridges, but they covered her forehead from temple to temple. Others had curling spikes or angular forks or curving branches, varying in color from pale orange to chestnut brown. Did Raymont have his mark on his skin alone because he was half Valley? Would her abomination have the mark? Now Rose had to worry about a deformed forehead as well as blue eyes.

At last Kitorl raised his palm toward the sky and spoke words Rose did not understand. He was about fifty, younger than she had thought when she first saw him; his long grey hair had misled her.

"We, the Council of Seven," he said, "sit in deliberation in these dire times. May the Eldest Deer grant us the imagination and wisdom to see truly." Then he smiled at Rose. "Please, will you honor us with your name?"

"It's Rose. Rose Chandler Brae."

"Ah! Delightful!" Kitorl rubbed his hands together. "My people have many legends about wild roses. Perhaps after today we will have another. Do you not think so, Sestine?" Kitorl asked a middle-aged woman beside him.

"I see nothing to inspire me, my friend." Sestine crossed her arms over her chest. Her eyes were midnight blue beneath thick, reddish-grey brows. "Didorieth, dirtdweller," she said to Rose, "I also speak your language, though it fouls my mouth." She spit on the ground. "I lead our forces in this region."

Rose pulled her cloak tighter.

"Mareck," Sestine said to a squat, red-haired man, "please translate for the others." The man nodded.

"Rose Chandler Brae," said Kitorl, "how I rejoice that our paths meet at last."

"But I don't understand," Rose said. "How did you know I was coming?"

Sestine rolled her eyes. "Our spies tracked you from the moment you left the cliffs east of Darrowdale. Do not follow a trail, even a secret trail, if you wish to remain hidden. Do your people teach their children nothing of woodcraft?"

"No," Rose said. "Do you teach your children to prune fruit trees?"

Sestine looked startled. Kitorl hid a smile. When Mareck finished translating, several of the other barbarians smiled, too.

"I asked our spies to watch for you," Kitorl said, "because I knew you were coming months ago. But I see that you are confused. I am a seer, you understand, and a bootmaker, too, which some say I do better, and so I often forget to begin at the beginning. After all, who can really say where a story begins? Are not all events middles? Are not—"

"Old friend," Sestine said, "if I might suggest beginning with the Dawning Hills?"

"Oh, yes, yes." Kitorl tapped one of the ridges on his forehead. "When I stood on the Dawning Hills two months ago, I looked out over the South Valley—oh, this land of yours is strangely wonderful, a green tale unfolding before the eye." He touched the eye of the peacock feather on the black patch. "To proceed, I looked out and saw a young Valley woman walking eastward, lost in her pain and fear, bearing a terrible burden. She was seeking us." He paused. "That was the first vision."

"A . . . vision?" Rose had never heard anyone admit to having visions before.

"I know that your people seldom have visions," Kitorl said, "and when they do, they think them a sign of madness or—"

"They aren't a sign of madness?" she asked.

Kitorl shook his head. "They are one way to see the truth, to hear a few notes of the Song in the World."

Rose recalled the dancing motes of darkness and her hands trembled. She fixed her eyes on a pine tree, something solid, of the earth. "I have . . . I have visions, too, sometimes." A bit frightened, she glanced at the council to see their reactions. They seemed surprised, but no one leapt up in alarm.

"Then the Eldest Deer has given you a great gift," Kitorl

said. "I would be honored to hear about your visions. As I am a seer, it is possible that I could help you understand their meaning, although I cannot promise anything, you understand. And I would be most interested in—"

"Perhaps later, Kitorl," Sestine interrupted.

Kitorl sighed. "The direct way is not usually the way of greatest truth, old friend."

"Perhaps not," Sestine said, "but I am urgently needed in Darrowdale."

"Then I will try your patience no longer." Kitorl rubbed his boot. "After that first vision, my intuition told me to come to this camp. As I journeyed, I saw you several more times. Once with a yoke around your neck, bringing water, bringing fire—bringing something to us, something vital to my people, though I could not see what. Peace perhaps?" He looked at Rose, his face full of hope.

Rose did not know what to say.

"Once," he added, "you wore the horns of an ox and danced on a stone wall around a large pool. Once, you danced with bone dancers. Another time, you walked through a long, red tunnel that was like the inside of a heart with—"

"Stop!" Rose exclaimed. "Stop it!" She climbed to her feet, ignoring the pain in her knee. "Here you are pretending to be nice to me when you're as mean as Raymont! What medicine did you give me so I would tell you those things in my sleep?"

The barbarians looked at each other.

"We gave you no medicine," Sestine said. "Sit down."

"Oh, dear," Kitorl said. "Oh, no! I am so sorry I have distressed you, though I do not understand how I have done so. Oh, I should only make boots! Then the only harm I can do is to give someone a blister or a bunion."

"But," Rose said, "some of those visions you described—they're my visions."

No one spoke. The flames danced, pink and gold and blue, throwing their light across the grey rocks that contained them.

"Extraordinary!" Kitorl whispered at last. "Marvelous! When a seer sees the visions of others, then a great truth is walking, trying very hard to reveal itself to us. Such seeing is rare, but not unheard of."

"It's hard to believe," Rose said slowly, but she sat down again and rubbed her knee.

"Seers have special training," Kitorl explained. "And you must have a stronger inward eye—intuition, I think you call it—than most of your people. Indeed, once in a vision, I saw you raise both your hands to the sky. A flame sprang from each fingertip on your left hand, and a leafy branch from each fingertip on your right hand. Oh, what gifts! It was marvelous! Truly, I could not wait to meet you." He rubbed his hands, delighted. "And here you are! With visions of your own! You might be seer to your own people."

Rose watched him in amazement. She had expected the barbarians to be savages, to be like Raymont—only worse. She had not expected this jolly, rambling man.

"Then a week ago . . ." Kitorl paused and shook his head, his delight fading. "One week ago, I saw you climbing the Wildcat Hills. In that final vision, I at last saw your face exactly as it is before me now. You had left all hope behind, left your heart behind," he said gently. "There was no light in you, no leafy green, only a black sorrow. And I see now that I saw truly."

In the silence that followed, Rose stared at Kitorl. She felt as if she were suddenly aware that she had been starving for months. Here was someone she could talk to, someone who would understand the strange things that had happened to her, the strange things she had seen. Here was someone who might help her. Help her? A raw surge of grief and hope swelled like a huge, sprouting seed in her throat, a seed so powerful that its roots shot down into her lungs and coiled around her heart, a seed so desperate that it pushed the rest of her body apart to make room for itself. All this happened in one breath, this transformation into pure emotion.

"Ah," Kitorl said softly, "you have endured too much alone. Held too much inside. What is so important that you would give up your heart to find us?" he asked.

Rose knew that if she spoke, all that sorrow, all that hope and despair and emotion would explode from her mouth and leak from her eyes. To contain it, she counted the rocks around the fire ring: one, two, three, four . . . twelve.

"You have brought us something," Kitorl said, "as I foresaw. But I am puzzled because it is less than I expected." He held out the pinnea brooch. "Where did you find this, Rose Chandler Brae? It is a Dalriada pin of mastery. This one is given to those who have mastered the art of negotiation." Kitorl's own silver, star-shaped brooch winked in the sun. It had the same workmanship as the pinnea brooch. Three of the barbarians wore similar silver brooches; only the shapes differed. "But," Kitorl added, "we know of no negotiator who has died in the war or even been taken prisoner."

"It belonged to Jaahdin Genhar," Rose said.

"To—" Sestine exchanged glances with Kitorl. All the barbarians murmured.

"And how did you get it?" Kitorl asked.

"Jaahdin's . . . wife, Amberly, gave it to her son," Rose said.

Kitorl's eyes lit up. "The Valley woman who married Jaahdin! They had a son?"

"Do they live?" Sestine leaned forward.

But Rose was staring at Kitorl. Married? Amberly had been married to Jaahdin?

"Answer!" Sestine said.

"Only their son, Raymont, is still alive," Rose said. "I brought the brooch to prove he is Jaahdin's son—and to tell you that he wants you to come and rescue him."

Sestine laughed. As Mareck translated, all the others laughed, too, except for Kitorl, who looked troubled.

"So the Didorieth think we are stupid enough to believe this fantastic tale?" Sestine's eyebrows raised, rumpling the antler mark, which emphasized her question. "If Jaahdin's son lives and wishes to join his people, let him come to us."

"He can't," Rose said. "He's been locked up in an attic since he was born. Hidden away from everybody."

The mark paled on Kitorl's forehead. "Why?"

"His grandfather hates him, but needed an heir for the land. If the Valley folk knew Raymont was part Dalriada, they'd kill him. He's never even been outside."

"Mud-eaters!" Sestine said. "Your people disgust me more each day. But Raymont is a man grown now. He would find a way to escape."

Rose shook her head. "We tried. He's locked in. There are bars on the window."

"If he has been hidden away, how do you know about him?" Kitorl asked.

"I'm his wife. I carry an abom—a baby. The heir to the land."

"Ah!" Kitorl nodded and rubbed his hands together. "We are moving closer now."

"Raymont's grandfather," Rose said, "has sworn that when the baby is born, he'll kill Raymont—and the baby, too, if it has blue eyes. Please, you must help them."

"The council will speak together now," Kitorl told her. While they talked in their own language, a man wearing three copper bracelets carried the big pot to the fire ring. He bowed to the others and then spoke, gesturing to the sky, where the light was softening as the sun surrendered the afternoon. Kitorl nodded. The man hung the pot on the three-legged stand;

a little liquid spilled out and hissed into the fire. Just as Rose was thinking that she could not imagine Kitorl eating people, he spoke.

"I fear that I alone believe your story." He sighed.

"Those who murdered Jaahdin could have given you his brooch," Sestine said, "so you could lead us into a trap. You dirtdwellers would rejoice to slaughter more of us."

Rose twisted her cloak. "You're the barbarians. You eat people."

"We do no such thing!" Sestine said.

"You killed my brother!" Rose exclaimed. "You destroy our farms and orchards—"

"The dirtdwellers began the war by mining for metal and jewels in our mountains," Sestine said.

"Lies," Rose said. "We fight only in self-defense."

"Peace!" Kitorl held up his hand. "This is not the time to debate the war. I was so certain, from my visions, that you were important to us, Rose Chandler Brae, desperately important. But from what you have told us, I do not see how. One Dalriada locked in an attic is terrible, of course, but not of vital importance to the war. Perhaps my hope for peace influenced me too much." He sighed. "I shall have to make more boots and be more humble."

"Because you know the location of this camp," Sestine said, "we cannot allow you to return home. Unlike your people, however, we do not kill those with whom we have sat in parley. We will send you to the Red Mountains."

"No!" Rose exclaimed. "No!" She had thought nothing could be worse than giving up Greengarden in order to save it, but giving up Greengarden without saving it was a nightmare beyond her imagining. It left her in a place without hope, without satisfaction; it left her with nothing. She saw herself floating forever with her arms outstretched on the surface of the black swamp, stuck to it like flypaper. Even her breath could not escape. To her shame, Rose began to cry.

"Dear child, I am so sorry," Kitorl said. "If only . . . I still sense something about you. What is it? Oh, what is it!" He shook his head. "I cannot see the way. It is dark."

"Yes," Rose cried, "it is dark. Darker than the attic." She took a deep breath and to comfort herself said, "To light a candle in the dark, close your eyes. See with your breath, your soul, your heart."

Kitorl stared at her, then closed his good eye. Because the peacock-feather eye continued to stare at her, it seemed as if Kitorl were winking. The other barbarians remained silent, watching him. Rose wondered what he saw, and out of which eye, and she felt the hunger rising inside her again.

"Do you see the dancing motes of darkness?" Rose asked him. Kitorl kept his eye closed. "Do you know about the dark well? About diving into the terrible and the beautiful? But what about the darkness that has no visions? The blackness that is only nothing—like the swamp at the bottom of the gorge. Do you know about the monsters that live in your mind? Can you see them?"

"The terrible and the beautiful," Kitorl murmured, his head slightly bowed. "I see you . . . standing in a room filled with burning candles. The light creates a shimmer of gold around you, a shimmer of gold . . . of gold . . . And now a man painting a slanted wall, painting it gold—but the light around him is dim. There you are again, outside with the same golden light burning around you." Kitorl smiled. "Now even the moon is gold. The edge of your light falls across a man, reveals him . . . Ah!" His eye opened. "Yes!"

"What is it, old friend?" Sestine asked.

"It is Raymont who is important!" Kitorl exclaimed. "We must rescue him."

Rose crushed her cloak in her hands.

"Why is he important?" Sestine asked.

"I don't know," Kitorl said. "Something to do with gold.

Perhaps it has to do with the mines. I only know we must rescue him. There is no doubt."

"This is not enough," Sestine said.

As the council began to discuss the matter, Rose thought of another way to persuade them that her story was true. She found the secret pocket in the lining of her skirt, picked out the stitches, and then pulled out the hank of red hair.

"Here's a bit of Raymont's hair," she said, holding it up. The wind fanned the long, thick strand, which blew backward over her wrist. In a ray of the setting sun, the streaks of gold in the hair shone with more brilliance than they ever had in the gloomy attic.

A quail chirped; the waterfall roared in the distance; and closer, the stew began to bubble. But the Dalriadas, their eyes fixed on Raymont's hair, seemed to have turned to stone. Rose feared she had offended them. They probably thought the hair had been cut from a Dalriada killed in battle.

Then Kitorl, Sestine, and the others sprang up, their faces wild. They all shouted at once.

"Rhohar!"

"Jaahdin *denau becla*!"

"Raymont da Rhohar!"

"Rhohar Genhar!"

Every barbarian in the camp came running toward Rose.

29

Saving Greengarden

Sestine grabbed the hank of hair from Rose and held it high while the other barbarians crowded around, talking and exclaiming. The man with the spiked hair ran to a horse, jumped on, and rode away fast. Kitorl reached toward the hair but pulled his hand away the moment he touched it. Then, with the lightest brush of his fingertips, he stroked the long strands.

"What is it?" Rose asked. "Why's everybody so excited?"

Kitorl held out his hands to her. Rose took them, and after helping her to her feet, he bowed to her.

"From this day forward," he said, "our people will honor and praise you. They will name their daughters Elanae—our word for rose—after you. And there will indeed be a new rose legend—do you agree now, Sestine?"

"Legends and tales and songs!" she said. "I shall never doubt you again, old friend."

"Then you believe me?" Rose asked. "Believe that Raymont is Jaahdin's son and that it's not a trap?"

"Yes, and much more." Sestine kissed the hair.

"Behold!" Kitorl said. "Raymont is our king!"

Rose's mouth fell open. "Your . . . king? Raymont? You can tell that from his . . . hair?"

"Yes." Kitorl took the hank from Sestine. "See these stripes of gold? They are the sign of royalty among our people. We have not had a queen or king since Queen Odara died ten years ago."

"But if Raymont is a king," Rose said, "then wasn't Jaahdin a king, too? You must have known his son would be a king."

Sestine shook her head. "The succession does not pass in a straight line, though it tends to run in certain families of high rank."

"Earth's Mercy," Rose said, horrified by the thought of Raymont having so much power. Even as she was pitying the barbarians, Rose realized that now she had another chance to save Greengarden, and her smile grew as wide as theirs.

"Oh, blessed day!" Kitorl said, clapping his hands. "Now, Rose Chandler Brae, tell us again what you told us before." After they all sat down, Rose answered their questions as best she could. She told them how Raymont had been feigned to be a monster, and their faces tightened. She told them how she had married him believing this, and their faces filled with wonder.

"It will be a legend worth telling," Sestine said.

Twenty minutes later, when the aromas of garlic, onion, and potato were wafting from the stew, Kitorl asked, "What of King Raymont's dreams and visions?"

"They haunt him," Rose said. "He paints some of them on the attic walls. In one, he searches for an apple growing from a special tree. If he could eat this apple, everything would be all right."

Several council members nodded. The cook, who stood

by the fire ostensibly to tend the stew, but really to listen, nodded also.

"That dream is another sign that Raymont is our king," Kitorl said. "We have a legend about a magic apple called a Firegold that grew back in the Golden Age, before the Great Rift."

"A magic apple?" Rose asked eagerly.

But Sestine waved one hand. "Later. Tell us more about our king—our king who is found!"

While Rose talked, Kitorl rubbed his hands over his antler mark, as though he had a headache or was trying to remember something.

"You speak of Raymont with fear," Kitorl said suddenly, "not love. You did not come to us in order to help him."

"No." Rose turned her wedding ring around and around.

" 'As mean as Raymont,' you said, when you were telling us about your visions." Kitorl added, "Our king is . . . mean?"

Rose felt trapped. She did not want to lie, but if she told the truth, the Dalriadas might not want Raymont, and then she would be unable to save Greengarden.

"Raymont's very . . . unhappy," Rose said at last. "Imagine how you might act if you'd been locked up all your life. And told you were a monster. Once you rescue him, though, I expect he'll be fine . . . well, better, anyway. And he might not crave the laudanum anymore either."

"Laudanum?" Kitorl asked. So Rose explained.

"This is grave news," Sestine said, "but we will soon cure him of that craving."

Kitorl looked at Rose hard, as if he knew she was not telling the whole truth. After she had answered a few more questions, the Dalriadas spoke among themselves. More people had ridden into the camp while she talked; nineteen now sat in a ring behind the council, passing Raymont's hair from hand to hand as they laughed and talked, their blue eyes shifting from Rose to the hair to Rose again.

A chill danced over her shoulders. She drew up her knees and looked at the sky. Night had fallen. She felt as if she were looking into the black well, then as if she were sitting at the bottom of the well looking up. Or was she in the bottom of the pot looking up? She smiled. Were the stars the pricks of light from popping bubbles? What would it be like to see dancing motes of light as well as dancing motes of darkness? Rose stared until her eyes hurt. A wild idea took shape in her mind, a huge idea, an impossible idea, one that would help the Dalriadas and the Valley folk.

Sestine turned to her. "We have sworn to rescue our king before this moon dies. It will be the greatest moment of my life. Tell us the name of this foul place where he is imprisoned so cruelly."

Rose plucked at the mat. Until now, she had been careful not to mention Greengarden or even Stonewater Vale by name.

"Kitorl," she said, watching the flames lick the side of the pot. "What is sacred to you—to the Dalriadas, I mean?"

Sestine frowned. "What has that to do with—"

"If you will permit me, old friend," Kitorl interrupted. "Many things are sacred to us, but chief among these are the sky, the mountains, and most of all, the Eldest Deer Who Runs on Kalivi Mountain."

"What if," Rose said, "what if a Dalriada did something evil while he was on your sacred mountain? That wouldn't make the mountain evil, would it?"

"No," Kitorl said.

Rose leaned forward, her hands outstretched. "The land didn't hurt Raymont. It's good; it feeds us. You saw how alive it is! How beautiful! The land is sacred to my people and me. If I tell you where to find Raymont, then you—all Dalriadas everywhere—must swear not to harm the land or the people on it. Forever. That's the first condition."

"Condition!" Sestine cried. "She dares set conditions!"

"This is why you came," Kitorl said softly, "to save your beloved land. Who among us would not do as much to save our mountains?"

After Mareck translated, many of the Dalriadas nodded.

"There's a second condition." Rose paused, seeking the courage to speak her wild idea, and she found it in the peacock eye stitched on Kitorl's black eye patch. She took a deep breath and said, "You must end the war."

No one spoke—not Sestine, not Kitorl, not even the translator. They looked stunned. Rose grinned at Kitorl.

"You saw truly, seer," she said. "I do come bringing peace—though I didn't know it until a few moments ago. Agree to this and think how much everyone will admire your foresight. You might never have to make another boot again!"

Kitorl smiled.

"You ask too much." Sestine frowned, and the antler mark on her forehead rumpled. "If we must, we will raid each farm until we find our king. You cannot have traveled far, with child and on foot—the king must be near Darrowdale. Both the dirtdweller who imprisoned him and the place where he has been imprisoned deserve to be destroyed."

"Whether you like it or not," Rose said, "your king is half Valley. Would you destroy the land of his mother and ancestors?"

Sestine and Kitorl exchanged glances. The crowd murmured. The cook stirred the stew, and the long wooden spoon banged against the pot.

"Besides," Rose said, pulling on her fingers, "wouldn't it be easier just to rescue Raymont? And skip all the fighting? Aren't the safety of an orchard and the end of a war a small price to pay for a king?" She sighed. "And then we could all just go home."

"Your words are wise, Wife of the King," Kitorl said. "We shall consult with the others."

While the council talked and argued, the cook raked embers away from the blaze and set another pot on top of them. Rose heard her stomach growl. Sestine had said the Dalriadas did not eat people. Rose was hungry enough to believe her.

Ten minutes later, the Dalriadas fell silent.

"The Council of Seven agrees to your conditions," Sestine announced. "Our rescue, too, shall inspire a legend. Since I was a girl, before my Ridgewalk, I have dreamed of serving the next ruler, but never that I would lead his rescue!"

"You are worthy of the honor, old friend," Kitorl said. "Now, Rose, tell us where to find our king."

"Swear first," Rose said.

Kitorl stood. He pulled a vial from his pocket and untwisted the top. "Behold the sacred water from the Great Snake Glacier on Kalivi Mountain." Kitorl turned in a circle, sprinkling the water toward the sky. "Hear us, Eldest Deer Who Runs on Kalivi Mountain, though we are far from you. The Dalriadas swear two things in your name. First, we swear we will not harm this woman's land or the people upon it. Second, we swear to end the war and make peace. Hear us, wind, stars, earth! Hear us, Eldest! Witness our oath to Rose Chandler Brae, who is her land walking."

Rose nodded. There was nothing more she could do. She only hoped Kitorl proved more trustworthy than Mr. Brae and her father. The Dalriadas waited, all those blue eyes, all those antler marks rippling their silent language, all those red heads like spots of flame in the forest.

"The name of the orchard is Greengarden," Rose said.

* * *

The day after she arrived back at Greengarden, Rose pushed up the sitting room window in the Bighouse and leaned out into the night. The scent of mint blew from the herb garden. To the left, a few late clematis blossoms clung to a withering vine. Mrs. Schill had hidden Rose's five-day absence so well that no one had realized she was gone. To keep her end of the bargain, Rose had sent Mrs. Schill to East Dale Ranch to find Adrena.

Rose leaned farther out the window, looking left and right, until she saw the full moon blazing across the sky. She winced and drew her head inside as the grandfather clock struck a quarter past one. Sestine was late. Had something gone wrong? In the dim light, Rose slid her fingers over the cold, bumpy rivets that fastened the maroon leather upholstery onto Mr. Brae's chair. She hoped he slept soundly.

To endure the waiting, she began counting the rivets. Up in the attic, Raymont was waiting, too. In the note Rose had sent up on the dumbwaiter, she had explained the rescue plan but nothing more. Sestine wished to tell Raymont he was the Dalriada king.

Something brushed Rose's arm. She started, then saw the green damask curtain billow in the wind. When she smelled the sweet fragrance of the late Ebullient apples, her heart contracted. Soon she would leave Greengarden forever. Frantic muttering came from the drawing room, where the portraits were raising an alarm. Fainter, and deeper down, came rumblings from the land itself. The barbarians must be near.

A blot of shadow skittered on the far wall, and a Dalriada slipped through the window, followed by another and another, until six of them surrounded Rose. Many more, she knew, waited outside the Bighouse and all over the orchard.

Rose clutched Mr. Brae's chair, sickened. What had she done? Why had she led the barbarians to the place she loved most? She told herself for the hundredth time that she had led them to Greengarden to save Greengarden. Then she told herself for the thousandth time that she had to give up Greengarden to save it, give up what she wanted more than anything else in the world. A taste like vinegar burned her mouth. What if the Dalriadas broke their oath? What if they freed Raymont and then raided the land anyway?

Sestine poked Rose's shoulder. With tears on her cheeks, Rose turned, crept up the stairs, and pointed to Mr. Brae's door. She waited in the dark hallway while the Dalriadas went inside. Sheets rustled, a bedspring creaked, and then— silence. A moment later, three Dalriadas came out, and Sestine gave Rose Mr. Brae's gold chain. The two keys on the end were still warm. How simple they looked, and yet how much she had endured to get them. And now that she had the keys, she only wanted to throw them away. Her mind darkened.

Don't let It out!

Sestine prodded her again. Rose led her up the attic stairs while the other two Dalriadas guarded the threshold. At the top, Rose took a candle from her pocket and lit it; the oak door loomed before her, flickering. Sestine lifted the iron bar, then took the candle. Rose inserted the longer key into the upper padlock and tried to turn it. Nothing happened. She turned harder, jiggling the lock until metal rasped against metal. Still nothing.

Sestine seized the keys. She tried them in both padlocks, but neither budged.

"You have tricked us, Didorieth!" Sestine's hands circled Rose's throat. "It's a trap!"

"I swear—" Rose choked, her breath cut off. She tried to pry open Sestine's fingers.

"Rose?" Raymont called. "Is that you? Have my people come?"

Sestine let go and Rose gasped, gulping in air, trying to hold down the nausea in her stomach.

"Yes, it's me," Rose said. "But the key won't work. Did he change the locks?"

"How should I know? Is that Sestine with you?"

"I am Sestine, yes. Are you truly a Dalriada?"

"Yes," Raymont said, "oh, yes. And I want to go home. I want to see the towering red peak. I want to see the horses whose hooves beat like my heart. I want to hear all the stories of my people. Let me out!" He pounded on the door. "Let me out!"

Sestine bowed her head.

"Hush, Raymont," Rose said. "Someone will hear." She was thinking about the night she had tried to steal the key. If Mr. Brae had guessed the truth, he might have worn a false key, a lure to catch her in case she tried again.

"We've got to search Mr. Brae's room for the real key," Rose said.

Sestine nodded.

Back in Mr. Brae's room, Rose closed the heavy drapes, then used the candle to light the lantern on the bedside table. The Dalriadas began tearing the room apart.

Mr. Brae, a strip of leather tied over his mouth, scowled up at her. Cords bound his wrists and ankles. Because the top placket on his nightshirt had three buttonholes but no buttons, it fell open, exposing his throat with its three-inch white-ribbed scar. Mrs. Schill had been right. Lower, Mr. Brae's nightshirt was hitched above his knees, revealing his pale, blue-veined shins and, on the left one, a purple splotch shaped like a leaf. Instead of feeling triumph at seeing Mr. Brae humiliated, Rose felt sick. She pulled the green robe off the oak headboard and draped it over his legs.

"They've sworn not to hurt Greengarden," Rose told him. "They only want Raymont. Once he's gone, Amberly's curse will end. I'm . . . I'm going with them to the Red Mountains. So the land will be free of both abominations."

Mr. Brae looked surprised.

"Now," Rose added, "tell me where the real key is so we can leave."

Mr. Brae shook his head.

Sestine unsheathed her knife.

"Tell or die, Didorieth, lower than dirt."

Mr. Brae merely raised his eyebrows.

"Don't hurt him!" Rose said. "We'll find it."

"We do not have much time," Sestine said. "If your people discover us, there will be fighting."

"But you swore—"

"We will defend ourselves."

Rose looked around the room. The Dalriadas had pulled everything out of the drawers; shirts, pants, socks, gloves, and several small portraits lay strewn across the rug. As usual, the walking stick leaned against the nightstand. The coyote's silver eyes flickered in the candlelight, and his tongue gibbered, *Fooled you! Fooled you! Fooled you!*

Rose picked up the stick. "I've had enough of you!" she said. She unscrewed the coyote's head, and a shiny new key fell into her hand.

Sestine seized the key and, with Rose following, ran back up to the attic. First the lower padlock sprang open, then the upper. Sestine flung wide the door. Raymont faced them, back-lit by the lantern light in the attic, his red and gold hair shimmering on his shoulders, his face petulant.

"My king!" cried Sestine, and she dropped to her knees.

30

The Sacrifice

Your king?" Raymont asked, staring down at Sestine. "I'm your king?"

"Yes," Sestine said. "Hail, King of the Dalriadas, Bearer of the Farlith. The Hart in the heart of the mountain will sing from the Caverns of Kalivi when you return to us."

Raymont's chin rose. In his pupils, pricks of diamond-shaped light darted forward like a storm unleashed. Rose stepped back.

"My dear Mouse," Raymont said, "how nice to see you in person again. It's been so long that I had fortunately forgotten how ugly you are. Tell me, did you get tired of writing notes?"

Sestine glanced from one of them to the other, puzzled. "Where are your belongings?" she asked Raymont. "Give them to me, quickly now, and we will go."

"The Mouse will carry my bag," Raymont said.

"I have to carry my own bag." Rose walked down the attic stairs to her room, where she lit another candle and then reached under her bed. The sack she dragged out felt as heavy as a stone. Her heart felt like a stone, too, which she would leave behind to fill one small hole in the Faredge Wall. She put on her cloak.

"Goodbye," she said, glancing at the white wrought-iron bed frame, the wardrobe, the red hat, and the folderol chest. Though covered with dust, the fantastic candles still ranged around the walls, still waiting for the seventy-seventh candle to complete the circle. At the door, Rose stopped. She walked back to the folderol chest, took two handfuls of Amberly's buttons from the bottom drawer, and dropped them into her pocket so that her baby would have something from his Valley grandmother.

Sestine stalked past the doorway with Raymont slung over her shoulder. *The Thing was out!* Rose held on to the chest, swaying a little, breathing too fast. "I insist on seeing him before we leave," she heard Raymont say. Alarmed, Rose followed them into Mr. Brae's room, where Sestine was lowering Raymont beside the bed.

Two feet taller than Raymont, taller than the tallest Dalriada guard, the oak headboard and footboard loomed up, intricately carved with grapevines, flowers, apples and pears, meadowlarks, and even a few ears of corn. As on the night she had tried to steal the key, Rose again saw the bed as a vast plain between towering cliffs. The contours of Mr. Brae's body were like those of the land, with valleys and hills, ravines and peaks.

"Why didn't you tell us the king is lame?" Sestine asked Rose. "He never would have survived our rites into adulthood. That must be why the Eldest Deer in his wisdom has kept the king here."

After staring down at Mr. Brae for perhaps a minute, Raymont slowly stretched out his white hand. From the expression on his face, Rose thought he was going to caress Mr. Brae, but with a swift dart, Raymont poked his shoulder instead. Then Raymont pulled his hand back fast—as though it might be bitten off. When Mr. Brae did not move, Raymont smiled and relaxed, the brown antler mark sharpening against his pale skin.

"Dear Grandfather," Raymont said. "Why, it seems I am your jailer now. And a king, too, with the Dalriadas eager to do my bidding."

Mr. Brae's eyes blinked above the gag.

"Come, Grandfather, amuse me," Raymont said. "I want to see you squirm and beg for mercy."

"My King, we must leave now," Sestine urged. "Many lives are at risk."

"Wait." Raymont picked up the candlestick from the bedside table. "Perhaps I can inspire my dear grandfather to be more entertaining." And he poured a drop of hot wax onto Mr. Brae's nose. Mr. Brae jerked back.

"Stop it, Raymont!" Rose cried.

Sestine gripped Raymont's wrist. "Torture is not our way, my King."

"But it is my way." Raymont set the candlestick down. "And his. Isn't it, dear Grandfather? Tell me, shall I lower the gag so you can tell them how you lamed me on purpose? So that I couldn't run away?"

Rose's mouth opened. Sestine grasped the hilt of the knife on her belt and bent over Mr. Brae.

"Is this true, dirtdweller?" she demanded. "Is it true!" After Mr. Brae nodded, Sestine looked hard at Rose.

"I didn't know," Rose said. "I swear on the land. I didn't know."

"Kill him." Raymont pinched Mr. Brae's hand. "I want to stare into his eyes while the life ebbs out of him."

"Leave him alone," Rose said. "You have what you want."

"My King," Sestine said, "we swore our highest oath,

swore by the Eldest Deer Who Runs on Kalivi Mountain, not to raid this place or to harm anyone here."

"But I swore no such oath." Raymont held out his hand. "Give me your knife, and I'll kill him myself. Finish what I started years ago—why, see, there is already a line to guide me! Don't you understand how long I have dreamed of this moment? Up in the attic, you will find paintings of all the ways I have imagined killing him."

"You represent our people," Sestine said. "You must honor our agreements and not disgrace us in the eyes of the Eldest Deer Who—"

"I don't know anything about any old deer!" Raymont shouted. "And I don't care! I want him dead!"

"Quiet!" Sestine's antler mark darkened from red to umber. "You will give away our presence!" All the joy that had lit her face earlier had vanished. The other Dalriadas, unable to understand, watched while their fingers slid up and down their bowstrings.

"Besides," Raymont said, "this agreement was made without my consent. I had planned that we would destroy this cursed Greengarden. Fell every tree. Burn every cottage, and kill all the livestock."

"What?" Rose gripped the footboard. "You would have . . . ? When you knew how much I . . . ? When I risked my life to free you? But why?"

"To punish you," Raymont said. "To punish you for betraying me."

"I've done nothing but help you!"

"You betrayed me by loving Greengarden more than you loved me."

Rose stared at him, stunned, then reached into her pocket, grabbed a handful of buttons, and flung them at Raymont. They bounced off him and struck the oak floor, where they pinged and wobbled and rolled in every direction around the room. Rose stood still for a moment, surprised at herself and at her sudden awareness that some things could never be forgiven.

"My, my," Raymont said. "Tell me, who's having tantrums now, Mouse? Tossing her little buttons around."

"They're your mother's buttons!" Rose exclaimed. "And it's her land you want to destroy."

He shrugged. "My grandfather's blood at least I'll extract from this cursed hole. If you don't give me your knife, Sestine, I shall swear an oath of my own. I shall gather Dalriadas who are loyal to their king, unlike you, and then return with them and destroy Greengarden."

Rose did not know which was greater, the disappointment or the rage in Sestine's face.

"There will be no glorious song about this rescue," Sestine muttered. She crossed her arms, cupping the points of her elbows, and turned her back on Raymont. The other Dalriadas gasped.

Don't give him the knife, Rose tried to say, but her voice stuck in her throat. Lock him up—lock it up! We should never have let the Thing out!

Sestine faced Raymont again. "Your spirit is twisted and lost from living so long among the dirtdwellers. But my first concern is to get as many people out of this alive as I can. We must leave. If I permit you to take this man's life, will you swear to abide by the oath we swore to your wife?"

"All right." Raymont shrugged. "I swear."

"You do not know your people, my king," Sestine warned, "so listen well. We do not hold with oath breakers, especially if they are kings." Then she looked at Mr. Brae. "Choose, dirtdweller. Death now and safety for your land and people. Or life now and the possible destruction of your land later."

As Mr. Brae's hands strained against the cord, Rose had the sudden impression of a cloud whirling between the headboard and footboard, a cloud stretching over the plain of the land. Suddenly she seemed to be outside, standing on the Faredge Wall as it wavered beneath her feet, waiting. All of Greengarden waited, too. The deer in the alfalfa field looked up; the coyote circling Opal's hen house paused; the swinging hammock stood still; the mouse and the rat and the red squirrel in the dairy froze; the sap sliding in the Golden Flames halted; the sleeping breath of all the children and their parents ceased; and, in the drawing room, even the portraits hushed.

Then Mr. Brae relaxed his hands. Greengarden shuddered, vibrating even up into the house, and when everything on the land began to move again, Rose bowed her head against the oak footboard because she knew what his answer would be.

Mr. Brae raised one finger.

"The first?" Sestine asked. When Mr. Brae nodded, Sestine sighed. "Very well. My King, you will do exactly as I say. I do not tolerate torture. Do you understand me?"

Raymont nodded.

Sestine gave him her knife. "Under the ear and across the throat—make it quick."

"No!" Rose lunged forward. "Raymont! If you do this, you really will be a Thing! Earth's Mercy, don't—" But a Dalriada grabbed her and clapped one hand over her mouth.

As Raymont raised the knife, Mr. Brae looked first into Rose's eyes, then down at her stomach; and then, arching his upper body toward her, he looked into her eyes again, beseeching. She nodded. Raymont struck.

Rose flinched, turned her head away, and threw up all over the Dalriada's hand. Down on the floor where it had fallen earlier, the coyote head lay with its mouth open in an eternal, silent howl.

* * *

Minutes later, Rose stumbled through the Redheart apples, swept along in the final part of the rescue—escaping without detection. Barbarians surrounded her, walking behind her and on either side of her in the adjoining orchard rows. Everyone moved silently, except Rose, who could not stop crying. Ahead of her, two men had joined their crossed hands to make a throne for Raymont, who sat with one arm flung around each man's shoulders. In the moonlight-mottled darkness, they looked like one man with three heads. They looked like the Thing.

Thing! Monster! Beast! Rose stifled a sob. All of Mrs. Schill's and Mr. Brae's warnings had proven correct, and because Rose had ignored them, Mr. Brae was dead. A branch scraped her cheek. She ducked, and her bag bumped the ground. Sestine, who was guarding Raymont, turned and glared.

Rose glared back. Oath breaker! Sestine must think little of this "Eldest Deer" on whom they swore. Rose felt as if her chest were going to explode—or collapse. Again she had trusted, again been deceived. She could rely on no one, least of all herself. One by one, she had overcome, or at least faced, the things she feared in order to save Greengarden. Yet all the choices she had made since the day she had chosen to work in the Bighouse had been wrong. They had led to murder.

Wooden props supporting the fruit-laden branches jutted out into the grass. Rose swung her bag at one, wanting to hit something, anything, hard. She had thought Mr. Brae evil, thought him as much a monster as Raymont, and yet he had died to save the land.

She heard a keening and froze, but the sound welled from inside her own head: a wail from the memory of the knife, from the raw act of murder, from the stink of vomit and blood—so much blood, much more than she could have imagined, and all of it running down into the quilt's valleys and hills, the ravines and peaks, running down along the plain of the bed into the land into the roots into the bones of her ancestors, and finally into the dark well at the heart of Greengarden.

Greengarden still rocked with the gift of Mr. Brae's sacrifice. Here in the Redhearts, Rose could see the news tossed from tree to tree by the quick, staccato wind-words of the leaves, and she could feel it in the dim murmuring of the earth beneath her feet. Everything everywhere knew what Rose knew: Greengarden was saved. Together, she and Mr. Brae—but mostly Mr. Brae—had saved it.

The price was high: one life, two souls. Rose picked a Redheart, cupping it in her hand as she walked. After she left Greengarden, who would look after the orchard and keep it from ruin? Who would see to the thinning, the pruning, the battles against blight and pests? Who would care for her parents and Verda and Mrs. Schill and Susa and all the people, bonded and free? Who would know how to speak the word *mine*? Oh, who would love the land as much as she did? Rose wanted another hour, another day, another summer. She wanted to wait until the Golden Flames bloomed, until the peaches were ripe; then she would be ready to leave, but not now, not yet.

Mr. Brae's last look had spoken as clearly as words. He had passed Rose a trust to care for the land and to continue the line of Braes through her child. But she had to leave. How would her child know who it was if it grew up far from Greengarden?

"How will I know who I am?" Rose whispered.

Then hooves drummed ahead and to the left. Rose dropped down in the tall grass, glad, for once, that it needed cutting. The barbarians dropped, too. Saddles creaked as the horses walked closer.

"How many more hours' watch we got?" a voice asked.

"About two, I'd guess, before you get your coffee, if that's what you're dreaming of, Joff," someone answered.

An orchard patrol in the next row was riding straight into the band of barbarians.

31

Abiding

Did you hear something?" Joff asked, stopping his horse. The other man stopped, too. No, Rose wanted to scream. Keep riding! Keep riding! The wind came up, and the tall grass tapped her face. Only a few yards away, moonlight dappled the withers of Joff's horse. The rest of the horse, and Joff, too, were hidden by Redheart leaves.

Rose glanced down the row, scanning for barbarians, but saw only the shadows of the trees. Her hand clenched into a fist. Sestine had already broken her oath once tonight. If she broke it again, and the barbarians attacked Joff, Rose would try to stop them, though her attempt would probably be futile.

"I don't hear nothing but your stomach growling," the other man said at last. "Come on, Joff, or you'll never get your coffee."

"Wait. Something's odd."

"Just the full moon, likely. Makes things queer."

"It feels like . . . I don't know, like someone I know is close by."

The man laughed. "I know who you're thinking about!"

"Who?"

"Susa."

"No."

"Well, she was working here in the Redhearts today. She's set her cap for you. She knows you pity sick animals and women in distress. Heck, you offered to marry Rose Chandler! Now, there was a pity case if I ever saw one."

"She's no pity case. I'd do it again in a minute."

"If you say so." The man paused. "Gonna do the decent thing and give Dorrick's baby a daddy?"

"No," Joff said. He jiggled the reins. "Enough of this. We're due in at the south watch station. Get along, Spire." As the horses walked forward, the two men rode close enough to their enemies to feel their breath, yet never saw them.

When the hoofbeats faded, and the only sounds were the leaves fluttering and an owl hooting in the canyon, Rose stood, still clutching the apple she had picked. The dark shapes of the Dalriadas rose around her. She walked on, trying to forget what Joff had said. Why rejoice in his words when with each step another word shouted in her head? *Leaving, leaving, leaving.*

Five times the Dalriadas cut across the irrigation ditches, under cover of the trees, before they at last reached the end of a row and stepped into the open. The light from the full moon slammed into Rose's face. She yanked her hood forward, fighting the urge to run back and hide in the orchard. To her left stood the northwest well. Donney's end of the wooden boom that attached to the pump lay in the dirt.

They had come out beside the eight-foot wooden fence on the western boundary line, near the northwest tip of the Faredge Wall. A section of the fence swung open, and four Dalriadas leading horses came around the hill. Ahead of her, the two men carrying Raymont crossed the boundary. When Rose reached it, she grasped the fence post and raised her foot to step off Greengarden forever.

A slow subterranean crooning vibrated through the wood into her fingers. Rose stopped, her hand tightening on the post. Was it the well gurgling? Or was it the dark root of the land? She thought of all she had learned from the darkness, not the flat, bleak darkness, but the fertile darkness with its dancing motes. She had dived into the dark well. She had been cloven by the dark plow. She had lit a candle in the dark attic—the candles! Yes! Where were the candles, brightly burning? Where were the dancing motes of light? Rose pictured the fantastic candles, unlit, standing in their dusty circle around her room. To her astonishment, she realized that she had never dived into the light.

Still grasping the fence, Rose looked back over her shoulder. All along the Faredge Wall, tiny flames winked on the trees, ten or twenty at first, then hundreds, then thousands glimmered, illuminating the old grey stones. A bone-wrenching, heart-wrenching lament poured through the air, swelled through the ground, through the trees and the rocks and the fence post she held. It resolved into a long, rolling cry:

Rose, abide.

Rose stood in shock. Greengarden was calling her! She inhaled, filling every bit of her lungs, and then exhaled, blowing toward the trees. The flames erupted into dancing motes of light—in green and gold and silver. Up into the sky billowed shining trills, cascading streams, and geysers of glorious light. When the glittering froth brushed the moon, Rose threw back her hood. If she wanted to be free, she had to stop hiding from the light, from the horrors it might reveal.

Look, she told herself. Look at it! And for the first time in her memory, she looked straight up at the moon. The dancing motes of light swept her toward the shining ball until she plunged through its surface. Inside, silvery light spilled over her arms, her hair, her cloak, and even the apple in her hand.

Her arms and legs stretched out, and Rose started spinning like a wheel. Her limbs began to grow—curling, looping, weaving in and out, and then hardening into black metal. She became the black wrought-iron rose on the attic window, except the moon was the window now. Light skittered and skipped along her bars, which turned from black to glowing gold.

Rose, abide!

As the love of the land glowed inside her, Rose burned with her own radiance. Pressure built in her lungs and all around her heart.

"Let it out!" she cried. A greenish-black cloud smoked from her stomach, disgorging a whirlpool of blackness. Out of it stretched white hands with claws that snaked around the bars, tapping them, scratching them. She screamed in pain. In the whirlpool's heart, a spinning mouth spewed out fangs, claws, and thorns.

Rose sobbed. She recognized the creature. It was the Thing—the true Thing. It was made of her fear of death, pain, light, and dark; of her hatred of her baby and others; of every single ugly thing she loathed about herself. As the wheel turned and the claws scratched and the creature howled, her own radiance—her joy, imagination, and love—revealed this part of her for the first time: she was a monstrous rose. A hundred times brighter than the moon's light, her radiance showed the terrible in herself and the world.

But the monster was neither all of the world nor all of her. What of her love for Greengarden and its people? What of the sacrifices she had made for them?

ROSE! ABIDE!

From the base of the black whirlwind, the dancing motes of light sparked and spiraled around the bars until the snaking fingers shriveled. The smoke vanished. Instead of a black whirlwind, there blazed a whirling cornucopia of light. Out of it flowed a fountain of apples and roses and grapes made of sparkling flurries. Swallows whisked in and out, leaving little starry explosions. Not only did her radiance bring the monstrous into greater view, it also brought the wondrous into greater view. Rose burned, but she was not consumed because she was a rose of light, kindled by love. She laughed and heard Greengarden laughing with her.

Again Rose felt the rough wood of the fence post against her fingers. She put her foot back on the ground, back inside the fence, back on Greengarden.

"Put me down!" Raymont was beating against the Dalriadas' shoulders. "Now!" They lowered him to his feet. No longer on Greengarden, Raymont turned to Rose. "I am free!" he exclaimed, stretching his arms wide. "Outside at last!" A breeze lifted his long hair. "Wind! That's wind! Funny how it feels colder against my eyes than my skin—I never imagined that." He looked up. "The stars! Oh, Mouse, you never told me how many there are!" Then, as he turned, still looking up, the expression on his face changed. He grabbed Rose's arm.

"The moon," they said together. Their eyes met, the pupils dark against the whites; their hands met; their terror met. It was the same terror, and for one moment, it made them the same. Then Rose remembered her radiance and let go of his hands.

"How can I?" Raymont said. "I'm frightened. Rose, help!"

"It's a light that shines," she said. "Only a light that shines on the dark."

"But terrible things—"

"—should be seen. You told me that dreams can take you to terrible places and wonderful places. Isn't light the same?"

"The dark's better. Safer."

"Only sometimes," Rose said. "When it's dark you can't

see the terrible things, but they're still there. You can hide in your mind for a while, but pretty soon there's no place left that's safe."

Sestine looked from one of them to the other, baffled, and then walked toward the horses. Up on the hill a coyote howled, and Raymont jumped.

"It's all too big!" he cried, shaking his head, lashing his red hair from side to side. "I can't breathe! I hate that moon; I hate it!"

"I know," Rose said. "The light makes everything worse. Once you've seen, you can't . . . you can't pretend the monster isn't there. Or that the terrible things don't happen. And then the fear is bigger."

Raymont moaned.

"But without the light," she added, "the roses have no color. And you love color, remember?"

Slowly he raised his head. Rose looked into the face of a murderer and did not know how to say what she now understood, that in this half-light, half-dark realm of the moon, the terrible and the beautiful stood face-to-face.

"Raymont," Rose said, "I'm not going with you."

"What? But you must! I need you. I—"

"You'll be all right. You have your people now." Rose nodded toward Sestine. "And this is where I belong. The Red Mountains would be a prison for me—just as the attic was for you. I'm staying here."

"If you don't come," he said, "I shall . . . I shall tell them to kill you."

Kill her? Rose stared. She was not surprised, though, because this was what always happened to her. Again, the Thing had come forward because of her determination to live as she chose.

"Well?" Raymont asked in a low voice. Rose knew that leaving Greengarden would be a greater darkness than death. It would mean living in fear again, under the shadow of the monstrous rose. If she were dead, at least her body would return to the earth, and she would still be part of Greengarden. At last Rose understood the words on Amberly's sampler, understood Amberly's choices.

"I shall abide," Rose said, "even if it means I'll die."

"She refuses to come," Raymont told Sestine, who had walked back to them. "Kill her, or force her to come!"

Sestine spoke quietly. "I will do neither. She has saved you. You should be grateful."

"You disobey your king?" Raymont scowled.

"You have much to learn about being a king," Sestine said. "And you are not anointed yet. You have endangered us all with your foolishness."

Raymont's mouth hung open. "But," he said at last, "I want my child with me. I want it raised in the Red Mountains. What if it has blue eyes?"

Rose thought quickly. "In seven months send a messenger to the camp in the hills. If the baby's blue-eyed, I'll smuggle it up there, and you can raise it in the Red Mountains. If it has brown eyes, I'll raise it here."

"That would be best for all," Sestine said.

An owl swooped overhead, and as Raymont watched, his eyes widened.

"You've given me this," he said to Rose without looking at her. "The world. Freedom. Very well, you may stay and squat on your little clod of dirt."

Sestine looked away.

Rose hefted her sack and walked back into the orchard before Raymont could change his mind. As soon as the branches closed around her, she ran through the trees, leaping the ribs of moonlight that lit her way home.

32

Speaking the Word

As the grandfather clock struck nine, six tiers of candles blazed in the chandeliers in the drawing room. Light slid down their crystal droplets and spattered onto Rose's back where she crouched on the dark red carpet with a match in her hand. Behind her, on the spinet, golden beeswax candles shone in the brackets on either side of the music rack. The spinet, like all the furniture, was not only free of its dustsheet but also clean and freshly polished. Even the air smelled fresh; all three windows stood open to the night.

Two more candles burned in the wall sconces in between the portraits, who were muttering softly to each other and occasionally to Rose. They had not once called her "upstart." In the middle of the room, on all four sides of a bier draped with green brocade, white candles burned in tall wrought-iron stands. On the bier lay Mr. Brae's body.

Rose had prepared his body for burial with her own hands, choosing his clothes, winding his neckscarf, laying the coyote stick beside him. The Dalriada raid, as people were calling it, seemed much longer ago than two days. On a chain around Rose's neck, hidden under her dress, hung the key to the attic door, which would remain locked until she finished repainting the walls and any blue-eyed barbarians in the stacks of canvases. No one had questioned either her right to make these decisions or her position as mistress, even when she had freed all the bondfolk.

Rose finished lighting the candle on the floor and stood up. In a circle around the bier, flames danced on the fantastic candles she had brought down from her room. This time, Rose had left no gap in the ring because she knew it was complete: she was the seventy-seventh candle. And within her—she put one hand on her stomach—the light of another life burned.

Rose went back to Mr. Brae's body and pulled a threaded needle from her pocket. Along the edge of the bier, eight of Amberly's buttons lined up end to end. Rose picked up the first, the carved bone button, and then held it against Mr. Brae's suit coat while she inserted the needle.

A gust of wind blew through the open windows, ruffling the fringe on the brocade. The crystal droplets on the chandeliers tinkled. The flames leapt and made the walls flicker with light and shadow. Rose looked up. She smelled sage from Greengarden's hills. Familiar voices came drifting through the window, someone laughing, someone calling.

Speak the word, said the pinch-nosed woman in the portrait.

Rose smiled, pulled the thread tight on the bone button, and said . . . "Ours."